QUICK CHANGE

By Jay Cronley

QUICK CHANGE
SCREWBALLS
GOOD VIBES
FALL GUY

Quick Change

«»

Jay Cronley

DOUBLEDAY & COMPANY, INC.

GARDEN CITY, NEW YORK

1981

All of the characters in this book are fictitious, and any resemblance
to actual persons, living or dead, is purely coincidental.

DESIGN BY NINA GILBERT

ISBN: 0-385-15180-2
Library of Congress Catalog Card Number: 80-5450
Copyright © 1981 by Jay Cronley
All Rights Reserved
Printed in the United States of America
First Edition

I would like to use this Dedication Page to express my admiration for John D. MacDonald, Ed McBain, Donald E. Westlake and other writers who have written an ungodly number of terrific novels. That these men are prolific *and* talented is obviously noteworthy. That they have come up with enough people to dedicate all their books to is the most astounding damn thing I have ever seen.

QUICK CHANGE

Grimm didn't feel like a clown, but he handed the kid a balloon, anyway.

"Is that a light bulb on your nose?" the kid asked.

"Get lost," Grimm said.

"That doesn't sound like clown talk to me."

"You want the balloon or not?"

"You're the meanest clown I ever met."

"Listen, kid. You're getting on my nerves."

The suit was hot and the makeup smelled like turpentine, and wearing tennis rackets would have been easier than the floppy shoes, but a plan is a plan.

One thing Grimm hadn't particularly counted on was the number of greedy children following him along the sidewalk. You can't think of *everything*. The children couldn't follow him into the bank, that was for sure.

"Hey mister clown, stand on one finger."

Grimm took some change out of his front pocket and threw it in the grass in front of the bank; so much for the children, they zeroed in on the money.

He walked into the bank, exactly the way it had been drawn on the practice paper.

You just don't *rob* a bank. You try that, without a well-conceived plan, and they'll gun you down—that is, if you aren't

electrocuted first. In the modern bank, there are wires hooked
to plants, and cameras behind clocks.

The plan is what separates the pros from the cons.

And whereas the plan might be that you rob the bank of
millions of dollars and live happily ever after, there are many
sub-plans that determine whether you will have to give the
money back, or live happily ever after in jail.

Grimm knew about a guy who lost a button on his pants at
a very bad time—when he was stealing some money. This guy
reaches down and his mask slips off and the next thing he
knows he is banging a tin cup on the bars, asking for more
swill.

A plan is equal to the sum of its parts. Somebody stubs his
toe at the wrong time, and this triggers an electronic device
that drops the bars around you.

For example, you have to start somewhere, like with the
mask.

It's obvious a man has to wear a mask so his face won't be
on the evening news. Money is no fun if you have to spend it
down in the sewer or somewhere as dark. You *don't* put a bur-
glar's mask on and walk three blocks to the bank. Somebody
might say, "That guy is going to rob the bank." You don't
put the mask on right outside the bank, either. This attracts
attention, and you might be clubbed by the guard. So
whereas a mask sounds like a simple proposition, it isn't. You
have to think it out.

It was Grimm's idea to go as a clown. Clowns don't rob
banks.

"Hi there, mister clown," the guard said.

"What's your name?" Grimm asked.

"Hugh," the guard said. "Hugh Estes."

"Have a balloon, Hugh."

"Thanks."

There was some doubt whether Hugh Estes could draw his
gun inside five minutes. And if he could get it out of his
holster, he would have to figure some way to get it over his

gut. A bank guard's primary responsibility is to keep rich old women from bumping into the windows.

"Hugh," Grimm said. "I have terrible news for you."

He frowned. "I don't get to keep the balloon?"

"Worse than that. Come over here."

Hugh Estes got up from his desk. Grimm put his arm around the old fellow and led him toward the door. "How's your heart, Hugh?"

"Never better. You with Easter Seals?"

"No."

"United Way?"

"Hugh," Grimm said. "I'm a criminal. I'm robbing this bank."

Grimm had his left arm tightly around the guard's neck.

"That's funny," Hugh Estes said. "You're one of the best clowns I ever saw."

"I'm no clown. Clowns don't talk. Underneath this calm is a guy who's getting a little nervous. I've got dynamite taped all over me, Hugh, so if you don't want all these people blown to bits, just do what I say."

Hugh Estes thought. They had taught him about this sort of thing in bank guard's school. One out of approximately 475 people who say they are loaded with explosives actually detonates himself or herself.

"I've got a terminal illness," Grimm said. "So it doesn't matter what happens to me."

That was the one who blows himself up!

Hugh Estes was getting real nervous real fast.

This would look very bad on his résumé.

"Lock the door," Grimm said.

Hugh Estes looked back at his desk, where the alarm button was. "You can't rob this bank. There's only one way out. This bank has never been robbed. It's foolproof."

"Yeah, but I'm no fool," Grimm said.

Hugh Estes slid the glass door shut and locked it. Several people in the lobby outside gave the guard and Grimm funny looks. Grimm made a face at them. They smiled. Grimm took the keys from Hugh Estes, pulled the curtains, and led the guard to the middle of the room.

"This is a robbery," Grimm said. He removed a pistol from the pocket of the clown suit.

A couple of customers smiled. One applauded.

Grimm shot the gun into the roof, for dramatic impact.

The bullet hit a sprinkler and it began raining.

Panic is your own worst enemy, Grimm decided, standing in the middle of the bank with sirens going off and much water falling from the ceiling.

A little water never hurt anybody.

One man, who had been standing at a table filling out a deposit ticket or something, fell to his knees and started weeping. "We're all going to die," he screamed.

"You idiot," Grimm said. "Shut the hell up."

He told the customers to be still and he quickly went behind the row of tellers and told them to march out to the middle of the room and stretch out on the floor, it was nap time.

"We'll drown," a girl said.

"Lie on your backs, then," Grimm said.

While this was happening, the vice-presidents and loan officers and other officials seated across the room were punching a number of buttons to notify the authorities what was happening, so by the time Grimm got the tellers on the floor, the big shots were smiling, confident that order would be restored shortly.

"Out here," Grimm said, waving his gun at the row of executive desks.

"Do as he says," a man named Princeton said. "This will all be over presently."

So within five minutes of when Grimm entered the bank wearing a clown suit, the bank was his.

Approximately ten employees were lying on their backs in the middle of the bank.

About that many customers had frozen in their tracks, as ordered.

Except for the water, the whole thing was playing.

Grimm had demanded that the customers place their hands on their heads.

He walked to the first teller's stall and picked up a stack of wrinkled money that was in front of a customer.

"That's *my* money," the customer said.

"It's insured," Grimm said, putting the stack of bills in a bag he had concealed beneath the clown suit. The clown suit was baggy, and it concealed many items.

The customer said his name was Gooch.

"Listen, damn it," Gooch said. "I didn't get a receipt. How can it be insured if it's not theirs yet?"

Grimm told one of the tellers to get up, and he had her go around behind the counter and accept Mr. Gooch's deposit. Grimm stuffed the receipt in Gooch's shirt pocket and had the teller resume her position on the floor.

"Thanks," Gooch said. "A lot."

Grimm put about a thousand bucks in his sack.

The customer by the table was still whimpering. Grimm walked over to him and said, "What in the hell is wrong with you?"

"It's this water. It's got to be stopped."

"What's your name, you coward?"

"Lackey," the customer whispered in Grimm's ear. Grimm shook his head, like he couldn't believe it.

"Shut up or I'll slug you. I've had enough of this crap."

"The water."

"I'm catching a cold," one of the tellers said.

Grimm noticed police cars gathering outside. You could see the flashing red lights through the curtains.

"We're all going to die," the nervous customer named Lackey said.

Grimm marched everybody into the vault, except Princeton, a vice-president.

"Get on the phone and get this water stopped," Grimm said.

"You'll never get away with this," Princeton said.

"Tell them if the water isn't off in ten minutes, I'll send your thumb out through the night depository. Tell them if anybody comes near this place, I will blow it up. Get everybody out of this building."

"Okay," Princeton said.

The bank was on the first floor of a fifteen-story office building.

It took them about thirty minutes to evacuate most of the building.

Some twenty police vehicles had set up a barricade in the street.

Princeton informed one of his superiors that there was a madman inside, with a gun and dynamite.

Grimm took the phone and told Princeton's superior that he wanted to speak with whomever was in charge, out front.

"I want to talk to my mom, too," Grimm said. "I hate her. She always called me stupid. Let's see what she says now."

Princeton had lost a little of his suntan.

Grimm sent him back into the vault with the others.

Grimm pushed the vault door to, but didn't lock it.

"If I see the door move, in comes a stick of dynamite."

As he pushed the door closed, Grimm heard some crying and praying.

"That man is crazy," Lackey was yelling. "I was in the war. I heard of guys like that. He's going to kill us all."

"Be quiet," Grimm heard Princeton tell Lackey.

"*Please* shut up," a woman also said.

"That guy is going to cut our arms and legs off, I know it," Lackey promised everybody in the vault.

Grimm walked to the center of the bank.

The water stopped.
The phone rang.
Grimm picked it up.
"This is Rotzinger," somebody said.
"Who are you?" Grimm asked.
"Chief of police. Get your butt out of there right now."
"Rotzinger, if you raise your voice again, you're going to get a woman out in pieces. I was in Vietnam with a jerk that sounded like you, with all the big-shot, official orders."

Grimm heard Rotzinger turn away from the phone and tell somebody, "We got a crazy in there. Stay the hell back."

Grimm told Rotzinger to call back in ten minutes. He would have specific information regarding the helicopters.

"Helicopter? What helicopter?"

"Plural. Two of them."

Grimm hung up.

Grimm had paid a man named Nottingham two hundred dollars for information concerning the electronic equipment in the bank. There were four elevated cameras, scanning and taking pictures, and two hidden cameras, one behind the tellers' counter, and one behind a mirror over the vice-president's—Princeton's—desk.

"Nice knowing you," Nottingham had said when Grimm paid him for the information. "I hate to work with guys who always wind up shot or in prison. Takes a little edge off the money."

Nottingham was the best wire man in the business. He explained everything to Grimm.

"They put the cameras way up, because this guy in Cleveland sprayed them with paint. They put them so high, you can't get at them."

This bank's alarm system was the finest.

"There are twenty-two places that trigger alarms," Nottingham had said. "There is one fake fountain pen inside teller window four. You raise the pen, that's it."

"Good," Grimm had said.

The guy was *definitely* suicidal, Nottingham decided.

Grimm used Nottingham's information to shoot the cameras out.

With the first shot, the people in the vault began screaming and Rotzinger outside got on a bullhorn and began screaming. The phone rang. Grimm answered.

"Daddy?" Grimm asked.

"No, son. This is Rotzinger again. Your friend."

"Oh."

"What's that shooting?"

"I'm shooting out cameras. You want me to shoot some people?"

"No."

"Okay," Grimm said.

"Listen, son, what's your name?"

"I forget."

Rotzinger said nothing for a moment.

"Son, we have sharpshooters out here."

"If they shoot, they might hit some dynamite. It's all over the place, you know. By doors, everywhere. I'm going to shoot some more cameras out. Give me a number where I can call you direct."

Rotzinger gave Grimm the number of the pay phone across the street.

"If anybody sets foot on the street, you get a body."

"Oh Christ!" Rotzinger said.

Grimm hung up.

It was a good thing he brought along a lot of bullets.

It took him eight shots to hit the first camera. The lens on the damn thing was small. Grimm had to stand on a desk to get a good shot.

The screaming in the vault continued.

He got the cameras knocked out after about ten minutes.

He made the rounds behind the tellers' windows, collecting money. It was about an hour before people got off work, on

Friday. Money was everywhere. Grimm stuffed only big bills in the sack.

He estimated that he got maybe a half million the first ten minutes.

Grimm was the only one in town who knew he had them where he wanted them—overconfident.

After collecting and putting the big numbers in his sack, he went to the front window and peeked out. It looked like a convention where the latest in law enforcement vehicles were displayed. There were about a dozen police cars, two trucks, an ambulance and three or four television news wagons.

While this clown was in here making an ass of himself trying to rob a bank, which couldn't be done, those clowns were out there coordinating things and dreaming of promotions and write-ups in the trade magazines.

We'll see who has the last laugh, Grimm thought, peeking through the curtains. It will be the clown, for a change, and not the audience.

The plan had gone swimmingly, which was a little joke that caused Grimm to smile.

The overall strength of his strategy had been so sound, certain nagging little diversions, like the water sprinkler, had been easily solved. Grimm never even thought about *looking* before he fired his pistol into the roof. That amazed him. He had been over the procedure so many times, it was hard to believe there was a single possibility he hadn't thought about.

One of the reasons he felt so comfortable standing in the middle of a robbery in progress was because it was like old home week. He had thought things out so meticulously, his plan was so thrillingly perfect, it didn't matter that there were guys outside, guys with guns, guys upstairs and downstairs and guys in helicopters and guys in bushes and probably even guys out there disguised as mail boxes carrying grenades, all of whom would get a gold star for capturing the robber, or two gold stars for winging him first.

It was like Grimm was in a protective time capsule like on those science-fiction movies.

The reason he felt so safe, in the face of what most people would consider adversity, was because he was in the process of outsmarting the entire town, and quite possibly the country.

Grimm had had other good ideas for making a lot of money with minimal effort, but nothing he had ever been a part of ever felt like this. This plan fit like a gigantic Baggie, which he would use to carry money with.

There was moaning from the vault.

One of the hostages stuck a hand out and said, "Excuse me."

It was a female hand.

Grimm went to the door, and said, "Get back."

The hand disappeared and when Grimm swung the door open, the hostages were huddled against the far corner, as ordered.

"What's the problem?" Grimm asked.

"It's him," a woman said. She was one of the customers. "He has to go to the bathroom." The customer named Phyllis pointed at the nervous one named Lackey, who had been crying earlier.

"He what?"

"I have to go to the bathroom," Lackey said. "Bad."

Grimm rubbed his forehead with his left hand and said, "This is not school. What's wrong with you people? Am I going to have to shoot somebody?"

"The bathroom is in the outside lobby," Princeton, the vice-president, said.

"Come here," Grimm said to customer Lackey, who got to his feet and walked slowly forward. Grimm grabbed the man by his collar and put the gun under his chin.

"You're causing me a lot of trouble."

"I can't help it," Lackey said.

"Either you control yourself, or I'm going to knock you out."

"You better not," Lackey said.

The others in the vault were watching this confrontation with interest. Grimm had to let them know who was running things, so he slapped Lackey.

"Stop that," Lackey said.

Grimm slapped him again.

"That's enough of that," Princeton said.

• Grimm walked over and slapped *him*.

"Oh my God," one of the tellers said. "He's going crazy. He's going to kill us all."

Grimm looked up, and then fired a round into the roof of the vault. The noise was deafening.

"Kill me," one of the bank officials said. "Shoot me right now."

His name was Buzz Murdock, and he said that he had just designed a multi-million dollar advertising campaign that would begin today with billboards and television spots. One of the television ads grandly bragged about the bank's invincibility.

"Blow my brains out," Buzz Murdock said. "Please."

Princeton said the campaign was not yet wasted. He said maybe the end result of this scenario would support the bank's advertising claim. "How do you plan to get out of here?" Princeton asked.

"Maybe shoot my way out," Grimm said. "With you as a shield."

Princeton nodded.

"Leave me a gun," Buzz Murdock said. "If you get away, *then* I'll kill myself."

Grimm said that the police would obviously request that some of the hostages be released before the negotiations continued, so the best way to get out of here, whole, would be to calm down.

"If I have to prove to them I'm serious, then I'll carve up the troublemakers first. I was in the war. I know how to make a person sit up and bark."

"The only possible way to do it is to send out the one with the most children," security guard Hugh Estes said. "I got *seven* children."

"Why don't you shut up," a teller named Teresa said. "I'm pregnant."

"No you're not," Estes said.

"I sure as hell am," Teresa said. "Look." She patted her tummy.

"I'm older. Everybody knows the oldest goes first."

"You're fired, Estes," Princeton said.

"Ha," Teresa said.

"This wasn't my fault," the guard said. "The damn clown comes in and grabs me. What could I have done?"

The customer named Phyllis said, "The phone is ringing out there."

"I'll keep them quiet," customer Gooch said. He was the one who barely got his cash deposited and insured. "If they want hostages, we'll figure it out among ourselves."

"I can't *believe* you hit me," Lackey said.

"Do you want me to hit you again?"

"No."

"Let me know how it's going out there," Buzz Murdock said.

Grimm told him there were cars and vans and wagons all over the place. SWAT teams were in the building across the way, and probably in the shrubbery.

"If you get away with the money, my professional life isn't worth a dime," Buzz Murdock said.

"He won't," Princeton said.

"It's official," Grimm said. "You're staying through the whole, bloody mess, Princeton."

Princeton paled.

"And *you*," Grimm said, pointing his pistol at the nervous customer named Lackey, "one more whimper and it's lights out."

The customer named Phyllis, who was incidentally very pretty, walked over to Lackey and put her arm around his shoulder. "It's okay. That guy is nuts. Just relax."

Grimm pushed the door to, and went to get the phone.

"Listen, pal," Rotzinger said. "We've about had it with these cheap theatrics."

The cop had evidently talked things over with his cohorts, and they had decided to break out the hard stuff.

"Okay," Grimm said. "I'm going to kill a woman."

"We hear one shot, we'll come in through the front glass."

"Then I'll blow everyone up. There is a pregnant teller named Teresa. I'll shoot somebody in the vault, so you won't hear anything, anyway."

"Well goddamn it," Rotzinger said.

Grimm asked if the television people were there.

Rotzinger said yes.

"I want to talk to somebody with TV."

"Impossible."

"Okay. Bye."

"Wait! I'll call you back," Rotzinger said.

"You get two minutes."

"Well goddamn it."

"One minute."

"I want that pregnant woman out of there."

"We'll talk about that when I get my helicopters. I want them in the street, empty. No pilot. I can drive a chopper." Grimm made a sound like a motor.

"We're working on it," Rotzinger said.

"Work harder," Grimm said. "And a motorcycle. I want a Harley, right next to the second chopper."

"What?" Rotzinger asked. "What?"

"And a city bus, down at the corner, facing west. Full tank. No driver."

"That's crazy."

"What did you say?"
"Nothing. Nothing."
"Get the TV guy."
Grimm smashed the phone down.

Some bank.
It looked as much like an insurance company or an accounting office or even a rest home. There were chairs and sofas, soft colors on the wall, and nice carpet on the floor—all sorts of comforts to take your mind off the fact you were in a bank.

The tellers' windows didn't even have bars.

Some of the modern branch banks had motifs, like Western or Early American, and a few gave trading stamps, like grocery stores.

These people tried so hard to make banks look homey, they forgot where in the hell they were. When Grimm had announced the robbery, everybody looked at him like he was going to steal some pens, not *money*.

While waiting for the call from some television person, Grimm put his feet up on a desk, with a view of the vault and the front window, in case the mayor or somebody got nervous and threw Police Chief Rotzinger through the plate glass, headfirst.

That wouldn't happen, though.

Nothing would happen except what Grimm dictated, because as he had concluded many months ago, when this idea stopped rattling around up there in his head, banks were a bunch of bull.

When it became obvious to Grimm that there was a simple reason why banks weren't being robbed of fortunes, he devoted his time to devising a method that would permit him to leave the bank with the money without getting the daylights shot into him.

It *was* true. Guys needing money would walk right by a

bank and try a liquor store and have some dog come out of the back room and bite them in the butt.

Banks are very smug.

They have fat men sitting at guard desks because of the cameras and wires and electrodes or whatever the hell else is in the walls and floor and roof. The guy in the corner liquor store, though, he has a Doberman underneath a box; or a trap door, or a net, something sneaky.

Grimm did a lot of research and interviewed a lot of guys and came up with a couple of sound theories.

The reason why big banks weren't being robbed of fortunes was because nobody was trying.

The last time somebody tried to rob a bank in this town was four months ago, and this attempt was made by a dope addict, who came in the front door, screaming, and was under about seven-hundred pounds of arrest fifteen minutes later, when three cops jumped on him.

It was in all the papers:

ROBBERY FOILED.

The guy's picture had been taken from six angles, and alarms had been sounded within one minute of the attempt, and people who had been considering a bank as a possible score went, "Oh boy, back to the drawing board. Those banks, they're too tough."

What everybody forgets is the guy was a dope addict with no brains.

What that attempt proved to Grimm was: Do not run into a bank wearing your own face.

Grimm found one man who was not afraid of banks, a man named Grigsby, who had come up with a great plan and was going to rob a bank, the day after he got out of the pen.

"That's the good thing about prison, you can think things out," Grigsby told Grimm.

Grimm estimated that Grigsby would be eighty-three years old when he got out.

They got him for robbing a bank five months ago.

It was a beautiful plan, and it was foul luck that Grigsby got caught. Dressed as a monk, he wiped out four tellers' windows, but lost a contact lens getting out. He had 20/210 vision.

"When I swear on my right eye, it don't mean much," Grigsby told Grimm.

The police found the lens, and checked with the eye doctors, and three weeks later matched the contact perfectly with Grigsby's weirdly shaped right eyeball.

"Do not take anything in that can fall out," Grigsby told Grimm. "Eyes are easier identification than teeth or prints. You think everything through, there's a way. Look at it like this, more people break out of prison than rob banks. Prisons are *much* harder. They expect it. Banks, hell, they've got real cute."

Grimm thanked him for his time.

The last word did not sit well with Grigsby.

"Don't worry, I'm breaking out of this son-of-a-bitch within the week. One more thing, don't take a leak. A guy I know named Martinelli, they got him in Kansas City because he went to the bathroom on the way out, and they matched the urine."

Grigsby said the reason "The FBI" went off television was because nobody but dope addicts were trying banks and kidnappings.

"Banks are an untapped natural resource," Grigsby said.

"Time's up," the guard said.

Grigsby had been right.

Grimm thought of the old boy, and decided to open an account in his name, with maybe five grand in it. Everybody else Grimm had talked to had likened robbing a bank to robbing a snake pit. Quite a few guys thought a better bet was playing a ten-team football parlay.

It was a shame, nobody would ever *know* how this bank had been robbed. It was a minor discomfort, one Grimm was

able to soothe by reaching down into his sack and fingering
the wads of money.

"Fort Knox," Grimm answered.
It was 4:35 P.M.
He had been in there a little more than a half hour.
The reporter's name was Lake Bodean. Where the hell are
your Walter Cronkites and Edward Murrows?
The reporter said, "This is Lake Bodean."
Grimm told him he had the wrong number, he hadn't or-
dered any minnows or stink bait.
"I'm with Channel Five."
"Oh," Grimm said. "I have a statement to make."
Lake Bodean said he was familiar with what had happened
so far.
"Okay," Grimm said. "Rotzinger is making a grandstand
play, and risking the lives of many innocent bystanders. There
is a pregnant woman in here, and unless my conditions are
met, fast, things are going to get rough."
"Got it," Lake Bodean said.
"I also want it known that Rotzinger is using profanity during our negotiations. He is using the Lord's name in vain,
among other things. Put that on the air. If my conditions are
met, nobody will be hurt. If that stupid police chief gets in
the way one more time, I'll send out the bank vice-president
in quarters."
Lake Bodean said, "My God!"
"What's going on out there?" Grimm asked.
"Well," Lake Bodean said, "they have psychologists draw-
ing up profiles."
"Kind of like the way artists illustrate the Olympics, in
progress?"
"Kind of."
"Tell them I was in the war," Grimm said. "Tell them I
used to sleep in trees. You ever do that, Bodean?"
"No."

"You ever had a snake wake you up?"

"Uh, no."

"You ever had the enemy throw snakes *on* you?"

"No."

"It's no fun, Bodean."

He guessed not.

"What else is going on?"

"They don't think you can get away."

"I got away from more people than that, over there."

"Over where?"

"Forget it, Bodean. I'll get away."

"Oh."

"Tell everybody Rotzinger better cooperate."

"He's here."

Rotzinger said that it was a nice try, but it was time to be mature adults about the whole thing. He said he knew how Grimm had planned to attempt his escape.

Grimm got slightly dizzy; a bluff does that to you. He quickly recovered, and laughed. Rotzinger said now that everything was out in the open, there was no need to go on with this exercise in futility.

"You plan to dress some of the hostages as clowns," Rotzinger said slowly, like he was talking to a naughty child. "And send a clown made up the same as you to a different vehicle, perhaps even a clown *with* a hostage. In the confusion, you would sneak off."

Grimm laughed loudly. "That's the dumbest thing I ever heard."

Rotzinger was immediately depressed.

"The helicopters and other vehicles are en route," he said. "Thirty minutes. You will never, *never* get out of there."

"Maybe I don't want to," Grimm said.

"We want some of the hostages when the first vehicle arrives," Rotzinger said.

"One hostage for every demand," Grimm said.

"We want them all."

"You don't *get* them all. You want *any* of them?"

"Yes."

"Thirty minutes," Grimm said.

"I'll follow you to hell if I have to," Rotzinger said.

Grimm crawled along the floor and peeked out the window. Guys with rifles were running back and forth behind the cars and trucks trying, it seemed, to cross in front of the paths of the television cameras.

Rotzinger was pointing in various directions and surrounding the building one more time. He was furious. He pounded his fist on the hood of a police car.

Rotzinger nodded, after speaking to a man in plain clothes.

This would be the mayor's office, informing Rotzinger that since the man inside was playing with a deck that didn't include the picture cards, every effort was to be made to insure the safety of the hostages.

Rotzinger nodded furiously now.

He was obviously saying, "Of *course* we will."

Grimm didn't feel like a mind reader.

He felt more like the conductor of an orchestra.

There was more trouble in the vault.

The attractive customer named Phyllis stuck her head out and made a face and said, "You-know-who is acting up again."

"You sure are cute," Grimm told Phyllis.

"Another time, another place," she said.

Phyllis was wearing black slacks and a white blouse. She had short, curly brown hair, and a figure that would create, then stop, traffic.

"You look like you're thinking about kissing me," she said.

"In times of great stress, I get romantic," Grimm said.

"I don't think that would be very smart."

They were standing outside the vault.

One of the hostages inside said, "Get away from me."

A woman said, "Don't come near *me*."

Grimm swung the heavy door open and saw Lackey standing in the middle of the vault with his hand over his mouth.

"He says he's going to throw up," Teresa, the pregnant teller, said.

"Take him with you," a male teller said.

"I'm okay now, I think," Lackey said.

Grimm asked Lackey what was wrong with him.

"I have a nervous stomach. It's getting bad again. Not terrible. Medium."

"Why don't you put him out there," Buzz Murdock, the advertising man, suggested. "He's starting to make me a little sick."

"Me too," said one of the woman customers.

"He *is* bad for morale in here," Phyllis said.

Lackey was wearing jeans and a T shirt.

"There," Lackey said, "it's better now."

Grimm closed his eyes. He hadn't counted on anybody being so foolish. It's because of problems like this, guys open up on innocent bystanders.

"It's bad again. It's very bad. It feels like there are waves in my stomach. I think I'm going to throw up right now."

"Oh *God*," Teresa, the pregnant teller, said. "I'm getting real queasy."

"It's an act," bank-guard Hugh Estes mumbled. "She just wants to get out first."

"It's bad, right?" Grimm asked.

"Bad, but a little better," Lackey admitted. "It comes and goes, real fast."

"You're not leaving this vault."

"This is inhuman," vice-president Princeton said.

A couple of the hostages told Lackey to breathe deeply, put his head between his legs, and a male teller suggested that Princeton open one of the safety deposit boxes so Lackey could throw up in that.

"It's being cramped in like this," Lackey said. "That's what's doing it. I need air."

Grimm told hostage Lackey that if he so much as *started* to get sick, he would get shot.

"You're staying in here and you're going to act like a normal human being."

"Maybe if we quit talking about it."

Grimm told everybody to sit down, there on the floor. They had something very important to talk about. He was standing in the doorway of the vault, so he could see the outside door and front window. Nothing would happen, except a television camera might creep in for a close look. Since Rotzinger was positive there was no way out—he had killer-cops up in the air ducts and plumbing, surely—the chief of police wasn't going to risk any lives.

This was a crucial time in the robbery.

If Rotzinger thought harm had been done to any of the customers or bank officials, he would come through the plate glass, headfirst. If, on the other hand, nobody had been harmed, Rotzinger would likely play along with the clown's folly, long enough to get him out in the open, whereby the justifiable violence would break out.

Grimm knew this.

Rotzinger knew this.

Everybody knew this.

Grimm brought the hostages up to date on the negotiations.

"*Two* helicopters?" Princeton asked. He still looked like he had just come from a board meeting. His pin-striped suit was in perfect shape. It must be made of steel, not cloth. His hair was slicked back.

"This is *not*," Grimm said, "a question-and-answer period. I'm *telling* you what is going on. I'm getting a little sick of your neat face."

"But they *do* have the area surrounded?" Buzz Murdock asked.

Grimm admitted there was enough hardware out there to

arm the starving children of India, so they could go shoot some food.

"They want a hostage released for each of my demands."

"How many demands do you have?" former guard Hugh Estes asked.

"Five, possibly six."

"That's not near enough," Estes said. "There's about eighteen of us in here."

"You're safer in here," Teresa Singleton said, "the way you blotched things. The president of this place is out there waiting for you with boxing gloves."

Hugh Estes said, "That one is faking pregnancy and *that* one is faking throwing up."

"Let the pregnant one go," customer Gooch said.

"I'll name the baby after you," Teresa Singleton said to Grimm.

"Bozo?" Lackey asked.

After the helicopter landed, Grimm let the teller go.

It was a terrible mistake, and one he regretted the moment he saw Teresa Singleton being interviewed on television.

"Son-of-a-bitch," Grimm said, watching the woman on the screen.

She had calmly walked outside and into the street, where a man armed with a machine gun met and escorted her to the far side of the street. Grimm was peeking through the curtains. It was about 5:30, just starting to get dark.

Rotzinger asked her some questions, and looked from the woman to the bank. He shrugged several times.

This is going very bad, Grimm thought. Sending the pregnant teller out had been the only decent thing to do, but what in the hell, Grimm wondered, had decency got to do with robbing a bank?

Nothing.

"Damn," he said, then he walked over to Princeton's desk and turned up the television set.

"No comment," Rotzinger was saying. "Things are under control. The man has made several demands. I've told you that. We're getting the hostages out. That's all there is to it. Now get the hell back where you belong."

Teresa Singleton was very calm, and said she had been instructed by the police not to deal in the specifics of what had gone on in there. Yeah, the guy was in a clown suit. Yes, he was armed. No, she had not seen explosives, but that didn't mean they weren't there. The clown suit was very baggy, and she had noticed sacks of stuff lying around. No, nobody had been injured.

"Damn," Grimm said to the television. She didn't look frightened at all.

"Turn it up," one of the hostages in the vault asked.

"Shut up," Grimm yelled back.

Teresa Singleton told the reporter she didn't know what the clown planned to do with the helicopter, he hadn't said.

"He was kind of weird," she said. "But I was never really scared."

The moronic reporter frowned at the camera and said, "That's the first good news we've had in a while, here from the scene."

Grimm could just see the headlines:

PREGNANT TELLER FOILS HEIST; CLOWN GETS LIFE.

He kicked a chair over and concentrated very hard.

Grimm had been close to making so much money you would have needed a rake to sort it, several times previously. Each time, something that bordered on the supernatural had caused the job to sour suddenly, and in a matter of seconds, Grimm and his men had gone from almost rich to almost maimed or imprisoned.

Grimm had always been regarded as one of the best idea men in town. In fact, his ideas were so good, they were negotiable. A man named Mountbatten, who was with Grimm on the Brown job, *did* borrow two grand on Grimm's idea. The loan shark concluded the plan was so good, it was worth something on the come. But as little, silly, seemingly insignificant problems continued to reduce Grimm's jobs to footsteps and screams, the important people started crossing the street at mid-block so Grimm wouldn't get close enough to whammy them. Being regarded as a hex is a tough image to shake.

The Brown job was where Grimm came up with a plan where an art gallery could be robbed of a painting worth $220,000. Art galleries were a lot like banks; they were wired to the hilt, and as overconfident.

The painting in question was in a room that was continually photographed by a closed-circuit camera. The camera didn't pan. It was still—and focused on the wall of paintings. A guard, armed to the teeth, sat monitoring the screens.

Grimm decided to have a photo made of the room where the prize painting was, scaled to the size of the monitoring screen, and when the guard was momentarily diverted, somebody would merely hold up the picture of the room in front of the camera. The reception on the monitoring screens wasn't so hot, and the guard would never know he was looking at a picture, not the actual room. And, as the guard glanced at the picture, Grimm's guys would be cutting the canvas out of the frame. It would be quickly replaced by a forgery that would look all right on the screen. A high school art student did the forgery for $19.95.

Some thought this was the greatest plan in the history of the world.

It was a shame the guy holding the photo of the room in front of the camera sneezed.

Mountbatten, the guy who sneezed, felt real bad about it.

The guard saw the one room shake violently, and at first thought it was an earthquake, but then knew otherwise. One of Grimm's men smashed the guard, but the guard hit an alarm, and within seconds, the gallery was in an uproar.

It was raining that day. Grimm and his men fought their way out the front door. Grimm slipped on the wet sidewalk and about lost his manhood on a parking meter. His men picked him up and carried him to a waiting car, and safety. The headline was:

GALLERY ROBBERY FOILED.

Yeah, sure. By a head cold.

Things like that, and the Gimp job, leave a sour taste in a person's mouth. The Gimp job was where Grimm and some guys kidnapped the president of an oil company and held him for ransom. The money drop was damn near brilliant. Grimm trained this old nag of a horse to return to a barn. The money was to be placed in the saddlebags, at night, and the horse was to be turned loose. The horse would cut through the darkness, eliminating any strategy of following the cash to the source.

But for God's sake, it lightninged and the old horse panicked and broke its leg.

Grimm and his men were watching from a checkpoint on a hill.

It wasn't *that* bad a break.

They had strapped a tiny cop on the far side of the horse, like a trick rider, and their plan was to ride right into Grimm's camp, shooting from the hip. When the old horse fell, it smashed the little cop pretty good, which was the only fun thing that happened that night.

They took $110 from old man Gimp's billfold, and let him go.

"They're hiring college people for cops," one of Grimm's men said after the Gimp job was aborted. "Strapping that tiny cop on the side of the horse was brilliant."

"Bull," Grimm had said. "We just didn't think of quite everything."

So whereas when guys used to be very excited when Grimm called, lately, they had been "busy."

Grimm's ideas had at least been so good, nobody ever got caught.

It was a matter of considering *every* possibility.

But as seriously and meticulously and calmly as he had thought out the bank job, he didn't once think there might be a pregnant hostage who wouldn't act scared.

It didn't feel hopeless, yet.

It just didn't feel perfect.

Rotzinger called, said the hostage was secure, and that the other helicopter and Harley-Davidson had arrived, so please send out two more people. Rotzinger's concentration seemed to be on something else.

"I can't talk," Grimm said.

"Why?" Rotzinger asked.

"It feels like there are snakes crawling around in my head."

"*What?*"

"You heard me."

"You owe us two hostages."

Grimm went to the vault, yanked the door open, and Princeton said, "We've decided Gooch goes next. He has a daughter graduating from high school tonight."

"What do you think this is, the Dating Game?"

Grimm grabbed the one named Lackey by the neck, yanked him to his feet, and threw him outside.

"You're getting on my nerves," Lackey said.

"Get your raincoat, you imbicile," Grimm said.

"Oh yeah. It's chilly out there." Lackey turned to the remaining hostages and said, "He's crazy."

The vault door was closed.

The hostages heard a considerable amount of banging.

Lackey *was* scared.

Grimm watched him fall off the curb. He was scraped up by two men who pointed guns at the bank building. Lackey broke free and ran down the middle of the street and crashed into a blockade of saw horses. He was waving his arms. They dragged him off behind the police cars.

The television people were shocked.

Grimm flicked the channels and caught the highlights of the second hostage release.

Lake Bodean, the reporter with whom Grimm had briefly conversed, was frankly repulsed. He said it was "a jungle in there," meaning the bank. The second hostage had been set free, but the poor fellow was on the verge of a complete emotional collapse. He was presently at the command post, under observation by a doctor.

All Lackey needed now, thought Grimm, was an agent.

The second hostage had said that the man who had taken over the bank was "a mental case from the word go." The second hostage had been in the war, too, and he had seen guys in better shape in padded cells chewing on their fingers. The second hostage spoke of torture and a "stink of death in the air."

This hostage said he worked in construction and he had seen it all. You have, he said, all kinds of people in construction—guys who hit women and throw poor little dogs out of car windows and guys who drink bourbon for breakfast. But never in his life had he ever been so frightened. The guy inside in the clown's suit, he was capable of ripping wings off of butterflies, maybe even *Madam* butterfly.

He never blinked, you know.

One of the reporters asked what that meant.

Insanity.

The robbery had turned into a big media event and the television stations were jockeying for position "A" outside. One station had a camera on a building across the way, for a panorama of the police activity. Somebody had put a Channel 2 bumper sticker on a police car.

Ten minutes after Lackey was released, guys with tear gas rifles were deployed up and down the street, but as Grimm had told Rotzinger, if the glass broke, the dynamite would reduce the block to cigarette butts and buttons and bones.

Was there dynamite? the hostage was asked. There was.

There was a jar of clear stuff, God knows how many fuses, and a huge box. There was also, Lackey reported as best he could remember, something live in one of the clown's sacks.

Rotzinger called three quick times after the idiot Lackey was released, twice in panic, threatening to have the building lifted by huge helicopters if a hostage was hurt, and the third time Rotzinger was back playing his old game of Name That Escape.

Rotzinger and his experts had concluded that if they exposed the robber's plan for escape, he would become depressed and come out with his hands up like a bad boy. It was the old if-you-have-them-by-the-ass-their-necks-will-follow theory.

Each time Rotzinger mentioned that he had just thought of Grimm's plan, things got slightly nauseating. Grimm supposed *anything* was possible, so he held his breath until the chief of police spoke his mind.

"Do you choose curtain number two, or curtain number three?" Grimm asked. "Or do you want to come back next week?"

Everything Grimm said was being fed to a police psychiatrist. Once they knew how his mind worked, Grimm guessed, they would know where to aim when he came outside. Who *really* knew what those jackasses were thinking?

"Yes," Rotzinger said, "it was a very nice try, nice in that it caused a few uncertain moments. Justice will out, however."

A TV camera and microphone were obviously nearby.

"As I said, no man is above the law, and the more heinous the crime, the more dedicated every member of the law enforcement community becomes."

These quotes went on for a few minutes.

"You have a tape recorder in there," Rotzinger said. "One you plan to hook to the phone. While *we* think you're communicating with us, *you* will be climbing out the air-conditioning vent."

Grimm said *that* was a damn nice try!

But *he* knew what it meant.

Rotzinger was supposed to tell this ludicrous story, and while Grimm was laughing himself sick because the story was so stupid, cops would crawl in through the air-conditioning vent and make the capture while the robber was convulsing with laughter.

"That's not funny," Rotzinger said.

Grimm told Rotzinger there were two things real wrong with that idea, and about 150 things kind of wrong, but he would deal with the 100 percent bullshit during this brief conversation.

"One, I have so much money, it wouldn't fit in the air-conditioning vent. Two, there are explosives in the air-conditioning vent."

Rotzinger was silent again.

"You better concentrate on listening to me," Grimm said. "I was one-tenth of an inch from putting that last hostage to sleep."

Rotzinger asked what had made the second hostage so upset.

"Knives," Grimm said. "Here's where we stand now. You have no idea what I'm doing. I know exactly what you're doing, which is nothing, except meeting my demands. You're getting a little nervous. The mayor and people like that are starting to bitch. Now you say if I send a hostage out in a sack, you'll storm the place. That will cost you many more lives. There *is* a difference between one basket case, and two. If you want *nobody* hurt, just do what I say. I think it's about time to break somebody's leg."

"Don't do that."

"Where in the hell is my bus?"

"It's coming."

"I also want a pizza—sausage and mushroom, extra cheese. Have one of the SWAT men put the box in through the night depository."

"This is no picnic."

"It is what I say it is."

"You son-of-a-bitch."

Grimm went to the vault and brought back the pretty hostage named Phyllis.

She was put on the phone and she told Rotzinger they better do what the clown says. She whispered. "He's foaming at the mouth a little."

"We want another hostage," Rotzinger said.

"When the pizza gets here," Grimm said.

"You crazy son-of-a-bitch."

Grimm called back and gave Lake Bodean an exclusive. Fifteen minutes later, the reporter announced, seriously and exclusively from the scene, that the chief of police had just called the man who was holding many helpless hostages in a vault, a "crazy son-of-a-bitch."

Lake Bodean said that if bones started breaking, the people of this town would know where to point the first splint.

The pizza was, of course, doctored. Grimm pitched it into a garbage can.

When Rotzinger called in a half hour to ask when the next hostages would be sent out, Grimm didn't say a word about the pizza, and he could tell the chief of police was upset. Grimm *did* tell Rotzinger that there was no point in sending some sort of sleeping gas in through the air conditioning.

"I have a mask on. If I see any hostage doze off, he won't wake up."

In his extensive precrime research, Grimm had come across an account of a robbery in Washington where hostages were used as leverage. Some knock-out fumes were funnelled in through the vents, and an hour later, the cops merely sauntered in and collected the crook. All the cops talk about things like that at their conventions in Las Vegas.

"I was not born yesterday," Grimm told Rotzinger.

"Did any of the hostages eat the pizza?" Rotzinger wondered.

"Why do you ask?"

Rotzinger was pissed. "Damn it, some people get sleepy after they eat, is all."

Grimm laughed Rotzinger off the line.

The third and fourth hostages, a man and woman, were released at twenty minutes of eight. It was dark and quiet, out there.

Grimm had demanded that all the police vehicles be removed from the street, leaving only the helicopters, the bus, and the motorcycle. Rotzinger, sensing an end to this nonsense was in sight, agreed. He had thought things inside out, upside down, and backward. There was no way on earth that psychopathic son-of-a-bitch could get more than a block. So he tries to fly the helicopter off, so the hell what. Rotzinger had it figured that the lunatic might dress two hostages in clown suits and have them accompany him to a vehicle, which would prevent one of the sharpshooters from opening up. The hell it would, for long. The minute somebody got behind the control stick of the helicopter, he would be blasted. Rotzinger had a marksman in an office over the bank, with a clear line right to the driver's seat. As for the bus, there was a cop trained in hand-to-hand combat concealed in the overhead luggage compartment, right by the driver's seat. Before that clown could get the ignition on, the cop would be on him with a death grip. The gasoline in the motorcycle had been fixed so that the engine would begin sputtering precisely 1.5 miles from the bank, and Rotzinger had guys in bushes, 1.5 miles from the bank, on every conceivable route. It had been decided that if *one* hostage was injured, forty-five trained officers would go right through the goddamn plate glass. Otherwise, the psycho would be allowed to play out his hand before having it trumped. The guy in there must think he's dealing with the Keystone Cops. Rotzinger hoped that the fruitcake wouldn't just give up, the way most of them do. They very seldom give commendations when that happens.

They give credit when lives are saved by alert police action. Rotzinger had crack shots deployed all over the place. An electric mat had even been placed outside the door, so the guy could be knocked on his ass with hardly any effort. The gas thing did piss him off a little. That was a close call. Rotzinger had guys with tanks down there ready to dope the air-conditioning system. Nobody had mentioned a mask.

Nobody fucks with me in prime time, Rotzinger concluded.

If they could capture the guy alive, like with the charge from the electric mat, Rotzinger planned to rough the guy up pretty good, on the way in. It's fun to pound crazies; nobody believes them.

They would be talking about this capture at *all* the conventions. The fine ladies and gentlemen of this fine community would once more be able to walk the fine streets and not worry about somebody stealing their damn hard-earned money, you can quote him on that.

The thing was, a watched crackpot never boils, and whereas Rotzinger's natural reaction was to go for that guy's neck, he had convinced himself that patience was the safest course of action; patience and preparation.

The second and third hostages walked out to a seemingly empty street. Everybody was across the way in the bush.

Rotzinger signaled the hostages with a flashlight.

"He's peeking through the curtains," the girl said. She was very attractive. She was holding her white blouse together. A button had been ripped off.

"He do that?"

"Yeah," the girl said. "It was a good thing I was wearing slacks."

Rotzinger stared at the torn blouse. It was evidence, and this stuff must be scrutinized.

"I think he might be using drugs," the male hostage said. "He was doing something with a needle."

"Damn," Rotzinger said.

"He is off and on, you know," the girl said. "One minute, he's calm and the next, crazy. Sometimes he's funny, and the next thing, he's threatening to rip somebody's ears off."

"He thinks you're coming in to get him," the male hostage said. "He's got tables turned over and some of the other hostages in front, as a shield. I wouldn't storm him, right now."

Rotzinger had a police officer write all this down.

"The other people inside seem to be all right," the girl said, "except for one guy with the bank, the public relations guy."

Rotzinger nodded. He had compiled a list of known hostages. The girl gave him other names.

It was confirmed that the guy was still wearing his clown suit. He had taken his funny, pointed hat off, but was wearing a red wig. You couldn't tell much about descriptions, with all that makeup.

No, the two hostages just released hadn't seen other clown suits, but the guy had a couple of sacks and you couldn't tell what was inside.

"Probably money," the girl said.

"Yeah," Rotzinger said.

And yes, he frequently mentioned the war. He had told these last two hostages that if he could sleep ten days and nights in a rice paddy, he certainly could maintain life in that lousy bank.

Food?

No, they hadn't seen any.

Rotzinger nodded again.

The guy had seemed to get edgy, lately. He *had* been watching the clock a little. It was reconfirmed that from all appearances, the electronic recording devices had been shot out.

Gas mask?

The girl said it looked like there was a mask on one of the desks, she couldn't be positive.

Visible explosives, like near the windows?

There *was* something taped to the main exit. The curtains were closed, so you couldn't tell, out front.

None of the hostages had been injured, except the second one released, the girl hostage said, the nervous one; he was slapped around pretty good.

"We got a tranquilizer in him," Rotzinger said. "He was pretty upset. The pregnant girl, the teller, is fine."

The third and fourth hostages had to agree, the clown could flip out.

"I saw him ripping some phones out," the male hostage said.

"Everything is under control," Rotzinger said. He praised their coolness under pressure.

"I'm a little cool on the outside, too," the girl said.

"Get this lady a coat," Rotzinger said.

"Some safety pins would help."

"You got it."

The male hostage had to go to the bathroom, bad.

A policeman took the hostages to a stand for some hot coffee.

Rotzinger called back inside the bank, to request the release of more hostages. There was no answer. He sure hoped the guy didn't start carving on anybody.

Grimm called back in twenty minutes. Rotzinger was relieved.

"I got a feeling you're coming up the hill," Grimm said.

"No, no," Rotzinger promised. "We're not."

"You better not."

"We need more hostages."

"The hell with you."

"The women. How many more are there?"

"Forget it," Grimm said.

"If you don't cooperate," Rotzinger said, "we'll remove the vehicles, one at a time."

"I wouldn't."

"I have the authority," Rotzinger said, "to come right through the goddamn glass to get you if you don't cooperate. We do what you say. You better not start the bullshit."

Grimm felt a wave of nausea, like when Mountbatten had sneezed, shaking the painting called "Man's Inner Struggles." How a bunch of dots and lines could have been worth almost a quarter of a million dollars was beyond him.

"Okay, okay," Grimm said. "You get a hostage."

"*All* the women. *Now.*"

"You're making me mad," Grimm said.

"You're through. Come out with your hands up."

Grimm needed a good laugh. "You watch too much television. You get another hostage, when *I* say."

Rotzinger looked at the phone. Something had happened during the conversation, a goddamn clue. He had heard something, a change in tone. This was not a normal ear. This was an ear that had been in the business a long time.

Rotzinger got the tape man and the voice analysis man, and he had the last conversation played back, maybe ten times.

You can measure a person's voice like you can measure a person's blood pressure. The portable voice analysis machine cost the taxpayers something like $65,000, but by God it was paying for itself, right now.

"There was more tension and anxiety in the man's voice this last time, than ever," the voice analysis man told Rotzinger. "Toward the latter part of the conversation, I would say the man was very near panic."

Rotzinger wanted to know what the funny noise had been.

At first nobody heard a funny noise.

When they put the earphones on, they confirmed the presence of something that went "beep."

"Maybe something like a horn," the voice analysis man guessed. "Who knows? Clowns carry horns, don't they?"

"You really get paid for crap like this?" Rotzinger asked the voice analysis man.

One thing did *not* lead to another, so they went through, as Rotzinger called it, the "plate goddamn glass."

No hostage had been released for almost an hour.

Things were getting out of control.

Grimm had called back twice, almost incoherently.

Cops had crawled on their stomachs up to the front window, and had heard nothing.

It was concluded by the city officials and police officials and innocent bystanders that this could not go on forever, so a man was sent forward with the most sophisticated glass cutters in the world, and he cut a one-foot square out of the front plate glass, and silently removed it.

Nothing happened.

The cop slowly stuck his head into the darkened bank. The cop was wearing special goggles so he could see great in the dark. Then he crawled on his gut sideways, away from the plate glass, and returned, full speed, to the command post.

His report was concise.

He had seen nothing in there.

"Nothing?" Rotzinger asked.

"Nothing."

"What do you mean nothing?"

"Nothing."

"No movement?"

"Nothing."

"No explosives?"

"Nothing."

"No *people?*"

"Nothing."

"You're telling me you saw nothing."

"Nothing."

"Maybe they're in the vault."

"There's nothing in the main part."

"Maybe the guy was behind a desk or something."

"If he was, then the hostages were all in the vault."

The president of the bank said the vault could be opened from the outside.

Rotzinger licked his lips.

When they went in, it sounded like a wreck. A *big* wreck.

One of the television reporters, trying desperately to better his life position at the station, described the sound as being similar to what you heard if you took a ball bat to a chandelier. Then the reporter thought about what he had said, and frowned. Not many people probably hit chandeliers with bats. How could the masses trust a person who might have done goofy things like that? The reporter quickly recovered and gave a simple play-by-play of the proceedings.

The police went in like gangbusters and captured a garbage can full of pizza.

"Where is everybody?" Rotzinger asked pitifully. He swung his fist in the air and turned red in the face and everybody thought he was going to have a coronary, which, as the mayor later said, "would be the easy way out."

The mayor wasn't particularly fond of the notion that despite the cultural, recreational, and educational opportunities in this city, the only thing visitors would think of for the next 150 years was the bank job where the robber disappeared with the loot.

Rotzinger was so stupefied, he had his men check the desk drawers for Grimm, only he didn't know it was Grimm he was looking for. Rotzinger didn't know who or whom he was looking for.

Things had suddenly gone to hell.

Television gave things a nice push. They started calling it the "Crime of the Century," and here the crime was only a few hours old. The cameras panned in, with the long lenses, and showed the police officers scratching their heads and kicking glass aside.

Rotzinger just about went berserk.

The vault was full of hostages.

Statements were taken.

"He looked like a clown," said Princeton. "How did you let the madman escape?"

Princeton did a fine job of shifting the blame from the bank to the cops.

Security guard Hugh Estes told the television people he was sucker-punched.

Buzz Murdock, the advertising man, heard that the robber had apparently escaped, and he fainted.

Rotzinger told the television people that if they came any closer, they would be arrested. Searches covering every square inch of the bank were launched.

Guys in Hollywood started writing scripts, so they could fill in the ending and have a made-for-TV movie ready within a few months, maybe even, praise God, while the guy was still loose!

Rotzinger had an assistant gather all the television people and tell them this was a cruel, wicked crime, and it should be treated as such. Leads were being followed and arrests could be expected shortly.

People found it hard to dislike a guy who had robbed a big-shot bank of its insured money, without hurting a soul, though. It wasn't like the guy had *mugged* anybody. Anybody smart enough to take advantage of a big, stuffy, impersonal company can't be all bad.

After Buzz Murdock was revived with smelling salts, vice-president Princeton told him, "Keep this to yourself, but this might not turn out all bad. If the guy gets away, look at the publicity we'll get. We'll get more guards, new systems, cameras impossible to wipe out. It's like lightning. *No place* gets robbed twice. We might lose a few customers, but we'll get more new ones. The bank will be a landmark."

Princeton said that the last bank he knew of that got

robbed of a fortune successfully many *many* years ago, in Chicago, it changed its name and within a couple of years, quadrupled its business!

It was estimated that the clown got away with approximately $800,000.

America had a new folk hero.

Grimm would have much rather been in Sherwood Forest, instead of in a damn jungle.

"Take a left," he said.

"Where?" Lackey asked.

"Back there," Grimm said.

Lackey swerved to miss a cab.

"Let me drive," Phyllis said. "For God's sake, you're going to kill us."

"I'm not going to kill anybody," Lackey said.

"This is ridiculous," Grimm said. "Absolutely the most unbelievable thing I've ever seen. You missed the turn."

"You think there's one entrance to the highway? Is that it? There are dozens." He continued straight. They were driving almost directly beneath the freeway.

Grimm looked out the window. He was in the back seat with the money. "I have a question."

"What?" Lackey wondered, swerving.

"Why are we starting to veer *away* from the freeway? You would think if there's another entrance ramp down this one-way service road, it would stay *near* the freeway."

"I didn't build these damn roads," Lackey said. He leaned forward over the wheel and looked right. "I can still see the freeway."

"Wave to it," Grimm said.

"We should have thought about this more," Phyllis said.

"We should have thought about this *some*."

"Why is the street going left?" Grimm held the sack of money on his lap, gently, like it was a stuffed animal.

"Where are we going?" He was so tired. "I want everybody
to know that, no matter what happens, this is the most unbelievable thing I've ever seen."

Phyllis rolled her window down and said, "I can't even *hear*
the freeway now."

"You people are making me nervous," Lackey said.

Grimm looked out of his window. "Lock your door," he
told Phyllis. "We're in the middle of a bad neighborhood."

Lackey came to a stop sign.

"Don't go left," Grimm said. "That street probably goes
back to the bank. Don't go straight. There's no light down
there. There are probably street gangs in the shadows."

Lackey swung right, narrowly avoiding a Volkswagen.

"The men around here don't wear shirts," Phyllis said.

"Try to keep the car moving forward at all times," Grimm
told Lackey.

"Don't worry," Lackey said.

"Why?" Grimm asked.

It was hard to feel cheated with hundreds of thousands of
dollars in your lap, but as Lackey blundered through the resi-
dential area, his head scanning right and left like he was
watching a tennis match, Grimm felt at least psychologically
deprived.

There had been no time for a celebration. That would
come later, like maybe when Lackey took a dead-end street
and drove into a vacant lot, then everybody could get out and
hug and kiss.

A person robs a bank, it seems that somebody should have
thought ahead and programmed five minutes for hugging and
jumping up and down. It's hard though, Grimm guessed, to
assume without a reasonable doubt that you're going to exe-
cute the perfect crime, no matter how perfectly exquisite it
seems on paper.

Grimm sat in the back seat and worried.

When you go on vacation, it's only natural to wonder if

you turned the microwave off, and let the dog out of the closet, things like that.

Grimm had left nothing in the bank, except the clown suit, which he stuffed in a drawer. They would find that, but who the hell cared, except the place where Grimm rented the suit. *Grimm* hadn't even rented the suit. He had paid a wino five dollars to rent it.

Every base had been touched, securely, and then when Grimm crossed home plate, they hadn't even found the damn ball yet!

It was a relief to be able to act sane again. Acting crazy had been awfully comfortable.

The plan had been bruised several times during its execution, but as Phyllis had said, "The concept is so utterly brilliant, nothing could screw it up," and then she should have said, "Not even Lackey."

Phyllis had been over Grimm's plan with a fine-toothed comb, then she pulled the plan up by the roots and put it under a microscope. In the past, she had found flaws in Grimm's ideas, big enough to drive a paddy wagon through. This time, though, after hearing about the bank proposition, Phyllis had looked at Grimm so lovingly and admiringly and proudly, Grimm turned around to see if Phyllis was staring at somebody else.

Phyllis *knew* Grimm had potential.

All those years of ducking under the long arm of the law so they wouldn't be clotheslined, finally paid off.

Phyllis said the Gimp and Brown jobs, and all the other prayer jobs, were a joke compared to the bank. The bank was genius. Grimm's name would be up in lights, someday. Hopefully, not over the electric chair, he said.

Grimm had been wrestling with the bank thing about two months before he mentioned it to Phyllis. He *thought* it was not bad, but when you've almost destroyed yourself on parking meters during other ideas you thought were good, you never knew. When Phyllis wrestled Grimm to the floor, ripped his shirt off, and began kissing him, it dawned on him, maybe it was a *real* good idea.

They talked and talked and talked.

They had contingency plans, like if, during the robbery, a meteor hit.

And once the plan was properly launched, the results were predestined.

Damned if Phyllis hadn't been right.

The irritations were minor. They were: Lackey, Lackey, and finally, surprising no one, Lackey.

Lackey said Grimm was so convincing in the bank it scared him. Lackey said there for a while, he thought Grimm was *really* robbing the bank. Well, sure he was, but Grimm was so good, it was like he was somebody else. Lackey had apologized for about throwing up. You had to admit, it lended credibility to matters. Throwing up is so natural, none of the other hostages thought a thing about it. Phyllis had nearly pinched a hole in Lackey, trying to shut him up.

And as throwing up was not on the blueprint, neither was getting tranquilized. Lackey had been so wild when he was released from the bank, they had a needle in him before he could object. Grimm suggested that was why Lackey had missed the damn freeway entrance ramp, but Lackey said the shot had worn off, and he was operating at 98 percent of his effectiveness.

The horn could have been catastrophic. When Grimm heard it, his heart bounced around inside his chest like it was trying to get out. The horn, that was almost as bad as when Mountbatten had sneezed during the art gallery job.

They had pulled into a convenience grocery. Grimm had used a pay phone to call the booth across from the bank, as planned, to create the illusion he was still in the bank.

They don't have cars in banks, though.

As Grimm was talking to Rotzinger, Lackey accidentally hit the car horn.

They had planned on a lead time of anywhere from an

hour to, if they got lucky, all night. There was no way of predicting when the cops would go in through the plate glass. The horn honk shortened things considerably.

That was still another grand thing about the plan: so?

The hostages had been questioned. They were told to stick around, obviously to identify the clown or his body, when it was all finished. The questioning was quick and disorganized. Lackey, Phyllis, and Grimm had used false identification, and, after they had been questioned, they just kind of wandered off, because who in his right mind would have figured the hostages for the robbers?

Nobody in *this* world.

They had taken the money out in the lining of coats and in their undershorts and shoes and Phyllis had taken maybe a hundred thousand out in her purse!

Grimm had removed the clown makeup and suit inside the bank without fear, with the cameras shot to hell.

He had first shut the others in the vault.

He and Phyllis had marched outside, carrying the money and stories of the crazy clown.

Rotzinger had not purposely batted an eye; his right one was twitching involuntarily.

Grimm and Phyllis had wandered off to the car, where Lackey was waiting.

Nobody would know Grimm was not a hostage until they got inside the vault. They wouldn't even know then. When they started adding up hostages, they would find there had been one too many, but it was dark, did anybody know what one guy looked like? What guy? The hostage. Which hostage? Where the hell is everybody? What's going on here?

When they finally put one and one together, and subtracted eight hundred thousand, they would *know* those three damn hostages took the money out. Phyllis wore a wig. Lackey wore a wig. Grimm had a fake moustache.

It could conceivably be days before they knew who to look for, and by that time, Grimm, Phyllis, and Lackey would be far, far away. By the time they matched names and addresses, the robbers would be snorkeling, tipping natives, and getting tan.

They might not ever know who stole the money. People come and go, in this city, hundreds and thousands of them a day.

All things do happen for the best. Since they had never gotten away with any crime, there was no computer to check for modus operandis or birthmarks or known associates.

It has been a spinoff of one of the oldest tricks in the book, where a guy showed up at the border every day with his donkey cart. Customs was sure the seedy-looking character was smuggling something, and they tore the saddlebags apart, and looked in the donkey's mouth and inside the boards, everywhere, but they never found a thing. The guy was, of course, smuggling donkeys.

Grimm's illusion obviously had worked beautifully.

God, he would have felt great, had they not been so stinking lost.

The neighborhood was full of apartments. The selling point for the better flats would be "has glass in windows." Tourism provides the principal economic thrust in neighborhoods like this. Guys hang around, leaning on buildings, waiting for some sucker's car to run out of gas.

Grimm wouldn't have been surprised if some of the neighborhood thugs were responsible for what seemed to be an inordinate amount of tourism this time of night. Lackey had *sworn* there should have been a sign about the freeway entrance, a *big* sign, with arrows. The Neighborhood Committee for Easy Pickings probably sent a crew down to remove the freeway sign twenty minutes after the highway department got it up.

They drove without much hope.

"This looks new," Lackey said.

"It looks that way because we're going a different direc-

9.. Use

tion," Grimm said. "This is the same street we've been on. You drove up it. Now you're driving down it."

"What we need to find," Lackey said, "is west. The freeway is west of here. I'd stake my life on it."

"That can be easily arranged," Grimm said. "You miss that next light by the Mass Acre Bar over there, and those guys will be on this car like piranhas."

"I wonder why it's called that?"

"Oh, probably the guy's name," Grimm said. "Massacre."

Lackey made the light. The people in front of the bar sized the car up, like it was Miss Texas in the swimsuit competition.

There were few street signs because, as Grimm had explained, they melt the metal down for the pellet guns.

"Maybe it was Mass Acre, you know, because of the way people name country homes and things."

"Yeah," Grimm said, "and maybe those were splotches of red paint on the door."

Phyllis had been enjoying the scenic tour, silently. Grimm had a feeling she was about ready to make a very serious point. Phyllis didn't like surprises. She liked things spelled out. There was no excuse for bungling something you could control, she believed. The reason she had fallen in love with the bank job, and Grimm, was because it had been planned in such detail. So she might have seemed a bit like a fortune hunter. Grimm was a bit of a calf hunter, himself. Phyllis had great legs.

"We *did* go over this," Grimm said, anticipating Phyllis' thoughts. "We checked it on the map, and everything."

Lackey pulled up next to a car going about thirty, and he rolled down his window.

"Excuse me," Lackey yelled out the window, steering with his right hand, "how do you get back on the freeway from here?"

"How the fuck am I supposed to know," the passenger of the other car answered.

"What direction are we going?" Lackey asked.

"Straight," the guy said.

Lackey made a smart right turn.

Phyllis looked at him with murderous contempt.

"I should have known," she said.

"Why don't you shut up," Lackey told her.

"Stop bitching," Grimm said. He kicked the backs of each seat.

"Damn it, don't," Lackey said.

"Don't *touch* me," Phyllis said. "I take back everything we've ever done."

Grimm felt as though they were trapped in a Hitchcock movie. It was inconceivable that they could rob a bank and outwit this city's finest, then succumb to something as menial as a wrong turn, and be threatened by this city's rattiest.

"We need directions," Grimm said.

"It's a distinct possibility," Lackey admitted.

They were passing through an area of small businesses. Whores stood in doors of hotels, displaying their wares.

"Look at that one," Lackey said. "She about tripped over her breasts."

"She's probably somebody's mother," Grimm said absent-mindedly.

"Yeah, a gang of killers' mother. I would like to have the bar concession in this neighborhood, the bars that go over windows."

"That's it," Grimm said.

"Look at that," Lackey said. "There was a sign on a window back there that said One Acre for Sale. How could that be? There's no land around here."

"That's it," Grimm said again.

"Why don't you watch the damn road?" Phyllis said.

"Maybe they meant an acre, straight down into the earth," Lackey figured. "What's it, Grimm?"

"If you see somebody who's pregnant," Grimm said, "stop. I'll ask directions."

"That's not bad," Lackey said. "Pregnant people should be harmless."

Phyllis said that Ma Barker used to be pregnant. Then she said "Dear God." She leaned up and put her head on the dash. Grimm asked what was wrong with his idea.

"The pregnant woman," Phyllis said.

"What pregnant woman?" Lackey asked. "We haven't spotted one yet. It's hard to tell who's pregnant and who's just big and strong, around here."

"The teller," Phyllis said.

"Who?" Lackey wondered.

"The pregnant teller at the bank. The first hostage you let go."

"What about her?" Grimm asked. He was getting that funny feeling in his stomach.

"Did you see her?"

"What?" Lackey asked. "Around here? Where? When? What would she be doing in *this* neighborhood?" Somebody walked off the curb in front of Lackey. He honked. "Where'd you learn to walk, the fun house?"

Grimm leaned back in the seat and rubbed his eyes. Phyllis turned around and gave Grimm a weak smile. She, too, had failed to thoroughly consider the pregnant teller's role in the post-robbery confusion. Grimm and Phyllis were united in their agony.

Lackey didn't understand what in the hell anybody was talking about and wished somebody would help him find west. He looked up, several times, trying to get a reading from the stars. Somebody had stolen the best stars, and all you could see were flickers.

"Don't worry, sweetie," Phyllis said, scratching Grimm's knee. He patted her hand and said he needed a couple of moments with his thoughts.

"You can't think of everything," Phyllis said.

"Those are famous last words," Grimm said.

Lackey wished he understood. He had a little bad news he

had wanted to mention, not *bad* bad news, just *unusual* bad news, but the proper moment hadn't presented itself. Since escaping, there had been the honk during Grimm's call, then they got lost, and now there was this thing about the pregnant teller, which made absolutely no sense. Lackey had a hunch he was going west. It was just a feeling in his bones. He maintained his present course, through a section of apartments where stereo noise from the buildings was so loud, you could hardly hear the gunshots in the background. As he idled at one light next to a place called the Boynton Arms, Lackey was *sure* he heard gunshots. He tried to write the noise off to a backfire. It was possible somebody was driving a motorcycle up and down the halls of the Boynton Arms, so maybe it *was* a backfire. He didn't mention the alleged gun fire to Grimm or Phyllis. He sure knew why that dump was named the Boynton Arms. There were obviously boxes of arms in the basement. Lackey was pleased when the light changed (somebody had stolen the yellow), and they drove on west, hopefully.

Grimm fought off the first wave of panic, which came up to around his neck, and he thought quietly as Lackey swore at the stop lights.

"There's a nice apartment," Lackey said. "Hot and cold running whores."

The pregnant teller. Damn. Grimm concentrated, better late than never.

The key was, had the pregnant teller, the first hostage released, seen Grimm? She would know he wasn't a *real* hostage.

"I never saw her," Phyllis said. "Maybe she went home. It was real confused out there. She probably wandered off, like we did—called home or something."

Grimm hadn't seen her either, at the questioning or while he and Phyllis were strolling around behind the lines, looking concerned and innocent.

Had the pregnant teller seen Grimm, she would have said something like, "Who's he?"

Rotzinger would have said, "The last hostage."

The pregnant teller would have said, "No, sir. He wasn't in the bank. I never saw him in my life."

Rotzinger would have shot Grimm in the neck.

"We could have gotten around the problem by keeping the hostages separated," Phyllis said. "Some in the vault, some out, so nobody would have known who was who."

"I can't believe we didn't think of that," Grimm said.

"Yeah," Phyllis said. "But it's obvious she didn't see you. Hell. That could have hurt. But, the point is, there was a way around it. Your plan was so good, anything could have been handled."

"I could have been shot," Grimm said.

It *had* been a good idea to release a real hostage, for a nice blend of emotion.

Lackey whistled. "That was almost a bigger screw up than my horn honk. Look at it this way, Grimm. It's better to stare death in the face from here, wherever we are, instead of out there on the sidewalk in front of the bank."

Grimm wondered what else they had forgotten.

"Nothing," Phyllis said. "We could have probably gotten around it, even if the pregnant teller saw you but didn't recognize you as a hostage. We *could* have said the clown kept somebody in the main area, somebody fainted under a table or something."

"Yeah," Grimm guessed.

"No, I don't think so," Lackey said. "They'd have cut us all down. It was almost a *big* mistake. We were *real* lucky."

Grimm felt some satisfaction because the plan *could* have handled any recognition problem with the first hostage, but because there had been something they hadn't considered, he wondered if he might have accidentally left behind his birth certificate.

Nothing of note had been on the radio, just that the bank had been secured and that an old pizza and a clown suit had been placed under arrest. A city-wide search was in progress, which Phyllis said was standard police public relations malarky. They couldn't say it's hopeless, we're searching for between one and thirty-five people, names and descriptions unknown. Nothing was said about hostages unaccounted for.

"We've got all night," Grimm said. "Maybe all week. Still, I would feel more comfortable if we were doing what we planned, instead of this idiotic driving."

As Grimm and Phyllis were consoling each other for having dropped their guard, even though nobody landed a jab, Lackey decided it was the proper time to release the bit of information that had been bothering him. He explained that when he was questioned, he had not given the name they had decided on, John Johnson, which would take years to trace. In the confusion and nervousness of the moment, Lackey had said the first thing that came into his mind, which would be enough to scare hell out of any psychiatrist:

Sam Billabong.

At first, Grimm thought it was a joke, that Lackey was trying to make everybody feel good because of the narrow escape from the pregnant teller.

But Sam Billabong made too much sense; rather, it made such little sense, hell, it made *minus* sense—it had to be the truth.

The panic was again choking Grimm.

Lackey explained that he had an uncle in Philadelphia named that. Grimm had to hang his head out the window, for air.

"My uncle is not named Billabong," Lackey said sheepishly. "He's named Sam. I made Billabong up." Grimm almost lunged for Lackey's neck. It would have been a wise move. Lackey would have lost control of the wheel, and they might have lucked onto the right street.

Lackey said that only one cop had made a comment about

Billabong. Lackey had told the inquisitive cop that Billabong was Irish and Pakistanian.

"Listen, they bought it," Lackey said. "Nobody raised an eyebrow."

The names they gave the cops outside the bank were different than the names on their airplane tickets, but still, how anybody could be capable of offering a name that would attract suspicion? Well, it was beyond Grimm.

"They got the damn tranquilizer in me before they asked my name. For a few minutes, it was kind of like a dream."

They drove and watched for a pregnant woman. Lackey wrestled with a city street map, which was the size of a quilt. Several times, it blocked his vision, so Grimm took the map. Lackey had concluded that, "We are somewhere in this area."

"If they see us with a map," Grimm said, "they'll just pick the car up and take it away."

"Well, hell," Lackey said at a fork. He chose right because he was right-handed. "We're lost. We'll never get out. We'll drive around until we run out of gas, then they'll skin us. There's no hope of ever getting out of here."

"Keep it up," Grimm said. "I hear something."

"They'll hang us to a clothesline feet first," Lackey said.

"Good, good. More."

"They'll burn the car. There's no possible escape."

"I see it!" Phyllis said.

"He's done it again," Grimm said.

"I don't believe it," Lackey said. "It's the freeway!"

"Yeah," Grimm said. "Now all we need is an elevator."

There was no entrance ramp, but by God now that they had found the expressway, there was no way they were going to let it out of their sight again. Lackey drove under the freeway. "I'll make a U-turn."

Grimm said, "Good plan."

In some parts of town, what they were on would have been called a cul-de-sac, which is a fancy way to say "dead end" in the real estate ads. As they drove, and it got darker, Grimm expected to hear a steel door shut behind them. The turn-around area was about two blocks past the freeway, just far enough away so the passing motorists couldn't distinguish gun play from, say, something natural like a loud TV.

There were bars across from each other at the turn-around area. The one on the right was the Last Will and Testament Club, and the one opposite was Margo's Fun Bar.

"We just cannot get a break," Lackey said, slowing to a near stop. Several men sitting at the curb in front of the Last Will and Testament Club got to their feet. A large man stepped in front of the car. Lackey stopped.

"Maybe we could pretend we're from the Health Department," Lackey said.

"Don't stop the car," Grimm said.

"You want me to run over that guy or what?"

"It's impossible," Phyllis said. "He's so big, you'd need a ramp."

The man stepped out of the way and looked in the driver's window. Lackey smiled and slowly rolled the car forward. A sign in the window of the Last Will and Testament Bar said: FREE BEER TOMORROW. Margo countered with a sign advertising CHEAP KNUCKLE SANDWICHES. A fat woman was standing in the doorway of Margo's. Her arms looked like loaves of bread.

"Maybe we should stop and go in, pretend we wanted to come here," Lackey suggested as several men walked along his side of the car, "for a knuckle sandwich."

Grimm said, "Keep the damn car moving. If we stop, we're dead men."

"And women," Phyllis said.

Lackey started the pass between the joints, turning slowly back toward the freeway. Big people were on all sides of the car, kind of like an escort, but not quite: They were looking inside the car, the way a cat looks inside a goldfish bowl.

Grimm didn't understand the whys and wherefores of vio-

lence. There are people in this world who would just as soon
slug you in the mouth as look up a word in the dictionary,
and several of this type were wrinkling their heavy brows at
Grimm. He had stuffed the sack of money under Phyllis' seat.
Grimm had been in one fight in his life, and it lasted three
and a half weeks. A kid named Mike Skelton kept coming at
him. It started at a spelling bee. Mike Skelton was the high-
light of the event, missing the word "dictionary" by four letters. Some people find the dictionary an illogical source of information because if you can't spell a word, how in the hell
can you look it up? Mike couldn't spell well enough to get
the dictionary off the rack. He'd try to look up words in the
Almanac. When Mike Skelton mangled "dictionary," Grimm
about passed out laughing. Mike swore revenge. He was an
ugly kid with a bad complexion. The only reason he came to
school was because of the concentration of hubcaps. Mike ran
with other thugs whose idea of a good time was cracking
heads. Grimm won the first round. He was taller and faster
afoot. It was no contest. Skelton kept coming, though, day
after day, head down, fists clenched. Grimm never understood why pain and bleeding were no factor in Skelton's fight
plan. The reason was, the kid had nothing to lose. He was
ugly as hell to start with and didn't have a girlfriend. Grimm
could have smashed him with a bottle or run over him with a
car, but it wouldn't have mattered. People like that just keep
getting up. Mike Skelton finally got Grimm and jumped up
and down on him and dragged him and punched him and sat
on him and rolled him in dog manure.
 A fair fight is one where looks, IQs, and risks are equal. If
one man doesn't fear jail or deformity, then you have to make
him the heavy favorite over a man who has a flight to catch.
It's no wonder ignorant, ugly guys like to fight; it beats
watching ants.
 The thing is, you don't want to piss the Mike Skeltons of
this world off. All they use their heads for is opening doors.
Blood is relative; there's always more. You would think that a

man with a quick mind could hold his own against a pack of blockheads. What you have to watch out for, though, is it doesn't take much to piss these kind of guys off.

Grimm told Lackey to stop the car.

"Are you sure?"

"Turn the headlights out."

"Then what? Get out and lie on the sidewalk?"

"Shut up, damn it."

Lackey killed the motor and pushed off the lights. Grimm told Phyllis to open the door and lean up. She did. Grimm crawled out of the car, stretched, and said to the nearest large brow, "We're here about the money."

There were three of them near Grimm. The tallest stepped forward. He had an enormous beer belly. He leaned forward and said, "You what?" Grimm noticed that the bottom of the man's right ear was gone.

"We're here about the money."

The man nodded. "You must have took the wrong turn. There's no money here."

"Who is it, Arnie?" the fat woman in the door yelled.

"This creep," Arnie yelled back.

"We want the money *now*," Grimm said. "It's up to you. I have to say it. You have to hear it. We each do our part, you understand?"

"No," Arnie said.

"What's the creep want, Arnie?" the fat woman yelled.

"The money," Arnie said.

"What money?" Margo asked.

"What money?" Arnie asked Grimm.

"Oh boy," Grimm said to himself. He leaned down to Phyllis' window and said to Lackey, "They're playing games."

Lackey's eyes were wide and white. "Yeah."

"I'll play games on your fucking head," Arnie said. "Dumb games."

"You must not like this area," Grimm said, "because tomorrow, this beautiful neighborhood is going to be a weenie roast, you understand? It's nothing personal. I don't make the rules."

Arnie told Grimm to wait there, and he walked to where Margo was standing all over the porch of her bar. One of the two men remaining by the car while Arnie and Margo put their heads together said, "The last person that spoke to Arnie in that tone got droven over."

"Grimm," Lackey whispered, "you're not only going to get us killed, these people will go after all our relatives, cousins, and everything."

"You're doing great," Phyllis said. Her eyes were bright. "You might be on a hot streak. You might be the best I ever saw, Grimm. You get us out of here, you've got it made for life."

Arnie was back.

"Margo don't know you."

"I don't know Margo," Grimm said.

Arnie nodded. "She says maybe I should knock you out."

Grimm said nothing. Arnie said nothing. Lackey sneezed.

"Why is it you want the money?" Arnie asked.

"You owe it," Grimm said.

"What Margo and I want to know is why we don't know you?"

"I'm new."

"Boatright send you?"

"What do you think?"

"I think," Arnie said, "you're pissing me off."

"It's in the sixth," Margo shouted.

"You hear that?" Arnie said. "Let's go."

"Sure," Grimm said. He leaned down and said into the car, "It's in the sixth."

"Oh my God!" Lackey whispered. "Oh dear sweet God!"

"Oh honey," Phyllis whispered.

Grimm went with Arnie and the boys into Margo's. The radio was on loud over the bar. Margo led the way. She went behind the bar and adjusted a fluorescent light. It stopped flicking. One of the men at the bar squinted and said, "It stop lightning?" It was a typical neighborhood bar, cramped and dusty and stale, and Grimm stepped on things on the floor that crunched. He did *not* look.

"It is starting to come down pretty good," the radio said.

"Yes, Bob, it is," somebody else on the radio said.

"The rain is blowing in from right field in sheets," the radio said.

"Yes, Bob, you can't even see Blackman out there, poor guy."

Margo hit her fist on the counter. "Come on, lightning. Hit somebody." Margo paced behind the bar. Grimm stood with his hands in his pockets. "What do you know about the Toronto Blue Jays?" Margo asked Grimm.

"The usual."

"We know a *lot* about the Blue Jays, right, Arnie?"

"Too much."

"That's for damn sure. Too much. Not one of them bastards can come within thirty minutes of guessing the time of day. That's how screwed up the Blue Jays are. Know when the Blue Jays won five in a row?"

"Never," Grimm said.

"He knows the Blue Jays," Margo said.

"*We* know the Blue Jays," Arnie said.

"Everybody knows the fucking Blue Jays," Margo said. "Why do you think I'm so fat? Betting the Blue Jays." She ate a handful of peanuts. "There's ten calories in every one of them little bastards, you know that? Three, four hundred calories a handful."

One of the customers asked Margo what was going on.

"It's raining in the sixth."

"Somebody ought to shoot the Blue Jays," the guy said.

"That's some way to talk. You got ten on them."

"I do?"

"Boatright probably didn't tell you I called in a hundred on the Blue Jays, did he?" Margo said.

"No," Grimm said.

"Well, we did. You were probably out making the rounds, right? Taking money from poor people. Breaking up homes. Ruining lives, that right?"

"Yeah," Grimm said. "Sometimes I give money out, too."

"Sure," Margo said. "So maybe you think we're lying about the hundred on the Blue Jays."

"No."

"That's good," Margo said. "We called the mother in. Right before it started."

"What happened to Maurice?" Arnie asked.

"He's sick," Grimm said.

"Good," Arnie said. "He's a punk."

"The rain seems to be letting up a little," the radio said.

"Yes, Bob, but the field is awfully wet."

"Baseball kills more people than wars ever have," Margo said, bombing in some more peanuts.

"It's a good thing you said who you was," Arnie said. "There is a lot of turnover in this neighborhood."

"After a Blue Jay game everybody goes out in the street and fights," Margo said.

"Who's in the car?" Arnie asked.

"New people," Grimm said. "Trainees."

"It's a good thing Boatright himself don't come around here. He did once, in that fancy Mercedes." Arnie pointed over the bar to a trophy. It was a Mercedes hubcap.

"You got us one, twenty down before this fiasco," Margo said.

"On the nose," Grimm said.

"We lose this, that would make it two, twenty."

Grimm nodded.

"That would hurt," Margo said. "We're poor people. The rotten Blue Jays. I hate their guts."

"I wonder what Boatright would do if we didn't pay?" Arnie asked.

Grimm shrugged.

"Something bad," Margo said. "Those Italian sons-of-bitches would sell their own mother out for a submarine sandwich."

"What's your name?" Arnie asked.

"Joe," Grimm said.

"Is that Italian?"

"No," Grimm said.

"Jesus, Arnie," Margo said. "You talk like a Blue Jay."

Margo put a plate in front of Grimm. While they were sweating out the Blue Jay game, they might as well get fatter. "You in a hurry?"

"Nope," Grimm said. "Nothing ever changes. No need to rush."

"Maurice, that little simp, he was always in a hurry. It's a good thing Boatright sent somebody else. A couple of the guys, they were about ready to throw Maurice up on the roof. Eat up."

"We like you better," Arnie said.

"I like you, too," Grimm said.

They were sandwiches.

"It's coming down again."

"Yes, Bob. That is rain, all right."

The sandwiches reminded Grimm of his uncle Lou, so he took a bite and smiled. Uncle Lou was dead, but not because of any sandwich he ate.

"Good, right?"

"Right."

Uncle Lou used to fish in this little pond a half mile from where he lived. Grimm visited there a couple of times. It was cold. As Grimm remembered, spring was six days and summer was three weeks. It snowed, the rest of the time. Uncle Lou lived on Pond Street, and down at the other end was a beautiful little circle of water with a statue in the middle where the birds sat. In the winter, kids ice skated and played hockey on this pond. You could tell it was spring at Uncle

Lou's when the ice broke and everybody fell in the water. Uncle Lou fished in this pond. He fished there a lot, even when it was cold and frozen. Grimm remembered the old guy sitting in the middle of Pond Lake, with a hole cut in the ice, fishing away, as kids played hockey around him. When it was warm, Uncle Lou sometimes fished in the pond the whole weekend.

"Want another one?" Margo asked.

"Sure," Grimm said.

"Good, huh," Arnie said.

"Great."

One day, the fountain on Pond Lake broke. Water was supposed to shoot out of the statue's hand, but it started gushing up through the top of the guy's head, which looked ridiculous. So the city came out and had a look and decided there was a bad situation with the pipes. Pond Lake was drained. This took a long time. They brought out some trucks and sucked the water out. It was the social event of the summer. All the kids and most of the adults watched them drain Pond Lake, and a woman named Mrs. Lock watched closer than most. Her husband had wandered off three years previously, and quite a few people thought he was down there in the mud. Mrs. Lock was overjoyed when they didn't find her husband at the bottom of Pond Lake. They found a lot of crazy things—hockey sticks and pucks, lawn chairs, tires, shoes, beer cans, whiskey bottles, a bicycle, a stuffed squirrel, softballs, skates, loose change, the remains of a hamster with a brick tied around its neck, and some girlie magazines in a little chest. What they *didn't* find was fish. There was not one damn fish in Pond Lake. This hit Uncle Lou hard. Once they got the water out, Uncle Lou put on galoshes and walked through the mud, picking up all the lures he had lost, trying to catch that big one. That *any* one. He hadn't even caught the damn lawn chair. It was hard to guess how many hours Uncle Lou had spent there, fishing. It was in the thousands, that was for sure. Maybe twenty-five thousand. That's three years or so of nonstop fishing. Everybody thought Uncle Lou was catching something when nobody was looking, or at least getting a nibble! Had they known there were no fish in Pond Lake, somebody would surely have tossed one in for Uncle Lou to catch. Now, having a dream is a very healthy thing. But it's awful to have somebody call you on it in the light of day. Uncle Lou died six months after they drained Pond Lake, of humiliation. One rotten, damn fish. Had there been one in there, everything would have been just great. God was right when he said that what you don't know won't hurt you.

That's why Grimm ate the sandwich, no questions asked.

"What I don't understand," Margo said heavily, "is how you can play baseball in the rain. How you can see. How you can bat. There's not ten people in the stands. Still, they're playing baseball."

"Maybe the ump had a bet on the Tigers," Arnie said.

"One hundred horses-ass dollars," Margo said. "Riding on a ump. I hope he drowns."

"Listen," Arnie said. "The Tigers got a guy on second."

The radio said a Detroit player looped one to right and the Blue Jay right fielder slipped.

"This is criminal," Margo said. "This is the most . . . most . . . whoring baseball game I ever heard." Margo made a fist and held it a foot from the radio. The radio's tubes chattered.

The Blue Jays were a run ahead in the bottom of the sixth.

"Water is now standing in our booth," the radio said.

"Yes, Bob, it's ankle deep to a tall Tiger."

"I can't see the scoreboard."

"No, Bob, neither can I."

Single. First and third.

Grimm had a feeling that if the Tigers scored, Margo would put the radio between bread and eat it. Other customers had gathered at the bar to hear how the Blue Jays were pissing away another one.

The Blue Jay manager called time out and went to the mound.

"I don't think he's stalling," the radio said.

"No, Bob, I think he's just going to high ground."

"There's a small-craft warning in right field."

"And white caps around third, Bob."

"We still got a chance," Arnie said. "The tide is against the hitters."

The Blue Jays got a break when the next Tiger batter fouled one off behind the plate. The Blue Jay catcher circled under the ball and took in about a pint of water and passed out. The game was stopped. Those who had invested five and ten dollars on the Blue Jays celebrated. Margo went to the cash register and removed a twenty dollar bill and gave it to Grimm.

"This squares it," Margo said.

"Right," Grimm said.

"This one game could have turned the whole decade around," Arnie said.

Grimm smiled.

"Tell Boatright we'll have some more bets tonight," Margo said. "Tell him we're hot. You going to be the one coming around?"

Grimm nodded.

"We'll put the word out," Arnie said. "So nobody will borrow your car."

"Maybe you're our good luck charm," Margo said. Grimm was pleased when he wasn't asked to leave a lucky foot or lock of hair behind. Lackey and Phyllis seemed surprised when Grimm approached the car under his own power. They halfway expected him to come out in installments. Arnie gave a couple of guys the word, this car was sacred.

"Got any Tums?" Grimm asked Lackey.

"See you, Joe," Arnie said.

Grimm handed Phyllis the twenty. "My stomach is on fire.

I ate something in there that was purple. Come on, Lackey, get the hell out of here."

"You're something," Phyllis said. "You're really something."

Grimm told them the story of the Blue Jays and the rain, and as impressive as the twenty bucks was, Grimm came away with something much more valuable—directions to the freeway ramp.

"You could have sent us word it was going all right in there," Lackey said. "It was touch and go out here. I had to give a guy fifty."

The guy Lackey gave fifty to had been hitting his palms on the hood of the car, like he was playing the bongos.

"So?" Grimm asked. "Go two blocks and make a right."

"It scared me. The man looked insane. I thought he was going to smash the glass out for no reason."

"So you gave him fifty."

"Yeah," Lackey said.

"For no reason."

"I had a reason."

"He bought a raffle ticket," Phyllis said. She had crawled into the back seat with Grimm to show how much she appreciated living.

"Do you want to hear this story or do you two just want to kiss?" Lackey asked.

"Four blocks and another right."

"You're the world's best," Phyllis said. She was sitting in Grimm's lap.

"It's a chance on a car," Lackey said.

"What kind?" Grimm asked.

"The guy didn't know yet, but he thought a Cadillac. He said he was going down to a showroom to test drive the new model. I guess that's why you see so many poor people at the Cadillac places. Thieves, checking out the instrument panel."

Lackey's chance in the raffle was the nine of hearts. Grimm

looked at the playing card. A phone number was written in red ink on the back. On the number side, a woman whose breasts looked like weights on a grandfather clock—one breast hung to her waist and the other about came to her knees—was holding her panties in the air, like she was auctioning them off.

"Very provocative," Grimm said. "I don't want to hear it."

"You call this number Sunday and the guy tells you what kind of car it is and the lucky suit. The final drawing is Sunday night. There's a door prize."

"Here it comes," Grimm told Phyllis, who was nibbling on his neck.

"Good," she said.

"The door prize is a door," Grimm guessed.

"Of course," Lackey said. "But not an average door. This one is a garage door. The runner-up gets a key to a place where a lot of calculators are stored."

"Turn left at the whorehouse," Grimm said.

"Which one?" Lackey asked.

"The one at the corner," Grimm answered.

"I guess a lot of guys wouldn't have bought the raffle chance, but the way I saw it, it was the fifty or have a knife fight with that maniac."

"You choked," Phyllis said. "The guy wouldn't have done a thing."

"Please don't get nervous and start throwing money out the window," Grimm asked.

Lackey said he would show them. "I'll win the damn raffle." He also said he would hate to be in Grimm's shoes when those hard-working, God-loving citizens found out that they hadn't given twenty bucks to a bookie, rather they had given it to a sharpie, just passing through.

"When they find out," Grimm smiled, "there won't be anything in my shoes except socks. You don't wear shoes on the beach."

There was what had once been a laundromat to the right of the freeway entrance ramp. Lackey pulled in and parked. People were inside the remains of the laundromat stealing the paint off the wall. Everything else of value was long gone. Lackey dialed the number on the nine of hearts on a pay phone, outside.

When he got back behind the wheel he said, "It was a funeral home."

As they drove up the ramp, the radio said there was nothing new on the bank robbery, but four people dressed as clowns had robbed two liquor stores in the last hour.

Phyllis said they should get residuals when Paris came out with polka-dotted evening dresses and pointed hats, next season.

There was a lot of thinking to be done.

Ordinary things like changing lanes and parking the car and riding the elevator and changing clothes became major projects. Keeping from being sideswiped on the miserable freeway was every bit as important as the robbery had been. The consequences of an accident, even a scrape, would be terrifying.

See your license there, buddy. This lady says you cut in front of her. Everybody out of the car. What the hell is in that sack under the seat, money?

Lackey drove with both hands on the wheel and both eyes on the road, but hardly anything on the gas pedal. Phyllis was on Grimm's lap, whispering his praises or he would have noticed the scenery was not flying by. He *did* notice the spotlight.

When the police car pulled even with Lackey, Grimm said, "Don't panic."

"Oh, dear God," Lackey said. "He wants us to follow him. They're taking us in."

The officer riding shotgun was, it seemed, motioning for Lackey to follow him.

Grimm was getting awfully tired of thinking so hard, so often.

The car had been meticulously serviced at the station where Mountbatten worked. Mountbatten had given up his life of crime to work for a cousin, draining crank cases and widows. Mountbatten had never technically been a criminal because all the jobs he had participated in with Grimm had failed. Mountbatten waived the Widow Rate because Grimm was an old friend. It cost a widow $110 to get her car serviced, if nothing was wrong. Plugs, hell, that was $180, more if you wanted new ones.

The taillights worked. The headlights worked. The brake lights worked. Mountbatten said the car was in great shape, but what did he know? He was only a mechanic. A card mechanic, at that.

There was no logical reason why the nice policeman wanted Lackey to follow along.

Nine times out of ten, logic is the common behavioral denominator.

There *was* an explanation for this. Cops don't just ride the freeway, waving at people, in the middle lane, no less, with the trucks.

Grimm looked at the speedometer.

Lackey was driving twenty-eight.

"You're acting like a double agent, Lackey," Grimm said. "Speed this damn car up. You're breaking the law by driving too slow. The guy is motioning for you to get going a little, for God's sake."

"Okay, okay," Lackey said, gunning it.

"Not eighty. Go fifty-five."

The cop tipped his hat and drove away.

"One more screw up, and you're docked ten percent," Phyllis said.

"Oh, you think so?"

"I *know* so."

Phyllis and Lackey had never gotten along too well. Grimm

had repeatedly explained that there was a place in an important job for somebody with guts and loyalty, and Phyllis said, "You sound like you're describing a cocker spaniel."

Grimm also felt like he owed Lackey a little something because on a couple of the previous jobs there was some doubt as to whether there would be survivors. A man puts his bones on the line for you, that means something. And, if they got caught, it would be better to be in prison with somebody you know, like for a roommate.

Grimm had not counted on Lackey's inability to coexist with success. Lackey was a real trooper when the holsters were unsnapped. He was having a devil of a time with the downhill part of this job, though.

"I was just being careful," Lackey said of the slow freeway speed.

"I've about had it with him," Phyllis said.

"Why don't you drive the bandwagon?" Lackey said. "All you're good for is bitching, after the fact."

"Excuse me for not mentioning only a nitwit would break the law with almost a million dollars in the back seat. But believe me, I *thought* you'd do something like this."

"Please," Grimm said. "I beg you two. I don't want to go to an insane asylum. Money is meaningless there. People put it on toast. Please."

The folly on the other side of the tracks, not the railroad tracks, the *rat* tracks, had taken an hour, but they still had a good three hours to make the flight that would elevate them above all this mediocrity. The hour of slack time had been reserved for something like a flat tire. They would go by Grimm's apartment, change, put the money in a suitcase, and make the forty-five-minute drive to the airport with an hour and a half to spare, time for a leisurely cocktail.

On the radio, Rotzinger's most recent statement was "Get the goddamn mike out of my face."

The freeways are boring people to death in a number of ways. All the street signs look alike. You can't tell one city from another. Lackey dedicated himself to staying awake, and he drove cautiously to Grimm's apartment. There was an uncomfortable moment when a semi moved from the left lane diagonally through the right lane and partially onto the shoulder. The driver woke up when he heard the gravel, and righted his rig. Another time, about a mile before the turn-off, a car had pulled even with Lackey. Lackey looked to his left and saw that the driver's head was tilted forward. Lackey honked. The driver's head snapped back.

"Thanks a lot," the guy waved.

"The idiot was asleep," Lackey said, "going sixty."

The possibility that such an ungodly thing could reduce a masterpiece to confetti kept everybody on the edge of the seat, all the way back.

Life's little irritations seemed to be magnified 800,000 times.

Lackey felt like he had just crawled through a mine field when he stopped in front of Grimm's apartment.

"Let's go," Grimm said. "We have two hours and forty-two minutes."

"I don't want to be rude," Lackey said, "but just where am I supposed to park the car?"

Phyllis straightened up and scooted to the far side of the back seat.

"You sure are fickle," Grimm said.

"I think we should meet at the airport," she said.

"Park the car in a no parking place," Grimm said. "Park the car on the sidewalk. Park it anywhere. If we get a ticket, we won't pay it. They don't come to Europe to collect tickets."

"I don't like it," Phyllis said. "We should have thought of this. It's things like this that come back to haunt you."

"Somebody might steal it," Lackey said. "Or tow it away."

"We're only going to be inside fifteen minutes. Park the damn car by the damn fire hydrant."

"I don't know," Lackey said.

"I know," Grimm said. "Trust me."

It's hard not to trust a man who just robbed a bank and conned an entire neighborhood of heathens.

Phyllis said this particular lack of preparation was unforgivable. She had taken it for granted Grimm would have considered a place to park while they changed clothes and containers.

"You two just bitched away four minutes," Grimm said.

They hurried inside, through the lobby of Grimm's medium-rise, to the elevator. Grimm hit the button and the doors opened. They stepped inside.

Grimm pushed six.

They looked at each other.

As the elevator doors slowly closed, Lackey stuck his foot out and hit the rubber bar that caused the doors to open again.

"Okay," Grimm said. "This way."

They went to the stairs and walked up six flights. Elevators do get stuck, you know.

"That's much, much better," Phyllis said to Lackey.

She said that as long as they anticipated every potential problem area and planned ahead, nothing could stop them. Control was the key.

"All we have to do is manipulate our destiny for a few little hours," she said.

Grimm put the key in his lock and was mildly surprised when the door didn't open from the hinge. When Grimm pushed the knob, the door fell into the apartment, top-first.

"Look who's here," Mountbatten said. "Me."

Lackey and Phyllis looked at Grimm, for the next move. Mountbatten was standing in Grimm's apartment, hands on his hips. Whatever Grimm did, Lackey and Phyllis would back him. They looked at him like a receiver looks at a quarterback after the play is called. I'll cut out instead of in; that kind of silent communication.

These people were pros. They had been through enough, they could almost read each other's thoughts.

They could charge Mountbatten. That was one possibility. They all seemed to be on the same wavelength, there. Charge and swing. Several possibilities made this strategy implausible. They would bounce off Mountbatten like he was a bumper. Say they did manage to land about fifteen sucker punches to Mountbatten's skull, that would be the minimum required, then what?

Whatever. Grimm was the man of the hour. The direction he took would be amply fortified by his associates.

"Mountbatten," Grimm said. "You old horse's ass."

"You must be the robber," Mountbatten said, "and this must be the money."

Grimm held the sack up and smiled.

He had obviously chosen a more subtle way out of this mess, which was fine with Phyllis and finer with Lackey. Violence never solved anything. When Grimm got through with Mountbatten, the big fellow would be standing there in his undershorts.

"It's the money, all right," Grimm said. He handed it to Mountbatten, who looked into the sack and smiled.

"Hit him," Phyllis said.

"Lie to him," Lackey said.

"I knew it was you from the second I saw it on television," Mountbatten said. "It had your signature."

"In invisible ink," Grimm said.

"Yeah," Mountbatten said. "That's very funny. Some bums leave a little something behind, you know? I knew a guy that every time he pulled a job, he left a silver dollar behind. Somebody leaves *nothing* behind, it's you."

Phyllis' lovely face turned into a hideous snarl.

"What I couldn't believe," Mountbatten said, shaking his enormous head, "was why you didn't call."

Grimm said he knew. It was rude.

"Rude? It was worse than rude. It was cheap."

Lackey put his hand on his chest and said he had pains. Mountbatten volunteered to put Lackey out of his misery.

They sat down at the dining-room table. Mountbatten put the sack of money in his lap. Grimm looked at his watch. Lackey looked out the window. Phyllis looked at her fingernails.

Grimm tried to think of something, but he was simply too tired. He deserved better. He had just brought off the greatest robbery of all time, but he couldn't even get to the damn airport. He looked at his watch again. In two hours and some minutes, the jet would leave. It was unreal. It was like he had just scored a touchdown, and when he spiked the football to the ground, it bounced up and hit him in the balls. You can't give the MVP award to anybody like that.

"We didn't need you, that's all," Grimm said.

"You were the first on our list," Lackey said.

"Oh really?" Mountbatten said.

Grimm said, "Not *you*. We didn't need *anybody*. That's all."

Lackey said it was nothing personal.

"Oh," Mountbatten said, "in that case, I'll give you the money back."

He didn't.

Lackey frowned.

Grimm looked at his watch.

The first thing was the car, Mountbatten said. A man brings in a car that has not been serviced in six years, this means he is planning a very important trip. He doesn't care about the motor, but he *does* care about the little lights, like he doesn't want to be stopped for something dumb. This means he is planning a short trip, like to the airport.

"Then you give thirty-days notice on this place, well, it added up."

Giving notice, snipping off the loose ends, had been Phyllis' idea.

"I'm the only one who didn't do a thing wrong," Lackey said.

"I'm no criminal," Mountbatten said, "though God knows I've tried, right Grimm?"

They talked about the old jobs, and Mountbatten concluded that whereby a man could be guilty by association, he therefore was entitled to be rich by association. Mountbatten wanted some tokens of appreciation.

"This is not blackmail," he said. "Think of it as flight insurance."

"The deal was," Grimm said, "you were too tall for this one, Mountbatten. Somebody six feet, eight is easier to find than somebody average."

"I could have driven."

"I did all right," Lackey said.

Grimm explained why they were an hour and a half late.

"To tell you the truth, I expected you back here sooner."

"I hear a siren," Lackey said.

"Only a killing or something," Mountbatten said, nodding at the window.

"So," Grimm said.

"So," Mountbatten said.

"The siren is coming closer."

"What do you think?" Grimm asked Mountbatten.

"He's right," Phyllis said. "The siren *is* coming closer."

"I was thinking thirty," Mountbatten said. Mountbatten said that the service station where he had been working was closed this afternoon when somebody from the Better Business Bureau posing as a woman named Romero came in for a lube job. Mountbatten gave her the Puerto Rican Rate, $320 including new gaskets, and damned if the woman didn't have this signed statement from *real* mechanics, saying the car was in perfect shape. Mountbatten needed a little more than walking around money. He needed trotting around money.

"Thirty is a lot," Grimm said.

"They say you got better than eight hundred big ones. You about got me killed six times, before. That's five grand, each."

Grimm nodded.

"How much time you got?"

"Couple of hours. Plus."

Mountbatten nodded. "You can make it."

"The siren is very close," Lackey said.

"It really is," Phyllis said.

"Doesn't sound like a police siren," Mountbatten said.

"I hope to God it's not," Lackey said. He got up and went to the window.

"So take the thirty," Grimm said weakly.

"Here it comes," Lackey said, sounding like a race announcer. Phyllis had joined him at the window. Lackey turned and said, "It's a fire engine."

"I told you," Mountbatten said. He was stacking and counting money on the table.

"Relax," Grimm told Lackey.

"That was a close one," Lackey said.

"There's smoke from the building across the way," Phyllis said. "Black smoke."

Grimm said he hoped the whole neighborhood burned to the ground. He joined Lackey and Phyllis at the window, and they watched the fire truck stop in the street. Men jumped off the truck and unwound a hose. One of the firemen talked with the doorman of Grimm's apartment. The doorman pointed up, in the direction of Grimm's apartment.

"Some fool parked a car by the hydrant," Mountbatten said. "I would hate to be in his handcuffs." Mountbatten returned to the table to count his share.

One of the firemen tried the door on Grimm's car. It was, naturally, locked. Another fireman jumped from the truck, carrying an ax. He smashed the driver's window, reached inside and opened the door. The car could not be put in neutral and rolled away from the fire hydrant without the key. The fireman got out and kicked the fender on Grimm's car.

"They'll be coming," Lackey said.

"Yes," Grimm said. "They will."

"That *your* car?" Mountbatten asked. He stuffed the money inside his shirt, went to the door and said, "Send me a postcard."

The fireman with the ax opened the hood of Grimm's car. The hose had been attached to the hydrant. They ran the hose over Grimm's car. The fireman with the ax leaned into Grimm's motor while another fireman worked from underneath. Presently, they had made the adjustments that caused the car to roll, even without putting it in neutral. The car was rolled down the street and it came to rest halfway up on the sidewalk.

Bolts and things fell from underneath the car.

"Do they have the right to do that?" Lackey asked. "I have never understood it. I left them plenty of room to hook the hose up."

"They need the room to sign autographs," Grimm said.

"Being arrested by a fireman," Phyllis said, shaking her lovely head. "I want my share. I want you to count it out right there on the table and give it to me. I'll slug it out on the street with the dope addicts before I'll go through any more of this."

Grimm looked at his watch and was pleased it was still there. Nobody had slipped it off his wrist, the last five minutes. This was a good sign.

"What bothers me is I don't *feel* rich," Lackey said. "I feel sick. Maybe I've got the flu. My bones ache. I'm dizzy."

"Here's where we stand," Phyllis said. The firemen had charged the building across the way. "You two are giving our money away as fast as possible, fifty dollars here, thirty thousand there. We have no car. The lummox you gave the thirty thousand to for no reason at all is out telling his friends. The pregnant teller may or may not have seen you without the clown suit and has or has not given an accurate description to the police artists. If she has, they'll be waiting for you at the airport, with machine guns."

"We could take a bus to California," Lackey said. "And catch a plane there."

"And finally," Phyllis said, nodding at Lackey, "he's having a nervous breakdown."

"I am not. It's only a touch of the flu."

Grimm said that there was still plenty of time to make the flight, two hours and many minutes, and that instead of leaving the car in a parking lot at the airport as planned, they would leave it over there on the sidewalk in pieces, and take a cab.

Maybe they were trying too hard.

"Thousands of people take cabs to the airport every day. Nothing happens. Let's just calmly sit down and think of anything that could go wrong."

"A wreck," Lackey said. "We could be in a wreck and be killed."

"We're supposed to think about *bad* things," Phyllis said.

There was a knock on the door.

Phyllis said it was probably Mountbatten, giving the jinxed money back so he wouldn't fall down any more stairs.

Lackey said maybe it was the census department.

"That's the spirit," Grimm said. He opened the door, and leaned it against the wall. It was a uniformed cop and two regular people.

"You the owner of a brown 1975 Ford two-door?" the cop asked.

"We want to see a lawyer," Lackey said.

"Yes," Grimm said.

"What?" the cop asked.

"We're the Edisons," the woman said.

"What's this door doing like this?" Mr. Edison asked. "Get the lease, honey. The door is supposed to be *on*. You think I am going to move into a place where there is no door?

Get the manager. We wouldn't last fifteen minutes in this city with no door."

"Now I can't even leave," Phyllis said wistfully.

"Who are you again?" the cop asked.

"The Edisons," the woman said.

"Are you the owner of a brown 1975 Ford two-door?"

"Hell, no, we're not," Mr. Edison said. "This is our apartment."

The cop frowned.

Lackey said, "Anybody want some root beer?"

"I want to know what in the hell is wrong with this door," Mr. Edison said. "I come up here to *my* apartment, and the door is off. I'm not paying $470 for an apartment with no door."

"I was only paying $420," Grimm said.

"Get the goddamn manager," Edison said.

"What are you people doing in our apartment?" Mrs. Edison asked. "It's after midnight. The manager said we could leave some luggage."

"This isn't our apartment," Mr. Edison said. "This is an apartment without a door. You want to leave bags where they can just come in and go through them any time they want?"

"I think I have the flu," Lackey said.

"I want this goddamn apartment fumigated," Edison said. "And I want the door fixed." He told his wife not to step into the apartment. That might constitute possession.

"Why don't you finish packing, dear," Grimm told Phyllis.

"You'll pay for this." She took the sack of money and went into the bedroom.

"We have a flight to catch," Lackey said. "In two hours. We'll never make it. We'll have to sleep in the airport."

"What kind of people *are* these?" Mrs. Edison asked.

As Phyllis was packing, stuffing the money in a suitcase and some clothes in a smaller bag, and as Lackey was pacing the floor and mumbling about the kinds of crazy people who preyed on tourists stranded in the airport, the cop and the apartment manager wrote Grimm tickets.

The cop said parking by a fire hydrant was potentially one of the most despicable crimes on the books. Babies could be inside some building frying while the firemen were trying to hook up the hose.

"I have bad eyes," Grimm said.

The fine was $250, plus a tow fee, and the city was not responsible for damages incurred while clearing the vehicle from the hydrant area.

"It is obstructing justice," the cop said. "I would not want the consequences hanging over my bed."

"What happened over there?" Grimm asked.

"Somebody burned a few pork chops."

"My car was destroyed because of a pork chop?"

"A *few* pork chops. It could have been a little girl burning up on that balcony, friend. You ought to feel damn lucky."

"Ha," Lackey said.

The manager charged Grimm for the door. Mountbatten had ripped the hinges from the woodwork, so you didn't just screw the thing back on. Oh, no. You hired a dozen carpenters to come in and take measurements, and six screwers to come in and secure the hinge to the frame as the carpenters took coffee breaks. Putting a door back on is a major project here in the bowels of the city. You see carpenter shops on the corner, the manager asked. No way. They live *way* out. Mileage. Overtime. Mental anguish. The whole damn bit. You see a store that sells hinges around here?

The door was $145.

A check?

At this time of night?

From a move-out tenant?

Who is kidding whom around here?

Grimm went to the bedroom where Phyllis was swearing and stuffing clothes in a suitcase, and he got $145. He wrinkled the money and rubbed dirt on the bills.

"The money in the suitcase?"

"Yeah," Phyllis said. "We need to talk about that. I have a real good question about the money in the suitcase. A beauty. You'll love it."

"Save it," Grimm whispered.

"I can't believe I ever sat on your lap."

"That's not all you did. Remember the night I told you about the plan? Remember that?"

"Oh God. I can't believe it. You were a man then."

"And just what am I now? It's quietening down out there."

"You're average."

"What about the suitcase?"

"The money is in it, right?" Phyllis asked.

"Right," Grimm said. "I hope. The brown one."

"It is. Let's pretend we get to the airport. They X-ray the suitcase and see nothing but money inside. Then what?"

"They arrest us," Grimm said.

"That's why I am *not* going to the airport."

"Hell," Grimm said.

"I am going somewhere else."

"I'll handle it," Grimm said.

"You're not handling *me*," Phyllis said. "Ever again. I'm repulsed by this whole thing. I thought you were a man who called his own shots. This is like a firing squad."

Grimm said maybe they could wrap the money in something.

"The X ray goes *through* anything."

"I know," Grimm said. "We could check the bag full of money through." He smiled pitifully.

"*That* makes more sense than carrying a suitcase full of money to an X-ray machine."

"There's a way," Grimm said.

"Right. Sure. You and that psychopath out there can have at it. Me, I'm going to my grandmother's house in Nebraska."

Will it never end? Grimm wondered, carrying the door

money to the manager, who was asking Lackey what in the world happened to the door, anyway.

"One of the neighbors stopped by to borrow the *TV Guide*," Lackey said.

"What kind of place *is* this?" Edison asked.

"A good place," the manager said. He gave Grimm what was left of the deposit he made when he leased the apartment. It came to $7.75.

"The deposit was a hundred dollars," Grimm said.

"That's the way it goes," the manager said.

"What's new with the robbery?" Lackey asked.

"Which robbery?" the cop asked.

"The bank robbery."

"Nothing is new."

"Oh," Lackey said.

"Whoever did it is long gone," the cop said. "They're on a plane somewhere, drinking wine, laughing it up. There's one thing you have to remember."

"What?" Lackey asked.

"It's no skin off my butt," the cop said. "Something like that keeps everybody on his toes. I'd hate to be the next joker that tried a bank. He gets blasted in two minutes."

"I wonder how they did it?" Lackey asked.

"Beats me," the cop said. "I hear the chief thinks the guy climbed down through the sewers. They're tearing up the floor. If you see anybody that stinks, let me know."

"I bet they get caught and go to prison for life."

"Who knows?" the cop said. "I'd take their chances. The guy that did it is a genius." He turned to leave. "Listen, you dummy," he said to Grimm, "don't be parking by any more hydrants."

"With what?" Grimm asked.

"You got a point there. Get a bike."

"We'll be out in a second," Grimm said to the Edisons. He picked the phone up to call a cab.

"Disconnected?" Phyllis asked.

Grimm nodded and replaced the receiver.

"The bag limit on cockroaches is ten a day," Lackey told the Edisons. He coughed and patted his chest.

"What kind of flu do you have?" Mrs. Edison asked.

"They weren't sure," Lackey said.

"I'm not going in there," Edison told his wife.

They beat it.

They rode the elevator down and walked through the lobby and into the street. They turned left, away from the fire truck and the remains of Grimm's car.

"Have you got the tickets?" Grimm asked Phyllis.

"Two months ago I was dating a guy who played for the Giants. He was on the second team. He made seventy-five grand a year."

"Do you mind," Grimm said.

"Was he white?" Lackey asked.

"Plus endorsements. Seventy-five plus endorsements."

"That's a lot of hot dogs," Lackey said.

"We could have been very happy. We might have even been delirious. And then *he* calls with this bank thing."

Lackey said, "Grimm will get me to the airport, won't you, Grimm?"

"I made a big mistake leaving Mickey."

"Love can't buy you money," Lackey said. "We're rich. We're going to Europe and play on the beach. This is the beginning of a whole new life."

They stopped at the corner and waved at a cab.

They were in the heart of the city. They had more than two hours to reach the appendix.

Ten minutes to catch a cab.

Forty-five minutes to the airport.

Fifteen minutes to the gate.

"We can make it, easy," Grimm said. "We take the money

through the X ray the same way we took it out of the bank. On our bodies. We carry the one suitcase and put the money back in a rest room on the other side of the X-ray machine."

"That's perfect," Lackey said. "Cab!"

"We send an empty suitcase through the X ray?" Phyllis asked. "Are you kidding? If they see an empty suitcase, they'll frisk us."

"I couldn't stand to be frisked, carrying all that money," Lackey said. "Cab! Please. We need a cab here."

"Then we put *papers* in the suitcase, okay? The X-ray machine can't read. Papers are papers. They could be important papers."

"That's five minutes for the rest room," Phyllis said.

"We've still got almost an hour," Grimm said.

"*We need a fucking cab,*" Lackey screamed from the curb. "*One lousy rotten fucking taxi cab.*"

One pulled to the curb.

Lackey opened the passenger's door and said, "Thanks."

Grimm looked at his watch and said that only took four minutes—they had six minutes extra time in the airport.

"Hit it," Lackey told the driver.

The taxi pulled from the curb.

"The airport," Grimm said.

"What do you think about that bank robbery?" Lackey asked. "Really something, wasn't it?"

Grimm kicked Lackey's seat.

Lackey winked.

The driver smiled and handed Lackey a map.

"Thanks," Lackey said.

"War do," the driver said.

"What?" Lackey asked.

"What?" Grimm asked from the back seat. "What did he say? I want to know what he said, right now."

"I want to see your goddamn driver's license," Lackey said.

The cab driver smiled and said, "War do?" and he motioned at the map.

"He's asking where to," Phyllis said, "I'm afraid."

"*The fucking airport,*" Lackey yelled. He was pale. "*Stop this fucking cab.*"

"Ah," the driver said, smiling. "Poured."

"Air *port,*" Lackey said. His head was shaking. He had the map rolled into a weapon.

"There are fifty airports in this area," Grimm said. "He wants you to point to the one we want on the map."

"Here," Lackey said, opening the map against the front window. "Here."

"Ah. Jersey poured."

"No," Lackey said. "Kennedy, for Christ's sake. Kennedy Poured."

"Easy, Lackey," Grimm said. "I think he's foreign."

"I miss Mickey so much," Phyllis said. "I think it's time I told you about what Mickey and I did. He loved my legs, you see. He thought I had the most beautiful legs in the world."

"I beg you," Grimm said.

Lackey had the map spread out in his lap and he was pointing at Kennedy and explaining to the driver how they had two hours to make a very important flight. He told the driver that if they weren't at Kennedy in forty-five minutes, something awful would happen to the cab, something bright and hot.

The cab driver's eyes were wide.

"Can you hear me?" Lackey asked.

"Gorn dry poured," the cab driver said.

"You don't understand a word I'm saying, do you?"

"Mickey liked to rub my legs," Phyllis said to Grimm, who was looking out the window.

The cab driver skimmed through a red light.

"You don't even understand colors, do you?" Lackey said. "You don't know red from hell."

"Biga poured," the cab driver said, imitating an airplane with his hand.

"That does it," Lackey said.

Charley English wasn't from Norway, he was from Chicago, he didn't even know where Norway was on the map, except north, but one of his friends, Sandersen, was from Norway and you should have heard some of the stories Sandersen told about his fares. Sandersen said it was amazing what some people in a hurry would do if they thought they were in a taxi with a man who didn't grasp the language. It was a real funny premise. A man needs a diversion on a dull night. One of the dispatchers, Nettie, talked a little dirty after her "coffee" break, but that was about it. Driving a cab can be unbelievably boring.

Charley English would have something special to tell the boys and girls when he checked it in tonight. He had been working with Sandersen with the accent, and by golly, it looked like the accent was just about perfect.

"The secret," Sandersen said, "is you have to look dumb, too. When somebody says airport, you have to look like you just got off the boat."

Sandersen had had a woman faint on him when he started those hand signals about the planes.

Sandersen would have to go some to top this.

Charley English's front-seat fare got out of the cab while it was still moving. The guy started shaking. He looked like a basket case from the beginning, and he tried to get out of the car, running, but as anybody who has seen a dog jump out of the back of a moving pick-up knows, it can't be done. The front-seat fare made a game try of it. He opened the door, Charley English thought to throw up or something, but the guy started moving his feet like he was riding a bicycle, and then he jumped. You learned about things like this in math if you cared, about what happens to things leaving various points going various speeds. The front-seat fare hit the pavement full stride. The cab was going maybe thirty, was all. The guy took about four steps, lunges, but his feet couldn't keep up with his head, because his head was going thirty miles per hour, see, and you don't have to be a scholar to guess what happens when one part of your body is going thirty and another part is going five.

You fall. Fast.

The front-seat fare veered from the street up onto the sidewalk and crashed into a newspaper stand.

Grimm realized that Charley English was not from Scandinavia when he heard the man say, "Holy Enchilada."

Grimm had been staring out the window wishing Phyllis would shut up about the football player and her legs when he saw the cab pass Lackey. Lackey had his hands out in front of him for support. Grimm looked out the back window and saw Lackey smash into the newspaper rack.

"Stop," Grimm said.

"Go," Phyllis said.

Charley English hit the brakes and put the cab in reverse and screeched back to where Lackey was stretched out on the sidewalk.

"Stop the meter," Phyllis said.

"Listen to me," Charley English said, "I was just trying to break the monotony. This is the loneliest job in the world."

"Consider yourself sued," Grimm said, getting out of the cab.

Phyllis said, "I'll tip you what he sues you."

A crowd had gathered around Lackey.

"Are you all right?" Grimm leaned over and asked.

"His neck is broken," somebody said.

"His back is broken."

"It looks to me like he has a punctured lung."

"You should try driving a cab all night," Charley English said. "You get punchy."

One of the ringside spectators volunteered to call an ambulance.

The sighting of blood was a big deal. It was like the people standing around Lackey had been on a raft all week. They said "Blood" like they might have said "Land," very enthusiastically.

Grimm didn't like this crowd. He wanted to take a broom to them. Seeing somebody bleed made them feel a lot better about their rotten day, he guessed.

"There's blood on his temple!"

"That's a bad place to bleed from."

"You bleed there, you're talking about the brain."

"The poor slob."

"The poor dog."

"He don't need an ambulance, he needs a basket."

"Concussion."

"Concussion, hell. It's paralysis."

Grimm told a couple of front-row people that Lackey was an escaping child molester, and that the police would be here momentarily for statements.

Several people wandered off.

"He's all right," Phyllis said. "Let's go."

"Three quarters of the fares you get after midnight never talk," Charley English said. "They just sit there. How is a man supposed to get a little conversation? I was only going to let it go on a few blocks. I never saw anything like that guy."

Lackey opened his eyes, as if on cue.

Somebody said, "The blood stopped," like they would have said from the raft, "That wasn't land, it was a mirage."

"Lackey," Grimm said.

"What happened?"

"You got out of the cab," Grimm said.

"Oh."

"While it was still moving."

"Oh."

"You flipped out," Charley English said.

"Oh."

Lackey squinted up at Charley English. "Is that who I think it is?"

"I'm lonely," Charley English said.

"Why is he talking like that?" Lackey asked.

"No hard feelings," Charley English said.

"He was playing games," Grimm said.

"He was not foreign?"

"I was born in Chicago," Charley English said.

"I'm going to kill you," Lackey said.

Grimm and Phyllis helped Lackey to his feet. Lackey said there was no feeling in his lower back. He took several steps without collapsing.

"I'll let you know if there's internal bleeding," he told the disappointed people on the curb.

Charley English was badly shaken. He said he was going off duty. He drove away before anybody could get any information for an insurance claim. Grimm and Phyllis stood on the curb. Lackey leaned against a stop light and said he couldn't make a fist with either hand.

Grimm sold real estate, once. He sold it for his uncle's cousin or his cousin's uncle, he never got it straight. This was many years ago, before it occurred to Grimm that there had to be a better way to make a living than working for idiots. Grimm worked for his uncle's cousin or cousin's uncle two years without selling as much as a lousy shack. It takes a special kind of hambone to sell things. Grimm didn't have that spark, the ability to lie. The best salesmen are the best liars. Grimm was so bad, they sent him to a positive-thinkers rally, where they gave him kits and recordings and books that contained the basic message: A person has to have goals. Thinking positively is a new religion. It is taught by ex-preachers. Money is the God. One fellow grabbed Grimm by the collar and shouted into his face "You can do it!"

"Do what?" Grimm asked.

"It," the positive thinker said. His name was Dr. Rountree. He had a degree in arm waving. He told cornball jokes and promised everybody they could do it if they had goals, and then he collected fifty dollars a head. People like this used to sell snake oil. Now they sell sugar-coated crap. Somebody ought to take it to the lab and have it analyzed, Grimm decided.

After Dr. Rountree grabbed Grimm by the shirt and told him he could do it, he could make money, he could be a community leader and help stamp out smut, he could lose weight, he could read faster, sell more and make love longer if only he had goals, Grimm said he had seen the light. He would no longer drift through life like a piece of dead wood. He would take charge, be firm, and march toward his goals. He told the fake his first goal was getting his fifty dollars back from this sideshow.

They threw Grimm out of the meeting.

But still, if somebody like Sinatra sings about an ant moving a plant, there might be something to it. They played that record as background music during collection. Those at the positive thinking rally—Grimm hung around by the door and listened through a crack, free—seemed united by their enthusiasm.

Grimm grabbed Lackey by his shirt and said, "We've got to keep our spirits up. We can do it."

"I can't even get amnesia," Lackey said.

"All we needed was a cripple," Phyllis said.

"Give me my share and a gun," Lackey said. "And prop me up against that grocery store. I'll hold them off while you make a run for it."

"We can do it," Grimm said to Phyllis.

"Who are you kidding?"

"Not me," Lackey said. "We can't do anything. The last time I felt like this, I failed English."

"I miss Mickey," Phyllis said.

"I miss anybody," Lackey said.

Grimm looked up the street for another cab. Charley English had probably put the word out about this group's tendencies to jump from a moving taxi, so neither of the two cabs that went past considered slowing down.

"How much time do we have?" Lackey asked.
"God only knows," Grimm answered.

Rotzinger got his second wind, and decided not to commit suicide just yet.

He had moved the command post from the bank to police headquarters, so he would at least have the opportunity of firing those who jeered at him.

They got a Valium in him after he slugged the reporter in the stomach, and it had calmed him immediately. Instead of killing himself with a gun, he began thinking of poison and drowning. As the Valium sped through his veins, Rotzinger regained control and dictated a memo to the radio station, apologizing for punching the reporter, but concluding the note, "He stepped over the area roped off for the press and probably deserved everything he got."

Rotzinger had left his Valium at home. In the future, he would tape some to his calf.

It had been some kind of putrid night, all right, having a bank robbed right there in front of you. It was worse than putrid; it was devastating. The mayor was calling every five minutes for an update. After they dug the bank floor up, at the city's expense, the mayor drew his fist back and said that if progress wasn't made in a very short time, a complete reevaluation of the department was imminent.

In the three years Rotzinger had been police chief, the city had been relatively safe, except for the occasional murder, rape, stabbing, mugging, hijacking, gang fight, assault, robbery, and theft of everything that is not cemented down. People are of the mistaken opinion that crime can be prevented. As Rotzinger has said to the civic groups, "If you're worried about crime prevention, talk to the parents, not me." Cops merely enforce the law.

Getting out-fought is one thing. Getting out-thought is another. When a criminal robs a grocery and shoots a cop in the leg and gets away, you don't hear, "What's wrong with our police department?"

It's different when somebody is surrounded by two hundred police officers. That's the kind of crime you *can* prevent.

"You fool," the governor told Rotzinger. "We're the laughing stock of the entire country."

Sadly, Rotzinger and his men *were* used to crimes where the perpetrator entered the scene with guns drawn, firing from the hip, crimes that were ill-conceived and left a trail of panic a block wide.

This was the first time Rotzinger and his staff had been confronted by somebody who had thought farther than fifteen minutes or feet ahead.

You *had* to admire the clown. Then you had to track him down like a mad dog and squash him.

"The guy is a genius, pure and simple," Wax said. Wax was Rotzinger's assistant. "He vanishes right under our noses with the cash. I've never seen anything like it."

"Wax?"

"Sir."

"It would be nice if we could temper our enthusiasm for this criminal, or else I could get you a goddamn cheerleader's uniform."

It was almost more than a fifty-eight-year-old heart could stand.

They had played it by the book. They had surrounded the bank. They had cooperated with the robber, to insure the safety of the hostages. When there was no contact, they had moved in swiftly and surely to capture an empty bank.

"Get me another Valium, Wax."

"Yes, sir."

They tore the place apart, looking for the clown. Officers were still there, in case the guy came up out of a drain. If Rotzinger didn't come up with a lead, there was no way of predicting the consequences.

There was an urgent call on line two. Rotzinger asked his secretary who it was. It was a reporter, who was ignored.

"Where are the hostages?" Rotzinger asked Wax.

"Downstairs."

"Get the ones he put in the vault and put them in the conference room."

"Yes, sir."

"Where's Gilbert?"

"Just outside."

"Get him in here."

"Yes, sir."

Gilbert, the artist, said that if it was possible, his kid wanted the robber's autograph.

"Better yet, I'll give you his hand," Rotzinger said.

Gilbert doodled.

It was to be his most meaningful work of the night.

Wax called from downstairs to report that because of the confusion and the darkness of the bank several of the witnesses had evidently wandered off, but they had phone numbers and addresses, and a car was being dispatched to bring in the hostage at this very moment.

"Confusion?" Rotzinger said.

"And darkness," Wax said.

"Hostage? Singular. Where are the others?"

"We talked with Teresa Singleton, the pregnant teller."

"And?"

"After giving her statement, she walked home."

Rotzinger raked material off his desk with his right arm. A lamp smashed against the floor.

"She says she is too tired to come in," Wax said.

"Get her here. Shoot the door and drag her if you have to. Take a gynecologist."

"Yes, sir."

"Were the other hostages brought to police headquarters?

Or were they given lollipops and kicked in the ass and told to run along?"

"We looked up Sam Billabong."

"And?" Rotzinger put his hand on the handle of his top drawer.

"There is no listing. The address he gave is a drug store."

Rotzinger yanked the drawer from his desk. Pills, pencils, and magazines bounced off the wall.

"The other female hostage, Mary Johnson?" Wax said.

"There are four thousand Mary Johnsons," Rotzinger guessed.

"Eighty-six. I have DeCamp and Mobra on it. They've gone through about twenty. Nothing so far."

"Who took the statements?"

"Stark took the statements from the released hostages. Skinner talked to the people in the vault."

"Get Stark up here."

"Yes, sir."

"Get the pregnant teller up here."

"Yes, sir."

Rotzinger gave his pistol to Gilbert when Stark knocked on the door.

Rotzinger told Stark to sit down.

There was a stapler in the chair. Stark handed it to Rotzinger, who threw it across the room. Stark was a family man and didn't want to be fired. He had a feeling he had done something very bad.

Wax leaned in the room and told Rotzinger that all of the hostages who had been locked in the vault were intact, in the conference room.

"Sit down, Wax," Rotzinger said.

"What am I supposed to do with this gun?" artist Gilbert wondered.

"Draw it," Rotzinger said. "Just don't give it to me until Stark leaves."

Stark flinched.

It is impossible for a police chief to know all that many of his men. Rotzinger was doing good to know the captains of the various precincts. As the robbery had occurred in Captain Block's area, he had assigned the officers to secure the area and interrogate the hostages and witnesses. Block was still at the bank, looking under rugs for the robber.

Block had only been a captain three weeks. He was a very bright young officer. Great things had been expected of him. The robbery had been a blow. When last seen, he had been whimpering in the shadows of the bank. Block had called in several times to report no evidence. The last time, Rotzinger said that Block should call in only if he *had* evidence.

"Jesus, I'm sorry," Block said. "I guess this will go on my record."

"Yes, we're all screwed," Rotzinger answered.

So Rotzinger had done young captain Block a favor, assisting him with the robbery, showing him who went where, explaining how you had to meet certain demands to protect the hostages, how you negotiated and got the women out first.

Rotzinger had worked in *dozens* of robberies in his thirty-three years, maybe *hundreds*.

He had helped talk guys out, and he had shot guys down, and in all those years, nobody ever robbed a bank successfully under Rotzinger's nose.

Do you think anybody remembers all those times he caught the robbers, like the time in 1956 when he was a punk lieutenant and he chased this crumb four blocks and tackled him on the pavement? Hell, no. You are only as good as your next job.

Rotzinger would be a hot item at the convention in Las Vegas this year. Wayne Newton would ask him to step up on the stage. They would put a spotlight on him.

"And now, ladies and gentlemen, here is the only police chief in the United States of America, including Puerto Rico, to have a bank robbed while he stood there and watched. Let's hear it, one more time."

They would be writing about this one in *Modern Detective*.

They would make little Rotzinger dolls that lost their guts.

Hell, they'd probably get kicked out of the country club. His son might get kicked out of college. Son-of-a-bitch!

Rotzinger silently pledged that if he got out of this mess he, as the police chief of the greatest city in the world, would never associate with a common officer again. He would never be caught dead at a crime.

At the convention in Las Vegas last year, they had charts and graphs showing that in the last five years .0015 percent of all attempted bank robberies where hostages were taken were successful. Some cowboy got away with eighty-five dollars in change from a bank in western Kansas.

Of all the possible crimes, bank robbery is about the easiest to prevent.

"Hell," Rotzinger said to Stark, who blinked.

Gilbert was playing connect-the-dots on his pad.

Wax looked at his watch and said, "It has been two hours and five minutes."

"Are you tracking a rocket?" Rotzinger asked Wax, who smiled. Wax was not married and he had a box of degrees and he was not worried about what he would do after the mayor ordered this floor hosed out by the fire department.

Rotzinger had one remaining hole card.

It was his mind.

He had been down there in the streets all those years, and he had the reputation for being able to outsmart any criminal son-of-a-bitch alive.

Rotzinger was the one who, five years ago, had busted the Gimp case wide open. The kidnapping. It was a seemingly unsolvable case, perpetrated by masterminds, who arranged for the enormous money-drop to be made with the use of a silly old horse, at night. The horse had been taught to return to a point. There was no way to bug or follow the horse, so as the captain in charge of the operation, Rotzinger got a midget cop and taped him to the side of the horse. Old man Gimp was rescued, without a scratch, and although the kidnappers got away, Rotzinger's idea for infiltrating the enemy camp had been so inspired he got very good write-ups in the trade magazines and became a minor celebrity. He even gave a talk about kidnappings at one of the conventions in Las Vegas.

God, those were the good old days.

Damn, these were the dogs.

Rotzinger had solved some nasty ones, like the subway-hostage case, where he suddenly darkened the tunnel and car and had guys leap down from the rafters and up from under the tracks to capture a loony.

There was never anything like this, though. The son or sons-of-bitches who did this would pay.

So whereas things looked a little dark around the edges, the matter was not entirely hopeless. Robbing a bank is one thing. Getting away is another.

I've still got my mind, Rotzinger thought. There is still a place in this world for a thinker.

The mayor called and said that the newspapers would have a field day.

Rotzinger said a break in the case was in the offing.

"You swear to God?" the mayor asked.

The governor called and said there was no reason to panic but that he would certainly appreciate an arrest within the next forty-eight hours, preferably of the guilty person or persons.

You don't *always* have to arrest the person who did the crime.

It was a case involving an arrest made in the "gray area" of the law that helped Rotzinger become chief. The Bizanti

Case happened about six months after the Gimp Case. Then-Captain Rotzinger arrested Mario Bizanti for the theft of the Picasso. This theft made everybody sick. The Picasso just disappeared. That Mario Bizanti wouldn't know a Picasso from a Caspisso was of little importance. At first, Mario Bizanti was very surprised to learn he had stolen this valuable "Pisscasto," but the more he listened to then-Captain Rotzinger's plan, the sneakier and more brilliant he felt.

Mario Bizanti was a run-of-the-mill sneak thief. In the average district in a big city, you turn over a hubcap and a half a dozen Mario Bizantis scurry out. He was from a family of five brothers, two sisters, three mothers, and two fathers. The Bizanti family ran numbers.

Rotzinger came across the Flying Bizantis when they started running numbers in a different Cadillac each day. So Mario informed on his brother, for stealing cars.

Running numbers is a very easy way to make a thousand dollars a week, much more if you're doubly crooked. Running numbers is a con game in the first place. You sell a person a number for a buck on a thousand-to-one chance on a grand. You find somebody and say, this is your lucky day, you win the number, only instead of giving him the thousand, you give him about fifty bucks, and keep the rest. The guy says, "This is America, I won the number, anybody can!" under the penalty of mutilation. People in some districts will do *anything* for fifty bucks, like steal, so you can imagine how quickly a person would *take* fifty, and say they won a thousand.

It was a variation of the numbers game Rotzinger worked on Mario Bizanti.

If a person takes the time, you can work up quite a sheet on somebody like Mario Bizanti, everything from jaywalking on up. Rotzinger had a guy follow Mario around for a couple of weeks, with a camera and recording devices, and he put together a nice package whereby Mario Bizanti could be

locked up for approximately twenty years. Mario Bizanti
about coughed up his teeth. He started informing on everybody he knew, even his grandmother, who stole bologna from
the grocery.

It was true, the police didn't usually bother with punks like
Mario, but times were tough and nobody was hijacking any
subways or kidnapping any politicians, so you had to make
ends meet, even if you had to stretch punks.

Rotzinger told Mario it was nothing personal, any punk
would do, but Mario was one of the handiest. Rotzinger told
Mario the only way he could see out of this revolting turn of
events was: the Picasso deal.

"But I don't get it," Mario Bizanti said.

"I got it," Rotzinger said.

Airport security had found the Picasso in one of those fifty-
cent lockers during a routine search. It is *amazing* what you
find in airport lockers.

Rotzinger explained to Mario Bizanti how recovering the
painting was half the battle; a place to hang it was as important.

Blundering into a painting does little to reassure the citi-
zenry that it is protected by a bunch of sharp police officers.
Sound investigatory technique is what pays the rent.

"You want me to take the fall so you can be a hero," Mario
Bizanti said. "So you can be a big shot."

"Basically," Rotzinger said.

"How much?"

"Twenty, plus we say something like you were an art lover
or a psycho, something nice that gets you out of prison in two
years, three at the outside."

"There's a lot of bad things in prison."

"Twenty thousand, in a bank, earning interest. The longer
you're in, Mario, the more interest you make."

"Thirty grand, plus you fix it I'm out in *two* stinking
years."

If Rotzinger made chief, the difference in captain's salary and chief's salary was $42,450. Even the thirty seemed like a wise investment.

"It's a gamble," Rotzinger said, of the chief's job.

Mario had shrugged. "There's bugs in prison. Rats and snakes and crap. Guys that want to bite your nose off. I got to have thirty."

"Or you go to prison for all this other various and sundry activity, with *no* money. I promise you, I can fix that."

"Twenty-five."

Rotzinger agreed.

"The five grand interest makes it about thirty," Mario said.

"You'll also be a hero," Rotzinger said.

"Yeah."

"Don't worry about prison, Mario. There is a special wing where they put embezzlers and geniuses, guys who can write."

"I got a cousin in the pen who says every night at eight, they start hitting each other on the head with ball bats."

Rotzinger assured Mario Bizanti that in the uptown wing, they had color televisions and libraries and everything, so a master criminal was born and then nailed.

Rotzinger fixed it with this judge who owed him one.

Mario got five and a half years. Not bad. He would come out in a couple, a fairly well-off gentleman.

A little of it was hard to wash; few people could understand how Mario Bizanti, former numbers runner, part-time pimp, hubcap thief, glue pusher, and jack-off of all trades, could suddenly become a master art thief.

But strange things happen in the city.

The rich people should have slept good the night they put Mario Bizanti away, knowing that if some sneaky bastard tried to creep off with a Currier and Ives, or even a Burl Ives *record*, Rotzinger was there to straighten things out.

It was hard for those who knew Mario Bizanti real well to accept the fact that he crammed himself into a file cabinet in this art gallery, waited until everybody was gone, and then hovered above the wired floor in a motorized flying device. Then he allegedly suctioned himself onto the wall, like a mountain climber, and razor-bladed the Picasso from the frame. Mario then glued a reproduction into the vacant frame, and hid until the gallery opened the next morning, and slipped out unnoticed, carrying the portable and light-weight flying device in a sack.

Those who knew Mario Bizanti, or knew of Mario Bizanti, or knew people who knew or knew of Mario Bizanti, thought it was a giant box of horse manure.

But for $25,000 (plus interest), you couldn't get a peep out of Mario Bizanti. He told the court he was an art lover and merely wanted the poor people in his neighborhood to enjoy seeing a Paul Castro painting, and that he was going to return the painting the very afternoon Captain Rotzinger made the pinch.

"Next," the judge said.

Several neighbors Mario had hit with twenties testified it was true, the man just wanted to enrich the neighborhood, so he was sent off to serve a couple of years of watching daytime television.

Being the police chief is a lot of work. The most work is keeping the job. You have about a thousand smart young guys out there with masters' in criminology running up your back, so it's nice every once in a while to dump the administrative work and get out there in the field with the real people.

Like hell.

Rotzinger again promised himself that if he escaped this one with his skin, he would never attend another crime the rest of his life.

It was hard to take, one insignificant uniformed cop, screwing so much up.

Rotzinger looked at Stark.

Stark was trying to figure what he had done wrong so he could lie his way out. All he had done was take statements from the hostages. He had done that brilliantly, with a tape recorder. Names. Addresses. He had played the tapes back before telling the hostages to have some coffee and doughnuts and a seat. Maybe he should have *charged* them for the coffee and doughnuts. Maybe that was why the chief was so upset.

Rotzinger's wife was on line two. A couple of girls from the club had called at this rude hour to ask whose fault this robbery had been. Helen was upset. The club *loathed* bad publicity. Any time a member's child married a foreigner, there was temporary probation until the divorce. Bad publicity was automatic expulsion. Rotzinger told his wife that if she called one more time, he would shoot the phone. He banged the phone down.

"You're thinking you're very close to this job, right, Wax?"

"Not at all, sir."

"You're thinking, the old boy has really blown it. Well, Wax, the way it works is you're a part of this. If I go, you go. You too, Gilbert. You'll be sketching profiles at the fair."

"I didn't do a damn thing," Gilbert said.

"And you, Stark. There's not a dark enough place in the world for you."

"We did all we could," Wax said. "Nobody would have done anything differently. They just outsmarted us."

"Wax," Rotzinger said, "do you think you could stop that for five minutes?"

"They?" Stark said. "They who?"

Rotzinger said that was the first intelligent thought Stark had had all night, the "they who?"

Stark frowned.

"Tell him," Rotzinger told Wax, who said, "Two of the hostages are unaccounted for."

Stark sniffed. "What about the other two?"

"Two?" Rotzinger said.

"He's right," Wax nodded. "There were four hostages. The wild one, Sam Billabong, the one they had to give a shot to.

The pregnant teller, Teresa Singleton. The last two, the man and woman, Mary Johnson and John Brown. Four."

"You guys forgot there were four hostages?" Stark said. He had regained his color. Whatever he had done was nothing compared to forgetting a hostage. "That's hard to believe. As crazy as things got, I always knew there were four."

Wax quickly had somebody check on the "John Brown," his address and phone number. The phone number was not in working order.

"I got statements from them all," Stark said, "and checked their names with their identification."

"The IDs were false," Gilbert said. "Obviously."

"And you waste your time drawing for a living?" Rotzinger was trying to think. Pieces were falling into place. It was a shame the pieces were blank.

"We have three missing hostages," Wax said. He repeated their phony names. Rotzinger winced at the sounds.

"I thought Billabong sounded fishy," Stark said.

"He did have the ID?" Wax shrugged.

Oops, Stark remembered. That was the one they jerked off for a shot, right after the statement. He didn't have time to check that one's identification. Who would have thought a hostage was a suspect? He did check the others, though. Let them try to prove he hadn't checked the first one's identification.

"They all had it," Stark said. "Licenses. Cards."

"Where did they go?" Rotzinger asked. "After you got the statements, where did they go?"

Stark scratched his head. "It was very busy, back there."

Rotzinger got up from his chair.

"Nobody told me to watch them. They were hostages, not criminals."

"The pregnant teller, Singleton, walked home," Wax said. "Her phone number was correct."

"Walked?" Rotzinger said. "She walked away from the scene of a crime?"

Gilbert the artist whistled.

"I told them to have a seat," Stark said.

Rotzinger walked around his desk. "You should have stayed with them, Stark. You let them walk away with the money."

"I sure as hell did not."

"The other three hostages were the robbers."

"That's easy to say now."

Gilbert whistled again.

"It was an honest oversight," Wax said. "It *was* confused, back where the statements were taken."

"They didn't even run off. They walked off." Rotzinger had Gilbert the artist go with Stark to prepare drawings of what the three missing hostages looked like when they left the bank, which was not necessarily what they looked like now, but at least three dots of the puzzle had been connected.

"It was dark, back there," Stark said. "I'll try."

"This one will make a fabulous research paper," Wax said. "You really have to hand it to them."

"We already did that," Rotzinger said. "Now it's time to make amends."

For the first time all evening, he felt like he was back in the hunt, and the foxes had best not pause to lift a leg. Knowing *how* the robbery had been committed was a big, big step.

"You might think," Wax said, "they're long gone."

"Keep it up, Wax."

Rotzinger buzzed Gilbert the artist and told him he wanted the drawings finished in six minutes, and then he wanted them taken to the conference room for verification from the hostages who had been locked in the vault. He buzzed another extension and had men standing by to rush the drawings to every airport, bus station, cab stand, train station, and transportation center within a hundred miles.

It was by the book, Wax nodded. Sound. A long-shot, but *something*. Wax looked at his watch. "They've had time to get to any number of countries. The way they worked the bank, they could be halfway, three quarters of the way, to South America. Forty-five minutes to the airport. Three hours in the air. Amazing."

Rotzinger smashed both fists on his desk and pencils jumped.

"Maybe the plane will crash," Wax said. "Something."

"I'll follow them to hell," Rotzinger said.

The bus was half full of the oddest assortment of people Grimm had ever seen. Phyllis had refused to sit with him, so Lackey had requested and received the window seat. Phyllis sat on the row one up.

Grimm felt like he had just bet his life savings on a one-card come with four hearts, and was now merely playing the hand out. The city, out there, had a pair of deuces and was calling Grimm's bluff.

Lackey was in pain. He held his right side with both hands. The bus driver made Lackey move his hands and prove he had not been shot. It was against some rule to bring bullets on board, even if they're inside you. Broken ribs? Fine.

"One thing, Grimm," Lackey said, straining up the steps on the bus. "They would never look for us here."

"No, pal, they wouldn't."

Although the escape had once been thought of in terms of *hours* until departure, it was now down to *minutes*. As the driver, Bud Heathcoat, said, if the creek didn't rise, he would have them to within nine blocks of Kennedy in one hour and thirteen and a half minutes.

Phyllis said that was nice, from that distance they would have a lovely view of their airplane taking off.

"Unless we have a shootout," Bud Heathcoat said, "I'll get you there."

They would have fifty-three minutes to walk, run, or crawl nine blocks, check into the airport, and make the flight, which Bud Heathcoat said was entirely possible.

Grimm promised Lackey they would get a motorized wheelchair or something to propel him painlessly to the gate.

"Do they have doctors in England?" Lackey asked. "My entire right side is numb."

"The best," Grimm said.

Bud Heathcoat's city bus had just appeared. When Lackey leaped from the moving cab, a car behind had slammed on its brakes and crashed into a curb, and the driver was threatening lawsuits and violence, so when the bus stopped, Grimm thought it might be a good idea to quickly relocate.

That the bus would sweep near the airport was a pleasant surprise. God may have sent it.

They happily climbed aboard, and things got complicated again.

Phyllis had the correct change. She placed it in the money box and moved on into the bus. Neither Grimm nor Lackey had a penny. Phyllis carried the suitcase with approximately $800,000 on board, and the bag of hastily collected clothes.

Grimm was carrying Lackey. He propped him against a seat and dug through all eleven pockets, but didn't have correct change, or *any* change, for that matter.

Lackey had no money.

Phyllis had no more money.

All the money was in the suitcase.

"You people look clean," Bud Heathcoat said, "but I gotta have the fare. It's a rule."

"Be right back," Grimm said.

Bud Heathcoat looked at his pocket watch and said, "In two minutes forty-eight seconds, I leave this stop."

Grimm went back to where Phyllis was sitting.

"Do I know you?"

"Give me," Grimm whispered into Phyllis' beautiful ear, "the fare."

"Use your head," she whispered back, nodding across the aisle.

Grimm looked.

A thug was unzipping and zipping pockets on his leather jacket, like he forgot where his blade was. "The damn thing was here somewhere," he said, unzipping a pocket on his left shoulder. He appeared seriously drugged. In front of the character in the leather jacket was a middle-aged woman who said, in response to Grimm's look, "Don't you come near me." Three rows behind Phyllis was a sizable lad with three combs stuck in his hair. The rest of the crowd was less appealing. Two men were shooting dice below the back seat. Grimm decided Phyllis was right, it would probably be unwise to open the suitcase full of money right now.

Grimm took off his watch and said, "How much?"

"Nothing, damn it," the guy in the leather jacket said, feeling around for hidden pockets.

"Ten dollars for the suitcase and what's in it," said the kid with the combs in his hair.

To refuse this offer would indicate to the passengers in the bus that maybe what was in the suitcase was worth as much as *twenty* dollars. Knowing that, somebody might attack.

"Don't take it," Phyllis hissed.

"Ten dollars against the watch, if it works," one of the dice players said.

"It's worth," Grimm said, but then Phyllis whispered, "Watch it!" so Grimm said, "Seventeen or eighteen bucks. It works."

"Ten against the watch, I don't care what it's worth or whose body you took it off of."

Grimm walked back and put the watch on the floor.

One of the men picked it up, and listened. "Works."

The other man said, "Your dice."

A ten dollar bill was placed next to the watch, which was worth a hundred, easy.

Grimm held the dice in his right palm. They were red, with white dots. They didn't move.

"Throw them," the man who had put the ten against the watch said. Only his right eye blinked. The other man sniffed all the time.

You toss a seven or eleven the first roll, you win. You hit two, three, or twelve the first roll, that's craps and not worth the time of day and you lose your watch. You fling something else, that's your number. You have to roll your number on subsequent rolls before you roll a seven. It's a fun game.

Grimm blew on the dice and rolled the babies.

One hit the sniffer's foot and rolled under the seat. He leaned down and said, "Craps, you lose."

"Wait a minute," Grimm said. He leaned under the seat for a look. His heart about quit. "This is a two. I rolled two twos. That's not craps. That's a hard four."

"Oh," the guy sniffed. "My mistake. Throw the dice. Four's the number."

The guy with the funny blink said, "Four is a bad number. You ever think about it? Nobody's lucky number is four. You want odds on the hard four? That coat against five dollars."

Grimm said he would just as soon go for any four, a three and an ace, or the hard way, two deuces.

"What's your number?" Lackey asked from the front.

"Four," Grimm answered.

"Five hundred says you don't make it," the lad with combs in his hair said.

Phyllis moved her head ever so slightly, side to side, don't call it.

Grimm quickly rolled the dice six times and the numbers that came up were:

Six, six, six, six, six, six.

"Interesting dice," Grimm said.

"Virgins," the sniffer said.

"Right off the assembly line," the other one blinked. He blinked his right eye on every other word.

"Let's go back there," Bud Heathcoat shouted.

"I've seen guys roll all night and not get a four, right, Jackie?"

"I've seen guys roll all *week* and not get a four, Lonnie."

"Four is hard."

"It's worse than hard, Lonnie. It's steel."

"Which kind of steel, Jackie?"

"Both kinds, Lonnie."

"I've seen people roll four in their sleep," Grimm said, rolling six again. Then he rolled a five.

"I need a watch." Lonnie picked it up.

"Give you fifty for it," Jackie said.

"No way," Lonnie said. "Throw the dice."

Grimm threw a hard four, a pair of deuces. Jackie and Lonnie and Grimm sat there blankly, like they were waiting for the numbers to change.

"Ha," Grimm said, picking up the ten-spot.

"Well, son-of-a-bitch," Jackie said.

"Can I have your autograph?" Lonnie asked Grimm, who rushed the ten bucks forward to Bud Heathcoat. Bud closed the doors and gunned it. He said they were one minute and forty-six, forty-seven, forty-eight, forty-nine, fifty seconds late, but he could make it up and get back on schedule, this time of night.

Grimm was given change and he put his and Lackey's fare in the machine. Bud Heathcoat had hand-lettered a sign that was taped to the money machine:

DON'T TRY ANYTHING—MONEY FALLS INTO SNAKE PIT.

There were scratch marks on the side of the fare machine.

"What did you ever do to deserve this run?" Grimm asked Bud Heathcoat.

"Oh, ran over a guy."

Grimm helped Lackey to a seat behind Phyllis. Lackey straightened up, with great pain, and looked around at the customers.

"Know what this looks like?"

"What?" Grimm asked back.

"A bus to prison."

A bus is not the *worst* way to get to the airport, all things considered.

To take his mind off the nauseating stops and starts, and rotten smell, Grimm made a list of sorrier ways they could have gone to the airport: on a skateboard; on a Brahma bull; in the back of a garbage truck; in a wheelbarrow; in a hearse; or they all could have rented pogo sticks and hopped, and that would have been a terrible trip.

Grimm played this game three blocks.

After a while, even thinking about torture couldn't take his mind off the bus.

No matter how you looked at it, this was the most uncomfortable moment in Grimm's life.

It was even harder on Lackey, the poor devil.

The ventilation system was hooked to the gas pedal, and when Bud Heathcoat gunned it, gasps of hot air shot from the overhead rack, and when the bus slowed, the air was cold. The variety of temperatures and speeds got to Lackey, and he turned moss-colored.

"Can't this miserable thing keep moving for more than thirty seconds?" Lackey wondered. "It's killing me. What's that smell?"

"Used wine, I think," Grimm said. He told Lackey to open the window and try some fresh air. It was one of the old buses with latches you press and the window is supposed to scoot open. Lackey pressed the button and tugged at the glass, but it didn't budge.

Bud Heathcoat swerved to the curb, hit the brakes, and picked up a passenger. Lackey nodded forward in the seat. When Bud rejoined traffic, Lackey was propelled backward against the chairback.

He clutched at the window again. "Please, God," he said, "let this window open. Is he stopping twice on some blocks,

Grimm? This is worse than a boat. Tell him to stop stopping."

The lunatic in the leather jacket was still unzipping and zipping pockets.

The kid with combs in his hair was cleaning his fingernails with somebody's credit card.

The dice game was still in progress.

Grimm lunged forward.

Bud Heathcoat whipped it to another curb, opened the doors, and sat there as a man with a guitar strapped to his back tried to climb aboard without much luck. "I want out of this stinking town," he said. He had a bottle of wine in his right hand. "I've had it up to here with this place." The man held his hand about a foot over his head. "What are you looking at?"

"You," Grimm said.

"That's better," the man said, trying again to get on the bus. The guitar was parallel with the ground, and therefore was too wide for the door on the bus.

Bud Heathcoat looked at his stop watch and said, "You got one, thirty."

"What does *that* mean?"

"In a minute, thirty, we're leaving."

"Oh really?"

"Really."

"My name is Gene Miller. That probably doesn't mean anything to you, does it?"

Bud Heathcoat explained quietly to Grimm as Gene Miller tried to swing his guitar sideways so it would fit onto the bus, that every so often somebody from Traffic Control made spot checks to see if the schedules were being met. They're real sneaky, Bud Heathcoat said. They check manners, driving habits, the whole bit. *That*, maybe this jerk was from Traffic, was why Bud Heathcoat didn't close the door on the passenger's neck.

"Why don't you take the guitar off?" Grimm said.

"You sound like my wife," Gene Miller said. "She makes me sick. She just threw me out. She can go to hell. Who needs company and kindness and security and all that you know what?"

Gene Miller told Bud Heathcoat to take him to the nearest bar.

"You have to get on, first."

Gene Miller backed off onto the sidewalk and spilled wine on his pants and tilted the guitar so it was upright and he charged the bus and crawled up the stairs. He reached in his pocket and brought out some change, spilling half of it, and he crammed the rest in the meter.

"This," Gene Miller said, squinting down the aisle, "is a night to remember." He bounced off the seats, about fell in Phyllis' lap, caused Lackey to gag at the wine smell, and fell into a seat opposite the youth with the combs in his hair.

Bud Heathcoat told Grimm they were right on schedule, not to worry, and he would try to keep things smoother for Lackey. The bus jerked forward, then promptly stopped at a light.

"Oh hell," Lackey moaned.

Gene Miller looked across the aisle. He leaned up and said to Grimm, "There's combs in that person's hair."

Grimm said nothing.

The kid with combs said nothing.

Lackey was still wrestling with the window latch and swearing.

"You *play* the combs?" Gene Miller asked the kid, who said nothing.

"I'm going to kick the window open," Lackey whined. "If I have to."

"You *sell* combs?" Gene Miller asked.

Nobody said anything.

"There has got to be a reason why a person would stick three combs in his hair. Does anybody in this bus know? I mean it."

When Gene Miller said the kid's head reminded him of a little Christmas tree, the kid reached over and removed the guitar from Gene Miller's lap.

"Hey," Gene Miller said. "That's too big to stick in your hair." He laughed.

The kid balanced the guitar upright in his lap, holding the neck with his left hand. He grabbed the strings with his right hand and yanked them. As the strings were ripped loose, they made little "ping" sounds. The kid threw the strings in the aisle and handed the naked guitar back to Gene Miller, who sat quietly until Bud Heathcoat deposited him near a bar a mile or so down the road.

Grimm and Lackey, pulling together, got the window open. Lackey managed to squeeze his head outside and was ill on a Toyota. Lackey fell back in his seat and was creepily quiet.

As the bus continued to bound toward the airport, Grimm leaned up and asked Phyllis how she was doing.

"Very, very bad." She had the suitcase full of money on her lap and was holding it tightly. "I'm doing the worst I've ever done in my life."

"We're making progress," Grimm said.

The Toyota Lackey had been so rude to was weaving at the front of Bud Heathcoat's bus, like a dog nips at something it is a little afraid of, and Bud Heathcoat, unaware of the motive, was weaving back at the Toyota and shaking his fist at the driver.

Because of the activity, Bud Heathcoat forgot to stop for a passenger, and Grimm told Phyllis, "See, everything happens for a reason. We made up some time."

"Glad I could help," Lackey said weakly, of his contribution.

Phyllis turned around and said, "You deceived me. I thought I was in good hands. Your idea was luck. We should have sold it to somebody who has brains."

She started to tell Grimm how she and the blockhead football player used to practice hiking, so Grimm sat back and watched the scenery go by in one- and two-block gushes.

Lackey, bless his heart, dozed off.

Grimm hoped.

There is nothing like the thrill of an investigation in progress. It *is* like a hunt. Rotzinger had a gut feeling the trail was not yet cold. You give the bastards the first move, and then you crown them.

One of the joys of policework is you can make five mistakes, ten mistakes, fifty, and you can still be in the chase. But the opposition, he makes one small error and he can go to prison. Prison is a bad place. There are not always suburbs for intelligent, sensitive criminals. A mastermind who wouldn't hurt a fly is liable to wind up in a cell next to an eyeball collector, a guy who would bash your brains in for a shoelace.

Rotzinger had had a few anxious moments with Mario Bizanti, the brilliant art thief, the one who lifted the Picasso. They put Mario next door to a lifer named Fitch, who was so mean he used to swear at a mirror.

Mario sent Rotzinger a memo, "God help me," and Rotzinger pulled a few strings and got the brilliant art thief transferred to a slightly better neighborhood. You can also *push* strings and have people located next to guys who teethed on cell bars.

The thought of sending the bank robbers to prison helped Rotzinger forget he had been hoodwinked in front of a national television audience. But again, executing a robbery is but a small piece of the overall pie of crime. Getting the hell away is the good part, the crust, and if any of it crumbles, you're asked to take a number and get in line for the pen.

Overall pie of crime.

Rotzinger liked that phrase and thought about using it in a brochure at the convention in Las Vegas.

He told Wax to keep accurate notes, there might even be a book in this.

He told his wife to tell the biddies at the club there was no reason to panic.

In a case like this, it all starts happening at once, so you have to keep a clear head and ignore things like Wax, who continued to theorize about the robbers' whereabouts. His last two guesses were Tahiti and Barbados. When Rotzinger captured those people, Wax would probably throw himself in front of the gun fire, or at the very least get them a lawyer.

"I'm not *for* them," Wax said. "They're just interesting."

Gilbert got the drawings made and a few adjustments were added by the vault hostages.

The lab called up to say that the strange noise on the last telephone conversation with the robber had been identified. It was a car horn. When this information was relayed to Wax, he smiled and said, "That is, without a doubt, the best I ever heard!"

Rotzinger said nothing.

"The guy called you on a pay phone from somewhere else!"

Rotzinger nodded.

"And you thought he was still in the bank!"

"We. *We* thought."

"Lord," Wax said.

Rotzinger removed a tape from his drawer and said, "It all goes in the book, Wax. Your jubilation, your joyful hysteria."

"Facts are facts," Wax said.

"The only fool *fact* that matters is they screwed up a little bit, with that horn in the background. They're slipping, Wax, I can feel it."

On the other hand, the phone call from God only knew where indicated that the robbers had a sizable head start, and for all anybody knew, the call had been placed from a ship-to-shore radio.

Rotzinger rubbed his hands together and waited for the

next bit of information, like the *kind* of car horn it had been, because things were starting to get interesting.

From the conference room came news that bank vice-president Princeton had launched a lawsuit against the city for destruction of property, and that Buzz Murdock, the public relations man, had tried to jump out of the window.

Rotzinger quickly stomped off to the conference room, glanced at the statements that had been taken and retaken, and he told the hostages that progress was being made.

"What about the floor of the bank?" Princeton asked.

Buzz Murdock had been handcuffed to a chair. The last television report had opened with a shot of one of Buzz Murdock's billboards proclaiming the bank's invincibility, then the camera quickly cut to a live shot of the bank. Cops were still walking in through the glassless windows.

"Got any real leads?" hostage Gooch asked. He was the one who almost got cheated out of the FDIC insurance because his deposit hadn't been on the record at the time of the robbery.

"Yes," Rotzinger said.

"Ah, hell," Gooch said.

"How would you like to be a police officer?" Rotzinger asked so Wax could hear, but Gooch didn't get it.

Gooch had done his part, putting a phony mole on the clown's chin.

Artist/officer Gilbert said the hostages weren't too interested in getting the description right, and that several of the people who had been locked in the vault seemed openly contemptuous of the police; especially that Gooch.

Rotzinger told Gooch that if there was no mole on the clown's chin, perjury charges were in the wings.

Gooch said he wouldn't stay awake worrying until the robbers were caught.

"They're probably halfway to Tahiti," Gooch said.

Teresa Singleton was in a bad mood.

She had been dragged from bed to say again what she had

already said. Officer Stark was somewhat vindicated. After the questioning, the pregnant teller had been told to "stay out of the way," which is a little like telling somebody to have a seat.

"Everything was so screwed up," she told Rotzinger, "it's amazing you people found the bank."

Teresa Singleton said that after her statement was taken, she simply walked home and then she went to bed. She had not seen any of the other hostages.

"Had she seen the clown, she could have identified him," Rotzinger told Wax. "She would have known he wasn't one of the hostages, and she could have given us a description, and that would have been it."

Wax had to admit, that would have helped.

"So you see, Wax, they were luckier than they were good."

"I want some water," Teresa Singleton said.

"In the hall," Rotzinger said.

"That was a bad mistake, almost," Wax said.

Rotzinger said it was a trend. At face value, this bank thing looked like a professional work of art that could never be solved, but when you scrutinized matters, maybe these people were a bunch of amateurs who tripped over an idea that would be hard to screw up. But they had *tried* to screw it up.

"We still don't know who they are or where they are," Wax said. "And we can't wait for them to drop the suitcase and have the money fly out."

Rotzinger went over what they had:

1. A bank had been robbed of upward of $800,000, the exact count was still being made.

2. A man dressed as a clown had taken the employees and customers hostage, holding them in the vault.

3. The cameras had been shot out, poorly, with many bullets wasted in the bank roof.

4. Four hostages had been released: one, Teresa Singleton, was accounted for; three of the hostages gave false names and addresses.

5. The three hostages unaccounted for were the robbers.

The last male hostage, who came out with the second female hostage, was the clown. The clown removed his costume and makeup safely because the cameras had been shot out, and he walked out, posing as a hostage.

6. The money was obviously under the hostages' clothing.

7. In the confusion, the hostages had merely walked off, after giving statements.

8. The robbers eventually left the area of the crime in a car.

9. A call was made from *outside* the bank, to the pay phone. It was mistakenly assumed the clown was still in the bank. A noise in the background had been identified as a car horn, thereby proving the call had been made from elsewhere.

10. The horn noise was identified too late, giving the robbers time to get wherever in the hell they were going. The portable sound analysis device would be traded for something more practical, like handcuffs.

11. A potentially captivating error had been made by the robbers. As all the hostages had been held together in one confined area, the vault, they were familiar with each other. Had Teresa Singleton seen the last male hostage, the clown, she would have been able to inform the authorities that this was no hostage, this was trouble. An arrest could have been made. The party would have been over.

It was now time to think.

When Rotzinger joined the force, there were no fancy noise recorders which, when plugged into a computer, two hours after the fact, identified a car horn. There were no computers, no police psychiatrists who, after hearing all the evidence, said, "The guy's nuts." When Rotzinger joined the department, criminals were not pampered; a person had the right to remain silent, though, and if he chose this tactic, he also had the right to free stitches and plasma and crutches.

You were not dealing with normal people, there. You were dealing with lousy criminals who would just as soon slice up a God-fearing, law-abiding citizen as look at him. If people wanted to be treated like human beings then they shouldn't break the law, it was that simple. When you crack an old man over the head with a gun butt and take his money, you give up your goddamn rights.

Rotzinger agreed, it was just terrible about the crowded prisons and the cold mashed potatoes and the crooked basketball rim out here in the yard. Doesn't it just make a person want to write his Congressman. Bad television reception. Catsup stains on the books. No room to *live*.

The thing is, all the people doing the bitching about capital punishment and rehabilitation and animalistic living conditions in prison have never had a rotten son-of-a-bitch come into your place of business with a gun or knife and take your money or crack you over the head or shoot you in the gut. Rotzinger was firmly convinced that getting knifed or shot or raped was much more dehumanizing than sleeping on a lumpy mattress or having only an hour a day to shoot baskets.

What the righteous legislators and pompous citizens' groups have forgotten is that nobody makes a person commit a crime, and once you have screwed up, you have to pay your dues. We're talking about hard crimes, here. Say a guy embezzles a little something. Fine. Put him on a farm that looks like a country club. But when somebody cuts up somebody, the only right this rotten bastard deserves is one to the chops.

Rotzinger hated it when crusades were launched concerning something idiotic like conditions on death row. You have to balance the books.

The electric chair is cruel and unusual? And just what is shooting some poor old man in the stomach, during a robbery? Very few killers concern themselves with letting a victim die with dignity. You take somebody out violently, that's the way you ought to go. Fair is fair. So some old lady poisons her five husbands, you put a couple of drops in her Wheaties some morning, and that's that. Nice and simple. But when some rotten bastard guns down a citizen and then complains about too many flies in his soup, it's almost time to pack your bags to someplace where crime *equals* punishment. That's the only formula there is. Don't get Rotzinger wrong. He doesn't believe in blanket punishment. Frying everybody doesn't make sense. But neither does giving a cold-blooded, filthy, rotten son-of-a-bitching killer the same rights as a jaywalker. That smells to high heaven.

There is no doubt that capital punishment is a deterrent to murder. None whatsoever. You charcoal-broil a killer, it is a scientific fact he will never kill again.

When there is a chance a guy can knock over a liquor store and be out in a year or so if he gets caught, you're going to have a lot of guys knocking over liquor stores. Prisons would not be as crowded if the punks *knew* crime equaled punishment. Period.

The thing to remember is that those bitching about how uncomfortable prisons are are either criminals or idiotic politicians or college brats. The politicians are after the votes from the criminals who haven't been caught yet and the college brats. Times of worldwide peace are very difficult on law enforcement agencies; the politicians and college students don't know what to do with their mouths.

"Excuse me," Wax said.

Rotzinger blinked. "What?"

"I hate to break your concentration."

"It's all right."

"She's gone."

"Who?"

"Singleton."

Teresa Singleton was caught going down the front steps. She verified artist Gilbert's drawings, said they were close enough, except the woman obviously wore a wig, and maybe the men did, too.

"I say they're idiots," Rotzinger told Wax. "I say they're on their last leg. Smart people don't let cars honk in the background."

Wax said, "Could be."

"They're going to do something real ignorant."

Rotzinger didn't put much faith in the drawings, because
of the obvious disguises, but knowing that there were three of
them was a big help, and knowing that they were capable of
mass stupidity was of *enormous* value. Rotzinger told Wax to
trot down to the computer and get a print-out of every damn
thing that had happened in the last two hours. Make it three.

Although there was a crime about every fifteen minutes in
prime-time on the weekend, the later it got, the more things
calmed down.

"I want *anything* that involved three people, two men and
a woman. Spitting on the sidewalk. Speeding tickets. Anything."

"We're assuming they stayed together," Wax said. "And
didn't split up and perhaps drive to another city, or perhaps
even embark on a cross-country driving trip which, if they
went north, puts them somewhere near Canada. On the other
hand, perhaps they will simply remain in the city, secure in
new identities."

"Speak your treason louder," Rotzinger said, holding up
the tape recorder.

Wax got up to check the computer. Violations, crimes, and
complaints are instantly recorded on a computer.

"The only thing we are assuming, Wax, is that they are idiots."

Police Chief Wax had a fabulous ring to it.

The old boy had things so fouled up, it was a definite possibility. It was a sobering thought that some day as chief, he
might come up against an adversary as brilliant as the robber.
Wax would *never* leave his office, that was for sure. He hadn't
earned a masters in business administration for nothing.

It was time for a little modern blood in the chief's chair.
Rotzinger was about as old and innovative as radio.

Grimm decided that it was a funny world.

His dearest female friend was sitting one row up in the bus

with $800,000 in a suitcase in her lap. Her nose was pressed to the window. She was looking for football players.

His fondest male friend was asleep or in a coma in the window seat, his ribs ravaged, his stomach churning.

Who would have ever thought it. It was a family curse, Grimm guessed, that placed him here.

He was born into a nest of people who appreciated the amenities of money, but didn't particularly care for work. His father and uncles had a very prosperous used-car lot, and Grimm worked a while selling lemons to newlyweds, running odometers back, painting over cracks in the block. Grimm had cousins who sold various types of insurance for like a dime a week, and he had aunts who cranked out fake Indian jewelry for a store in New Mexico. Cheating people is hard work, though. When Grimm was attempting to sell real estate, he tried to unload this one shed to some foreigners, and put a quick paint job on some beams. He missed the sale because the termites flew off, leaving bare beams. Somewhere in this city there are about four million red termites.

As his Uncle Lonnie said, "There's five born every minute."

"Suckers, Uncle Lonnie?" Grimm had asked.

"No, crooks," Uncle Lonnie had said.

Uncle Lonnie believed that the way you kept your head above water was by standing on somebody's shoulders.

If *one* of Grimm's relatives had been a hard-working, government-fearing citizen, maybe Grimm wouldn't be sitting on this stupid bus right now. He would be in a home in the suburbs, with a wife, a dog, 1.8 cars, a job, credit cards, 1.35 color televisions, central air, children, within five or ten grand of even, but with *security!*

The thing was, though, he was even *now.* He didn't owe a cent. He was sitting on one-third of 800 grand. Granted, matters had not been proceeding swiftly to the predicted conclusion, but Grimm wondered how many people in this great country would have traded places with him.

Thirty, forty million, he decided.

"Come on, Bud," he shouted forward. "Drive hell out of things. You're doing a great job."

Grimm had a chance. What more could anybody ask out of life than a shot? Two shots? That's pushing it.

He hadn't hurt anybody, except poor Lackey there, rolled in a ball in the seat, and there was still time. They weren't standing as straight as planned, but they were still competitive.

The game is not over until you crap out. So the number you have to make is something debatable, like a four, so what, it's been done.

"We've still got the dice," Grimm said.

That's what this whole thing was like—a dice game. They had come to the table with a good plan of money management. They had made four or five passes and now, they were shooting the whole damn stake!

"We still have the damn dice."

Bud Heathcoat stomped on the brakes and said over his shoulder, "Airport."

Grimm leaned over Lackey and stuck his head out of the window and heard the beautiful sounds of jets taking off and landing.

"Lackey," Grimm said. "Wake up." He shook him gently by the shoulders. "I know this is going to come as a shock, but we made it. We're at the airport."

"We're *near* the airport," Phyllis said.

Lackey opened his eyes. "I had a nightmare. A bad nightmare."

"It's okay."

"I dreamed they shot us out of the air. We're about to land in Europe and jet fighters gunned us down."

"Let's go," Phyllis said.

"I also dreamed I was bad sick and threw up out the window of the airplane."

Grimm asked how Lackey's side was. He stretched and said

it felt like things were floating around in there, ribs and joints.

"Listen, Lackey. We'll get you a wheelchair at the airport. They'll take you right up to the gate and help you on board. In less than an hour and a half, we'll be in the air. In the morning, Lackey, we'll be on a beach, swimming."

"I doubt that, Grimm," Lackey said.

"Wading. Whatever. You have to be brave, Lackey. We're almost there."

"I'll do it for you, Grimm."

Grimm placed his hands on Lackey's shoulders and said he appreciated it.

"We go way back, Grimm."

"Yeah, pal, we do."

"I can do it."

"Attaboy."

"You people are making me sick," Phyllis said. She got up with the suitcases and walked to the front, and exited Bud Heathcoat's bus.

Grimm helped Lackey to his feet and guided him down the stairs.

Lackey looked sideways and then up. "I thought you said we were there. I thought you said we were *at* the airport."

Bud Heathcoat leaned over and nodded up and said, "Follow that airplane." He closed the doors and lurched into the night. As Bud Heathcoat had explained, to get to the airport from this exact spot involved driving approximately 1.3 miles on a freeway. This bus was not supposed to drive on the freeway. There were all kinds of buses in the fleet, Bud explained; good buses, bad buses, freeway buses, neighborhood buses. His was a bad neighborhood bus. If he put this bus on the freeway and went forty-five miles an hour, the sides would fall off, the motor would conk out, and three or more tires would explode. And, Bud said, the only remaining passenger, the guy in the leather jacket, could always be from Traffic Control. In her fury, Phyllis had offered to pay Bud Heathcoat

$1,000 for the idiotic mile ride to the terminal, but rules were rules and a certified route was a certified route. When Phyllis made the offer, Bud squinted and seemed very suspicious. People riding buses don't usually tip grands.

"That was a foolish thing to do," Grimm said after they had been deposited on the curb. "Offering him a thousand."

Phyllis said ignorance must be contagious.

They stood there, on the curb, 1.3 miles from the airport, listening to planes, and they checked their watches, like commandos or something, and Grimm told them what to do in any emergency, for example, if they were separated.

If we get separated, Phyllis thought, it will be the happiest moment of my life. I will stand on my head and click my heels. Grimm was such a hard one to figure. It never fails—the cute ones are dangerous. Phyllis had dated approximately eight hundred guys in her thirty years, and the ones who had a clearly defined future, the guys putting a little something away each week, they were the oafs and dullards. The cute ones, like Grimm, they are always on the verge. Phyllis could just see it—the day she dumped Grimm would be the day he hit it tremendously, and all that time and energy grooming him would be wasted. It was a little hard to believe she had given up a second-team pro-football player and a job in a travel agency for *this*, but then, there is something to be said for a cute guy and a suitcase full of money. Working in a travel agency, air-mailing widows to Greece and the Yucatan and Spain, was not all that hot a job. Sometimes the widows would call Phyllis in the middle of the night, collect, complaining because the hamburgers in Limerick, Ireland, were made of ham, not beef, or because the Bay of Fundy was late coming in, or because at the bullfight in Spain, they were using croquet mallets on calves. That's where Phyllis met Grimm, at the agency. It's a shame cute matters so much, but it does. Grimm stood there grinning, mumbling about a tour to England that he might want to take, maybe, but he didn't want to put a deposit down, and then have to cancel and lose it. All told, Grimm made and canceled eight travel packages, after aborted "business deals." Phyllis had not exactly quit the agency. She was taking two weeks of vacation. If this thing got off the ground, she could always wire in her resignation. If it failed, Phyllis could always be back at her desk next week, telling widows how lovely India was this time of year.

Now Grimm, he was a little more committed. At the moment, he had no car, no place to live, no job, and no hope for the future.

Phyllis hugged Grimm's neck, right there in the night.

"What was *that* all about?" he asked.

"You're just cute."

"This is very romantic," Lackey said, "but it isn't doing much for my side."

They had an hour and three minutes to walk to the airport, check their baggage and board the plane.

Lackey was in a hell of a shape. He had to bend right to keep his ribs from stinging, and the bus ride had caused his right leg to stiffen. His knee wouldn't flex so well. Lackey swung his right leg out in great, stiff circles, and propelled himself forward, like he was a pole vaulter. Each time he dug his right heel into the ground, he moaned, but he had the thought of the cash to fall back on, and also, as Grimm mentioned, the English make the best wooden legs in the business.

Many people schedule flights at bizarre departure times on purpose. The airport is less crowded at 3 A.M., and consequently you can get on about your business without having to worry about enormous lines everywhere. But the bad thing about flying at three in the morning is the same thing wrong with, say, catching a cab or a bus at three in the morning— those working the graveyard shifts are generally less competent than the eight-to-fivers. People working all night are usually moonlighting to make ends meet, and they're *always* in a bad mood.

"Is that so," the man at the curb said to Grimm.

"Yes," said Grimm. "It's so."

Grimm had requested a wheelchair for Lackey. Grimm had been at airports in prime time, and he had seen curb-side porters courteously and efficiently request and receive wheelchairs for the infirm. It was obvious that this guy had problems of his own, though, problems that far overshadowed Lackey's.

Harvey was the curb-side porter's name.

He had to *look up* the wheelchair number.

They were so happy to have walked to the airport without incident, they weren't too upset when Harvey opened the drawer where the wheelchair number was, spilling the contents onto the sidewalk.

"I doubt if you get a wheelchair," Harvey said. "This time of night, they work on wheelchairs."

"Work on wheelchairs?" Grimm said.

"You think them things just *run?*" Harvey scooped up some papers and sifted through phone numbers. "How about I get you a nice pizza, instead?" Harvey carefully replaced the number of the pizza joint. "The way it works is, some of the guys live in that apartment joint up the way, and the way gas is, some of the guys, they *ride* them motorized wheelchairs home on them service roads. Just rips the guts out of them chairs."

Grimm put the suitcase full of clothing by the stand and asked that Harvey please check the luggage through to London.

"We have our seat numbers," Phyllis said. "So just check the bag, all right?"

"England," Harvey said. "That's pretty fancy." He found the wheelchair number and spoke with a man named Rollo. Harvey looked at Lackey and told Rollo no, the passenger was not prone, it just looked like he was a hunchback, was all. Then, to Grimm, Harvey said, "An hour on the chair."

"Our flight leaves in forty minutes," Grimm said.

Harvey said, "Well, then, you've got to make a choice. The wheelchair or the flight."

Grimm, Phyllis, and Lackey chose the flight. Lackey had to think about it, though.

"Check the bag," Phyllis said, "and we'll be on our way."

"I have high blood pressure," Harvey said. "Unless I take these pills, I just might keel over, any time, anywhere. The reason I have high blood pressure is I don't get enough money. You worry about things like that."

"To England," Phyllis said. "Check the bag to England."

"England is going to be there," Harvey said. "I may not."

He sorted through more papers and said he couldn't check the bag to England.

"So to cure my high blood pressure, I take the pills and work here so I will get enough money so I won't have to worry."

"Why can't you check the bags?" Phyllis asked.

"There's a problem with the flight," Harvey said. "It says so right here. When there's a problem with the flight, the counter sends you this little yellow ticket that says there is a problem with the flight, don't check no more bags."

"What problem?" Phyllis asked.

Lackey was leaning on a NO PARKING sign.

Grimm was rubbing his face.

"Check the counter," Harvey said. "They know."

"We have our tickets," Phyllis said. "What problem?"

"Lady, there was a time when I acted like you. Got upset. Got mad. But now, see, I don't give one fuck about one thing. They say there's a problem, there's a problem. Maybe the wing fell off. Who knows. Just take your bag and go inside to the counter and tell them Harvey said there was a problem. You want me to check your bag to Cleveland? We got a flight to Cleveland in one hour. There's no problem on that one. London? There's a problem."

Harvey held up the yellow ticket.

He said he could check the bag to England, but maybe they wouldn't be going to England.

"What do you mean by that?" Grimm asked.

Harvey said that sometimes when there was a problem, it meant people didn't go where they wanted to go.

He looked at his watch. "You people got forty-six minutes. You can solve *any* problem in forty-six minutes. Unless you want to stand here and bitch at me."

Lackey lunged at the electric-eye door and stumbled into the airport. Phyllis carried the suitcase with the cash and Grimm carried the suitcase with the clothes.

There were about a dozen people at the counter. One window was open. The airline ticket agent was casually flipping through a book, shrugging occasionally. Grimm left Lackey and Phyllis with the bags at the back of the line, and he walked to the counter.

The ticket agent was meticulously groomed. His hair was perfectly parted and his moustache was beautifully squared. The prospective passengers were not as tidy.

"Get the hell back there," a man third in line said to Grimm. He had removed his tie and it was draped around his shoulders.

"What's going on here," Grimm said to the ticket agent, whose name tag read Milt Tune. "Is there something wrong with the airplane?"

Agent Tune slowly looked up from his book and said to Grimm, "There is nothing wrong with the airplane."

"Then," Grimm said.

"There *is* something wrong with the passengers. There are too many of them." Agent Tune smiled broadly. Then he said, "I'm sorry. I know this is no laughing matter. If you please get in line, we will be able to serve you more efficiently."

The man third in line said to agent Tune, "You creepy son-of-a-bitch, you just wasted fifteen seconds."

Agent Tune glared at the man third in line, then he played a number on the computer, shook his head, and told the passenger first in line that nothing was available on the noon flight to London except standby.

"This stinking flight is overbooked," the passenger third in line said to Grimm, loudly. "And that *flunkie* up there, that glorified *stewardess*, is doing nothing about it."

Ticket agent Milt Tune again looked up from his work at the passenger third in line.

"You heard me," the passenger third in line said. "Flunkie glorified stewardess who is afraid to do a man's work."

Agent Tune licked his lips and glanced back at his computer.

The man third in line was named Russ Crane and his wife's name was Norma and they had to be in England tomorrow for a big business deal. "If I am *not* in London tomorrow," Russ Crane said, very loudly, "a certain glorified stewardess is going to be looking for a new nose."

"We've had our tickets almost a month," Grimm said.

"Honey," Norma Crane said, "We've had our tickets *seven* months. Huh, Russ."

"Right, sweetheart. Seven stinking months."

Norma Crane wore her hair in a bouffant arrangement that looked like a little tornado. Her hair was starting to tilt slightly to the starboard side.

"We even have our seat numbers assigned," Grimm said.

"Honey, *everybody* has seat numbers. There are four and five people booked in some seats. They screwed this up real bad."

Russ Crane was looking more like a bulldog every second. He was even growling slightly in the direction of ticket agent Milt Tune, who was fingering the computer and flipping pages in a book. Other passengers were wandering back from the gate, and asking what was going on here.

"This stinking airline is going to pay if I'm not in London tomorrow, and not on any stinking *noon* flight."

"The noon flight is all standby," ticket agent Milt Tune said. "There are eight, no nine, seats on the 6:30 P.M. flight."

Somebody toward the back said, "I'll take two seats on that one!"

"That's tomorrow night," Grimm said to himself. "This is this morning."

"Listen," a girl behind allegedly important passenger Russ Crane said, "I got every bit as much right to be on this flight as you."

"You have no rights," Russ Crane said.

"Nobody has rights," Norma Crane said.

"The toxins must be backing up in your body," the girl said.

"Listen, you little hag," Russ Crane said to insignificant passenger Rose Miller, who appeared to be wearing a body stocking and had to be in London to study art, "The only way you'll get to England ahead of us is feet first."

"Jesus Christ," Rose Miller said. "You have got a very big problem." She tapped her temples. "You know, it's people like you that make this world so hyper." Rose Miller whipped out a tablet from her tote and began sketching Russ Crane.

"She's drawing you, Russ," Norma Crane said. "She's putting on a nose big as a cantaloupe. Russ, she's putting on long, floppy ears."

Russ Crane ripped the page from Rose Miller's tablet, wadded it into a ball, and flung the scrap in the direction of ticket agent Milt Tune, who was dialing numbers on a phone. The wad of paper bounced off agent Tune's forehead.

Totally worthless passenger Rose Miller bit her lip and moved her neck in circles, with her eyes closed.

She was breathing fast.

"Russ," Norma Crane said nervously to her husband, who was *praying* ticket agent Tune would make a move after getting hit with the wad of paper.

"What," Russ Crane said.

"Russ, look at that girl."

Rose Miller was still rolling her head.

"So?" Russ Crane said.

"Russ, I think she's putting some kind of spell on you. I saw a show on television about modern witches, and Russ, they did stuff like that." Norma Crane's hair seemed about to fall completely off her head. She straightened it, like it was a hat. "Russ, she's scaring me."

"Stop that," Russ Crane said to Rose Miller, who was now groaning softly.

"Make her stop, Russ. I'm not getting on an airplane if she puts a hex on you. I don't want her on *our* plane, Russ."

"Knock that crap off, you," Russ Crane said.

Russ Crane leaned out of line and told ticket agent Milt Tune there were now *three* people who had to make that flight. Others in line said, the hell.

Grimm walked back and explained the situation to Lackey, who was sitting on a suitcase, and Phyllis, who was searching her purse for some travel agency credentials she was going to flash on ticket agent Milt Tune, and the situation did not sound so good.

The computer indicated that the flight to London had been overbooked by approximately twenty-two bodies, but three passengers had opted for other flights, so it was about nineteen overbooked, at the moment, which was thirty-nine moments before the scheduled departure. Ticket agent Milt Tune was acting like he was out for a walk in the park and was smirking away valuable time. Artist Rose Miller had put some horrible spell on Russ and Norma Crane. Things, clearly, were out of control up toward the front of the line.

"It ought to be illegal," Lackey said.

"Everybody overbooks," Phyllis said. "It's policy. There's no rule against it. When there are no no-shows, it can be trouble."

"The pain in my side ought to be illegal, I meant," Lackey said.

"It must be a computer error," Phyllis said sternly. "Passengers with reserved seats, with seat numbers, are guaranteed a place." Phyllis waved the boarding passes she had procured three weeks and two days ago.

"What seats you got?" somebody in the middle of the line asked.

"Row thirteen, seats A, B, and C."

"Hey, me too," a voice from the mob shouted back. "I'm row thirteen, seat B."

"Why would you get row thirteen?" Lackey asked. "That's so unlucky."

"Well, crap," Phyllis said.

"Come on, Grimm," Lackey begged. "Get us out of this one. Think of something."

"The bank job pales in comparison," Grimm sighed. "It's like a lynch mob. If anybody tried anything, those people up there would stomp you into the floor."

It looked like the end of the hand.

There the goddamn city sat with a pair of deuces, calling right along. Grimm, Lackey, and Phyllis had hung in there after the first heart, and the second heart, and the third and the fourth, and they shot it all on the come, and caught a club. Four hearts and a club don't pay the rent.

"We could always try for a later flight," Lackey suggested. His former spunk was about gone. He sat like a skeleton, the life drained from his limbs.

"I have a feeling," Phyllis said, "that would be a mistake. I have a feeling, we better get out of this town, now."

She made the point that they had left behind a trail of cars by fire hydrants and broken newspaper stands and suspicious bus drivers which, if connected, would lead to this very spot.

But for the first time all evening, and morning—God this had been going on a long time—nobody was angry with another. This was nobody's fault. Precautions, the boarding passes, had been taken. They *had* arrived in enough time. By all rights, they should be getting on the airplane at this instant. This was merely bad luck, foul luck, and since it was unfair and not human error, Grimm, Lackey, and Phyllis more or less stuck together because three heads were better than one, even if one of the heads ached a little.

"This is the worst luck," Lackey said. "I mean, *hell!*"

Several of the people in the line turned to look at Lackey, as he struggled to his feet.

"She's right," Lackey said to nobody, but nodding at Phyllis. "We've got to get the hell out of here. *Now!*"

Others turned around.

"We deserve to get out of here. It's our right."

"Easy," Grimm said.

"Sit down and let us think," Phyllis said.

They were no longer last in line. About twenty people had been sent back from the gate.

"We can't just sit around, waiting," Lackey said.

"Why are you going to London," a woman in front of Lackey asked. "Vacation?"

"We have got to make a move!"

Lackey summoned up his remaining energy, it was a courageous effort, and he staggered toward the counter, where ticket agent Tune was fiddling around, calling here, punching there, being a disinterested spectator. Lackey stumbled to the counter and almost fell on it.

"If you will take a place in line, sir," Tune said, "we will be able to serve you more efficiently. I have called upstairs for assistance. Another agent is en route. The flight will be delayed, I assume, until this matter with the computer is resolved."

Lackey held out his ticket and boarding pass.

"To hell with London," he said. "I want to trade this ticket in for one to Cleveland."

"Oh God," Phyllis said.

"Get the hell out of here," Russ Crane said.

Ticket agent Milt Tune blinked once.

Everybody in line looked and listened as Lackey again said he didn't want to go to Europe anymore, he wanted to go to Cleveland.

"They will be here with handcuffs and nets at any second," Phyllis said.

Ticket agent Tune swallowed and said to Lackey, "If that's what you want, it's the next window."

Lackey supported himself against the counter and squinted at the next window, the one for "Passengers Without Tickets."

"But I have a ticket."

"To London."

"Yes," Lackey said. "But I hate London."

"But you have no ticket to Cleveland."

"No. I love it there, though."

"You need that window," Tune said.

The line parted and Lackey limped to the proper window, but there was no agent on duty. Lackey just stood there, dazed.

"I guess that about does it," Phyllis said.

Grimm said nothing. He watched passenger Russ Crane become enraged because Milt Tune just wasted one minute dealing with an insignificant madman (poor Lackey), and Grimm continued to watch as Russ Crane left his place in line and rumbled toward the counter. Everybody watched as agent Tune pointed at passenger Crane. Then somebody said, "My God."

Artist Rose Miller said, "This country is going to the dogs," and she began sketching the fight, which was not really much of a fight, it was more like a whipping. Russ Crane grabbed agent Tune's arm, and wrung it like a towel. Agent Tune screamed. Russ Crane then slugged agent Tune in the nose, and agent Tune fell over backward.

Several, more than that, about 80 percent of those in line, cheered Russ Crane's punch, but his wife said, "Now you've gone and done it. That guy will be all day getting things straightened out."

"Get up, you sissy," Russ Crane said, leaning over the counter.

"Hit him again," somebody suggested.

Grimm predicted the looting would start momentarily.

Harvey the bag man looked inside, shook his head, took a blood pressure pill, and got on his walkie-talkie to see if the entire fleet of wheelchairs could be rushed to the counter in question.

Agent Tune got up, holding his nose, which was bleeding. He had lost much of his smug exterior. It looked like he was about to cry. He disappeared through a door behind the counter.

Russ Crane nodded once, a that's-that nod.

Then everybody wondered, now what?

In several minutes, a different airline official came from the back room and asked that all the passengers with seats on the flight to London scheduled to leave in twenty-nine minutes please step this way, to a lounge area.

"We don't want any static from you, either," Russ Crane said.

Others in line said, "Yeah."

The new agent licked his lips and said there would be no static. He said the matter of too many passengers for too few seats would be resolved as equitably as possible.

Phyllis went to the window where Lackey was hunched.

Well, Grimm decided, it's time to check the cards again.

What do you know? The club they caught to go with the four hearts paired them up. They had a pair of sixes! Grimm was so excited at the prospect of a flush, he hadn't considered anything less. But a pair of sixes beats the city's pair of deuces, unless, of course, the city has three deuces or two pair. It was all on the table. You bet almost everything on the first four cards, you can't fold when somebody raises. There was not a damn thing left to do but call.

"Let's go," Grimm said to Lackey and Phyllis.

Lackey apologized for trying to swap London for Cleveland in front of all those people.

Grimm told him to forget it.
Nobody could have thought he was serious.

While Rotzinger was waiting for the computer print-out of crimes and complaints registered within the last few hours, the mayor dropped by for an update and to inform the chief that calls would be coming in from such places as Halifax, Lima, Moscow, and Chicken Livers, Idaho, requesting information on what was now being called The Crime of the Eon.

The mayor's name was Sands, and he had been elected on an equal-rights platform, and the mayor said his platform now was resembling a gallows.

There were obviously repercussions of this monstrosity that Rotzinger hadn't considered.

Rotzinger was certain he had considered *everything*—the boat, the third car, the club membership, the home entertainment center—but he listened obediently as the mayor expressed his thoughts.

The mayor scraped debris off a chair and sat down. He said he had just finished reading all the reports, and was shocked, humiliated, angered, tired, and depressed. Rotzinger asked the mayor, other than that, how did he feel?

"This thing has been bungled from the start," the mayor said, "and the press is going to castrate us."

Mayors are people, too. They are political people, but they have emotions. The average person thinks that a mayor or similarly well-placed public official operates mostly on remote control, and has stock answers for everything. But mayors get pissed, just like everybody else. The mayor called Rotzinger an incompetent ass.

Rotzinger started to call Wax and call *him* an incompetent ass, but instead he simply broke a pencil.

"We have two problems here," the mayor said. "The first is one of public relations. We are, at the moment, being laughed at by hundreds of thousands of people. It's like

Dallas being remembered as the city where Kennedy was killed. This city will be remembered as the place where the clown robbed the bank while police officers stood around playing with themselves."

Rotzinger said the game was never over until the last dog was dead.

"We cannot afford extra innings here," the mayor said. "Are you aware of the fact that right now there are people dressed as clowns robbing convenience stores and gas stations?"

They were aware.

"Are you aware that, if we don't apprehend these people, a motion picture will be made, and your role will be played by somebody like Elmer Fudd?"

Rotzinger said that officer Stark would be dragged through the park for letting the hostages disperse.

"The second problem," the mayor said, "is more personal. You have a great job. Every job carries with it some risk, this more than others. We belong to the city, the people."

The mayor walked to the window and he pulled the curtains open.

"Look at all those crazy bastards out there at three in the morning."

Rotzinger took a call from Wax, who said he had the computer print-out of recent activity, and would be right up.

"They pay us," the mayor said, "and we owe them."

Rotzinger sincerely wished the mayor would go away.

"It would be like me dumping garbage on the street," the mayor continued, heavily.

"The robbery?"

"Yes," the mayor said. "The robbery."

"I understand," Rotzinger said.

"Do you really understand what I'm saying?"

"Yes."

"It's all a matter of risk, Rotzinger, life is. I love this job.

Mayor of a big, important city. It's a lot of work, but the rewards are great. But if I screw it up, if I let the sanitation department start hurling garbage in the parks, I'm gone."

The mayor searched through the rubble on Rotzinger's floor for an ash tray. He frowned before continuing. "It's like this cigarette. It feels good to smoke, but is it worth the risk?"

Rotzinger's wife called and said she couldn't sleep and wondered how things were going because at noon there was a meeting of the Valentine Committee and she wanted to be able to tell the members that everything was okay and that there was no need to call an executive session of the Probation Committee, huh honey. Furthermore, Rotzinger's wife said, she had voted to put the Scotts on probation three weeks ago because of Henry Scott's driving while intoxicated arrest, and that meant Shirley Scott's friends might hold a grudge and try a power play because of this bank robbery thing, which was really nobody's fault, but then, The Club is a hard, cruel place, huh sweetie. So could she tell them at the Valentine Committee meeting that a lot of progress was being made because after all The Club was about the only thing in the whole world Mrs. Rotzinger cared about. So how was it going?

"Thank you," Rotzinger said, hanging up.

Perspiration beaded on his forehead.

"And?" the mayor asked.

"The lab," Rotzinger said.

"Let's don't tear up any more banks," the mayor suggested solemnly, "because in the first place it makes us look like fools, and in the second place, it costs a lot of money to replace five Italian marble sections of floor."

"Italian marble?"

"Italian marble," the mayor said. "Perhaps we need to enroll our law enforcement branch in art class."

Perhaps, Rotzinger guessed.

"We need to reestablish ourselves as deserving of public trust," the mayor said, holding a match precariously near the end of his cigarette. He had made a campaign promise to stop smoking if elected, as proof of his dedication. "You revert to bad habits when the pressure is on," the mayor smiled. "Right now, I'd like to smoke an entire tobacco plant."

Rotzinger brought the mayor up to date, and said he was hoping for some insight when the computer print-out arrived. The mayor listened to the progress report and theorized that Rotzinger was pissing in the wind.

Rotzinger blinked.

"Correct me if I'm wrong. We have sent out descriptions of people wearing disguises. The entire goddamn crew of Ringling Brothers will be arrested."

"Bone structure," Rotzinger wheezed. "Height. Weight."

"We don't know who did it or where they are. A common criminal hoodwinked us, and for all we know, he could be halfway around the world."

Rotzinger looked at his watch. No, a fifth of the way, he started to say, but didn't.

"We have all this equipment at our fingertips, and all the damn experts in the world, but can't stop a damn robber who starts out trapped, to begin with!" The mayor struck a match and moved it toward the end of his cigarette.

Rotzinger started to tell the mayor that the staff psychologist had issued his report. The conclusion was, the robber had more than likely been in need of money at the time of the alleged crime. But he didn't.

"Turn your head," the mayor said.

Rotzinger did. When he turned back, the mayor's cigarette was charred on the end, and a wisp of smoke was floating toward the air-conditioning vent.

"There are two ways for me to take care of this. Wait until you catch them. Wait until you don't catch them, and relieve you of your duties. Either way, order is restored. We cannot

have every thug in the world flying to this city to have a crack
at a bank. Look at it this way. You really screwed up."

Wax entered without knocking, and exchanged a knowing
look with the mayor. He held the print-out.

"Everybody is entitled to a mistake," the mayor concluded.
"And yours might cost you your future."

"We'll get them," Rotzinger said.

"One can only hope," the mayor said. "Hello, Wax."

"Sir."

Wax had just talked with his girlfriend, Irene, and she had,
in turn, gotten her brother out of bed, and he was rushing
some building plans over at this very moment because there
was a lot within a stone's throw of a road that led to a highway that led to the beach, which was a steal, and all they
needed was ten grand down on the lot. Irene's brother had
the inside track on a load of logs, which would make a great
almost-beach house. On the $42,500 salary, Wax had been
able to save an average of only $1.95 a week, but if he got the
chief's job, that would be another fifty grand a year to play
with. Wax was jubilant, so it was hard for him to look down
in the mouth. The word was all through the building, old
Rotzinger was hanging by a brass knuckle.

"What's this?" the mayor asked.

Wax told him it was the computer print-out of this evening's activity.

"So?"

Wax shrugged and nodded his head slightly at Rotzinger,
who was wondering how he could get a half a Valium from
his drawer to his mouth, unnoticed.

"There may be clues in there," Rotzinger said. He realized
he sounded a little like Basil Rathbone, so he changed "clues"
to "trends," and explained his theory about dealing with amateurs. One thing leads to another.

"Let's pray it doesn't," the mayor said, "or at this very moment, that clown might be going through your bedroom."

"One *bad* thing," Rotzinger said. "Amateurs panic."

"Maybe they got hit by a truck," Wax suggested, winking slightly to the mayor.

"Keep me informed," the mayor told Rotzinger. He said he would be in his office, keeping the members of the press, all eight billion of them, current. The mayor said he heard Ripley's Believe It or Not was sending a team to the scene, and that the bank would be on the cover of the next book.

Rotzinger coughed and licked the tranquilizer off his palm.

The mayor left.

Rotzinger took the print-out from Wax. It was about three feet long. "I have an important assignment for you, Wax."

"Sir?"

"Something you'll be great at."

Wax nodded.

"Go get me a cheeseburger and fries."

Who knew, after he caught these bastards, *he* might run for mayor. This ex-college frat rat of a mayor had the city jail looking like the YMCA. The gut-shooters and sneak thieves deserved their "living space," all right, and so do the god-damn cockroaches. Once this was over, Rotzinger decided to call the mayor and his intellectual phonies right out onto Main Street for a showdown.

Rotzinger's wife called yet again. He told her that if she bothered him one more time, he'd wear a string tie to the next dinner at the fool club.

It had been calm, as Friday nights go.

It's a bit overwhelming to sit with the arrest-and-complaint report in front of you, but after you've been in the business all those years, you get immune to all the pain and heartache. These things are, after all, jobs. The people investigating the complaints are officers, not social workers. If you take every flesh wound home with you, you'd crack up inside of a month.

It was like looking at the city's EKG.

The needle went off the paper with the bank robbery.

Major advances *have* been made in the field of crime prevention, for example, the department spent $125,000 last year on a study that proved conclusively that the weather influences human behavior. It's a nice thing to know—that a low pressure system causes people to get mean. There was a terrific paragraph in that report about how fish won't bite when the wind is from the east. So when the barometer drops, two extra people are put on the switchboard, how's that for getting maximum use out of a hundred plus grand? Calls are handled quicker and we can get the blood off the walls approximately six minutes faster, knowing that weather influences behavior. What we *really* need to know, Rotzinger mumbled to himself, running his finger down the arrest printout, is where a person plans to murder another person, so we can have an officer there. At last count, there were some 13.5 million street corners, not counting alley corners, and as Rotzinger tells the civic groups, it's a little hard getting a cop on every crosswalk.

Rotzinger knew what affected behavior more than weather: money.

If a man has to sleep on a fire escape, it's obvious he is going to get a lot more pissed off when it rains than a man who can afford a couple of weeks in Miami.

It's the dope addicts doing the killing and robbing, and when they get caught there are these wonderful government-funded projects that help the poor, unfortunate dope addict so he won't puke his guts up. Those programs are like giving beer to alcoholics so they won't get as drunk as they did on bourbon.

Rotzinger decided the world was in a hell of a shape.

Between the hours of 10 P.M. and 2 A.M., there had been a murder and a half—one guy stabbed in the stomach in a porno movie was hanging on by a thread—twenty-six rob-

beries, eleven burglaries, nineteen stolen cars, ninety-four acts
of vandalism, six rapes, and eight outbreaks by child molesters.

The computer gives you a play-by-play.

You can scan the overall crimes, or dial a specific category,
and hit a button for the complete arrest report. It's very
cheap entertainment. Rotzinger pressed the button and
scanned the recent child-molester file. You can quickly tell
what areas are hot. Rotzinger made a note to himself to send
extra people to this one block over by a strip joint, if he still
had a job, that was, because the child molesters were having a
field night. Three children had molested strippers, going off
work.

There were an average number of laughers—attempted
crimes that didn't come off the way they had been drawn on
the subway wall.

While attempting to rob a liquor store, a criminal had a
net dropped on him, and he panicked and ran through a glass
door, into the path of an automobile. The netting became en-
tangled on the bumper, and the robber was dragged a block.
The owner of the liquor store had hit a foot switch, releasing
the net from the rafters.

Another liquor store robbery was aborted when the owner
hit the trap-door button, and the criminal was deposited into
the basement, just like in the old movies, where he suffered a
broken neck. This would obviously be a lawsuit. Criminals
with guns have the right to be calmly arrested. Before you
bash them, you have to ask, "May I?"

A man sleeping in his apartment had been shot in the leg.
The shot had come from the next apartment, during a domestic argument. A woman tried to scare her husband. The bullet
went through the cheap wall and hit a man named Jeffries
near the ass.

It was doubtful the bank robbers would try to hold up a
liquor store to get a drink, so Rotzinger kept scanning the
"real" crimes, quickly, and then he called up the "Fruitcake

File," which is a record of time-wasting crap that constitutes about 90 percent of police work, things like:

9/15, 030, 1:05 A.M., 72ND & CPW—COMPLAINT CALLED IN BY OLLIE TROOST RE NEIGHBOR MAY PRUITT THROWING CAT NAMED FIFI OUT 10TH FLOOR WINDOW. SEE ARR RPT #6-62-B.

Or:

9/15, 115 & 114, 1:11 A.M., MAX'S BAR ON 200 BLK 6TH—CUSTOMER COMPLAINS BARTENDER SERVING WEEK-OLD TUNA. REFERRED TO HEATH D AND BBBUREAU. NO ARR. SEE REPORT 801-NR-4.

Or:

9/15, 222 BEAT, 1:22 A.M., 400 BLK 72—75 MDL 4-DR PKD BY FIRE HYDRANT, REMOVED AND CITED. DAMAGES. SEE ARR RPT PBH-20014-R.

Wax interrupted Rotzinger to report that the drawings of the robbers were in the final stages of being copied, and that any hour, they would be dispatched to the logical sites. At any one time, there are perhaps twenty-five drawings of badly wanted criminals in circulation at airports and other jumping-off places. These profiles are usually neatly stacked in drawers by ticket agents too busy getting people to Toronto and Paris and Miami to bother with matching faces with bad drawings. About the last time a ticket agent identified an escaping criminal was in 1956, when a guy nailed his brother.

Still, it's procedure.

Officer Ledbetter who shot a kid in the leg and was transferred to the copying machine pending the complete investigation of this shooting had to have something to do except put together homemade porno books.

Sending out drawings to airports and bus stations is a formality. It takes about six hours to get the damn things to the right people. What the hell. It beats work.

"Look at this, Wax," Rotzinger said, nodding at his computer.

NOTE TO 33RD: WORLD'S BIGGEST TITS NOW LIVING IN APT 1705 AT BLAIR APARTMENTS. TELL HER 201 SENT YOU.

Wax frowned.

"It looks like there is a pimp in our midst," Rotzinger said. "Find out who officer 201 is, get him out of bed, get him down here."

Rotzinger hit the ERASE button, and the world's biggest disappeared from the computer.

"We've got a half a dozen possibilities," Rotzinger said to Wax, who had mixed feelings about the old boy. He was making a damn game last stand, that was for sure. Rotzinger rubbed his hands together and scooted back from the computer terminal, after calling for the complete reports on six incidents that had occurred within the proper time span.

"The secret, Wax, is never to give your opponent too much credit. It is human nature to screw up, particularly in a pressurized situation. Instead of looking for them on some island, we should check the gutter first."

Wax glanced at each file.

A car containing two men and a woman had been driven into the lobby of a hotel. The passengers had fled before police arrived.

A party of two men and a woman had walked a check of $425 in a ritzy restaurant. Five bottles of champagne had been consumed.

"A victory party," Wax said.

"Who knows."

A taxi carrying two men and a woman had created a scene when one of the passengers leaped out of the moving vehicle and crashed into a newspaper rack, causing a car to the rear to ram a post. The passengers disappeared before the police arrived.

Three people, two men and a woman, had jumped from the window of a slowly moving subway.

Two men and a woman were ticketed for riding three on a motorcycle.

Three people, two men and a woman, called for an ambulance. Upon examining the alleged sick party, it was determined that the customer was in perfect health. The three admitted to the ambulance driver it was a play, because taxi and limo service was so rotten this time of night. They offered the ambulance $100 for a quick ride to the airport. He said no, he could make more than that on an ordinary emergency run. The three people were not in their motel room when officers acted on the ambulance driver's report.

"I want the manager of the hotel where the car ran in the lobby first," Rotzinger said, "then in order, somebody at the restaurant, the taxi driver, whoever turned in the subway complaint, the officer that handled the motorcycle, and the ambulance driver. I want all of these calls placed within five minutes, and I want the responsible party who can tell me about each incident involving two men and a woman on the phone, on hold, within 10 minutes."

Wax said that was a tall order.

Rotzinger looked at his right palm and squeezed an imaginary ball.

"Wax?"

"Sir."

"We have four hundred forty-four telephones in this building."

"We do?"

"If necessary, I want every one of these phones busy, and I want people carrying out my instructions. After I talk to the people who reported the problems, I want fifty people on stand-by for follow-up calls. I want every two-man, one-woman group involved in *anything* checked out, right down to their eye-teeth."

Oh God, Wax thought. What if he gets lucky, and the people who *did* rob the bank *did* panic and run a car into a building. Rotzinger would be a hero. He'd *emcee* the convention in Las Vegas next year. But, nobody would have been ignorant enough to have walked a big tab or jumped from a subway or a cab or tried to bribe an ambulance driver, after stealing $800,000.

If those people were stupid enough to get caught, Wax would personally see to it that each robber shared a cell with a cannibal.

All they had to do was stay calm, for heaven's sake.

"Wax?"

"Sir."

"More fries."

"Yes, sir."

"Get the calls set up, and send out for another order of french fries."

There's always natural causes, Wax thought, of the chief's job.

The night manager of the Jackson Brothers Hotel was named Bernard Overby.

Bernard Overby had a degree from a junior college, but that was about it. This degree was worth the frame it was encased in. The frame was worth four dollars. He had no wealthy or well-placed relatives. He had led a normal, middle-class life, and it all added up.

A degree from junior college doesn't make a damn, and experience as a night clerk in a flea bag—it was that or paint yellow stripes on the streets—doesn't make a double damn.

The good thing, the only good thing, about being a night manager of a flea bag hotel is you have plenty of time to work on your novel. Bernard Overby's novel was going pretty good. He was on page 850. The first chapter was seventy-five pages. He had an agent and everything. It was Bernard Overby's plan to write himself out of this trap. The thing was, everybody Bernard Overby knew was also writing a novel—bartenders, hash slingers, cab drivers, whores. Writing is a very competitive field these days; it's a way out of the salt mines. Bernard Overby's project was a Sweeping Novel of the North. It had started out as a Sweeping Novel of the South, but as his agent, Fuzzy Steinberger, said, "Jesus Christ, kid, there are already four hundred thousand of them things on the market. Move the goddamn thing, to like Buffalo, right? Buffalo, Trenton. Like that. The hell with the South. Bring it north, and I'll sell it for you."

Bernard Overby paid Fuzzy Steinberger $47.50 a month to be his agent. "Listen to me. It's normal," Steinberger said when Bernard Overby questioned the fee. "I got to read this crap, you understand? Not your crap. Your crap is not garbage. Other crap."

Fuzzy Steinberger read the first 400 pages of Bernard Overby's Sweeping Novel of the North in one night and loved it, which is about all you can ask out of life—hope. Bernard Overby was motivated and wrote sixty-nine pages the very next night. Steinberger's recent instructions had been encouraging. "I like the part where the guy gets it on with his wife's girlfriend. That's real choice material. Give me more of this, kid. Just remember, keep it north. You go south, and there's people down there living on twenty-five hundred dollars a year. You expect them to buy big, expensive books?"

The agent also suggested that Bernard Overby toss in a nice little chapter on how great the Mafia was. "We get them buying the book, hell, there's five million of them up here, we're in, kid. By the way, I got to go up with my fee to seventy-five dollars a month. The other garbage I got to read is killing me."

Fuzzy Steinberger said his crack staff was currently working on a title, something like Gone with the Tide, something with class.

A title was $150 extra.

The reason Bernard Overby's novel was going so well—he expected it to crest at 1,000 pages, and then start on the conclusion—was because he was living the role played by his lead character. You cannot simulate intrigue or lust. You can write about what you have experienced. The premise of the novel was that his lead character was unable to find happiness

or satisfaction with one woman, and therefore had rela-
tionships with *four* women, each with her redeeming value.

The wife with the good mind, for conversation.

The girlfriend with the good legs, for days on the beach.

The wife's sister with the good bottom.

The girlfriend's girlfriend with the large breasts for strolls
down the street in see-through blouses.

Fuzzy Steinberger's first idea for a title had been *Ms.
Frankenfuck.* "What separates porno from literature is a
plot," Steinberger said. "With this good story line, we start
taking their clothes off and we got it made."

And you wonder why guys sometimes take rifles to busy
street corners and open up on innocent bystanders?

Rotzinger knew why: despair.

You take away a person's hope, it's all over.

So Rotzinger listened as Bernard Overby explained how his
lead character might have to murder two of his girlfriends
near the end of the book, maybe even on the last page.

"The people in the car," Rotzinger said, proceeding cautiously when Bernard Overby paused to catch his breath.
Forced information is usually erratic.

"Oh, them. They ran. The car came up over the curb I
guess and busted into the door and front window."

Bernard Overby said it was still a big mess in the lobby. A
Mrs. Eskridge had stepped on a splinter and was threatening
to sue the hotel for $400,000,000.

"Two men and a woman?" Rotzinger asked. "In the car."

"Yeah," Bernard Overby said. "Two and one."

"They say anything?"

"A love scene requires total concentration, Mr. Rotzinger.
You do any writing?"

"No."

"Glad to meet you. It's very hard to duplicate a love-mak-
ing scene with glass flying. Somebody from the car said,
'Let's go,' I think. That was about it."

"What did they look like, roughly?"

"Tell me the truth. Does a Sweeping Novel of the North interest you in the least?"

"Sure," Rotzinger said. "You don't see too many of them."

"Greenbriar, the main character, can't find the perfect woman, so he goes after parts, legs, breasts, you know?"

"Interesting concept," Rotzinger said, tapping his finger on his desk.

"You're just saying that," Bernard Overby said.

"No I'm not."

"You're just saying that so I won't be depressed and do something insane."

Rotzinger insisted the setting and plot were . . . um, right up there.

Bernard Overby said he would inform his agent that Rotzinger wanted to buy a copy, at twenty-three dollars.

"Hell," Rotzinger said.

"Printing costs. Paper. I've been working on this four years. When I started, we were going to come out with the novel for six ninety-five. If I don't get it finished in a couple of years, the price might be up to thirty."

"Hurry," Rotzinger said.

"Got any title ideas?" Bernard Overby asked.

"Mr. Overby," Rotzinger said, through a sigh.

"Sweeping Novel of the North. Power. Lust. Greed. Corruption."

Rotzinger thought a moment and said, "From Here to Maternity."

"Not bad," Bernard Overby said.

"It was a joke."

"Oh."

"What kind of factories does this Greenbriar own?"

"Aluminum siding."

"Jesus Christ, Overby."

"I knew you didn't like it," he said.

"It's not that," Rotzinger said. "Aluminum siding just isn't too interesting."

"I guess I could go back and change it. To what?"

"Hell, Overby. Anything. Toys."

"Toys? That's not bad. That's one way he could get caught in an affair. His wife could see this doll that looked like his wife's sister."

"Yeah, sure."

"I love it. I absolutely love it."

"Tell me about the people in the car."

"One of them, a man, weighed about two-eighty, a fat slob. He looked inside the lobby and waddled off down the street. The other guy was very dark, like an Arab. The woman was more like a girl, like sixteen or seventeen."

"Thanks," Rotzinger said. He hated policework.

"Toys. That's great. It's going to be a lot of rewriting."

"You can do it, Overby."

Rotzinger heard typing in the background before Overby put the receiver down. He drew a line through the car-in-the-hotel-lobby incident.

You can live with the hard-cores, but guys like Overby can knock the wind out of you. There are millions of them out there, trying to root their way out of the trenches. But for the grace of God, Rotzinger thought, staring at the phone. Rotzinger mixed himself a tidy little vodka and tonic.

Valium, vodka and tonic, and french fries, Wax thought. Interesting.

"Cigarette?" Wax asked.

"Why not," Rotzinger nodded.

They had trouble getting taxi driver and impressionist Charley English because he was still on duty, but when Rotzinger got on the horn and identified himself as the chief, paper was shuffled faster, and the dispatcher promised to locate Charley and have him call Rotzinger, immediately.

The episode of a man jumping out of a moving cab was

third on the list of two-men, one-woman possibilities. Wax
was checking on the restaurant where the large tab had been
walked.

"Just keep in mind, I got a wife and three or four kids to
support," Charley English said, to open the conversation with
Rotzinger. Then, "What's the big deal? Granted, guys don't
jump out of moving cabs every day, but hell, the *chief*?"

Rotzinger calmly explained the inquiry was routine.

"Oh sure," Charley English said. "You check on everything
weird that happens in a cab."

"English," Rotzinger said, "it's none of your damn business
why I'm calling you. All you need to know is that I'm interested in those fares. Another thing, if you don't cooperate,
English, you'll be driving a crap truck."

"I should be so lucky. They make a fortune."

Charley English said the act of a man jumping from a moving vehicle was one of the more freakish things he had been
involved with in the nineteen years he had been driving a cab.
The guy was not even drunk. Once, Charley English got a
fare to Rhode Island, and another time, a woman sprayed
some Mace on her husband in the back seat, and he had
hauled people dressed as rabbits and things, but jumping
from a speeding cab was pretty strong.

"Speeding?"

"Not speeding. *Moving*. Going *exactly* the speed limit."

Rotzinger asked about the whole trip.

"The weird guy is in the front with me. He's nervous. A
man and a woman are in the back. She's very nice, by the
way. Good legs."

"Go on," Rotzinger said.

"The guy in front jumps out, no warning, no nothing. He
hits the pavement like a dog or something and goes headfirst
into a paper stand. I thought he was dead. He was all right,
though."

"Why in the world," Rotzinger asked firmly, "would the
guy in the front seat jump out?"

Charley English said nothing. He considered, for one tenth of a second, telling Rotzinger about his famous Scandinavian accent, but decided against it, and merely said, "Beats me, maybe he wanted to buy a newspaper real bad."

Rotzinger asked for the specifics and Charley English gave them.

"Where'd you pick them up?"

"By the park."

"At a residence? An apartment? A bar? You get a call?"

"On the street. The nervous one flagged me down. He was using profanity, screaming, jumping up and down on the sidewalk. They looked like they were in a hurry. People in a hurry usually give good, big tips."

"Where were they going?" Rotzinger asked.

"Airport."

Rotzinger covered the phone and told Wax this looked very good. Wax smiled.

"Which airport?"

"Kennedy."

"When?"

Charley English checked his records and said, "An hour and twenty minutes ago."

"Hell," Rotzinger said. "Two men and a woman?"

"Yeah."

"Describe them."

"Who can describe? They were wearing clothes. The woman was in a dress. Good to great legs. Sandy hair. Round face. Good teeth. One of the guys was nervous, and the other guy sat in the back and frowned."

Rotzinger said that Charley English was much better at describing women. It's the price you pay, Charley English said.

"What about the luggage?"

"What about it?"

"How many bags?"

"Two. They put one in the trunk and kept one in the back seat."

Rotzinger again covered the phone and told Wax, "This does not look good. This looks great. Get a car ready."

"Have some more fries," Wax said.

"What's this all about?" Charley English asked. "The bank thing?"

"What bank thing?" Rotzinger said. He got Charley English's location and said a car would be there in ten minutes to bring him down here so he could give descriptions to the police artist. "I want to know why the guy jumped out of your cab, English, and then I want to know where they went. This is very important. It is the most important thing you've ever been involved with."

"It *is* the bank thing. I had the damn robbers in my cab! They seemed like all-right people to me. I can't believe it."

Rotzinger told Charley English that he was not starting a fan club.

"They weren't mean at all," Charley English said. "They looked like average people, hell, like me."

Rotzinger explained that unless Charley English began producing critical information, he would no longer be average, he would be inferior, he would be unemployed, on food stamps, on welfare, on the ropes.

"They didn't hurt anybody," Charley English said, "if it *was* them."

"Obstructing justice is a felony," Rotzinger said. "You love your wife and kids?"

"No."

Charley English admitted that he had been working on his famous Scandinavian accent, and he assumed the nervous one in the front seat misunderstood the joke and was worried about being in a cab with a foreigner, so maybe that was why he jumped out. "I think they got on a bus," Charley English said.

"What bus?"

"A bus, a bus."

"A city bus?"

"Yeah, I guess."

"To where?"

"Who knows?"

"Stay at that phone booth," Rotzinger said. "Don't move."

Rotzinger told Wax to get the bus company and check the schedules within the proper time and location boundaries; and he sent a car after Charley English. "It's them," he told Wax. "I know it, by God!" Rotzinger smashed both fists on his desk. This one would not only be in the trade magazines— it would be in the history books! It's very seldom a crime is solved with sound, creative investigatory technique. Most stuff is handled when a rat comes in and says, "My dumb husband done it," or when you follow blood.

Rotzinger had a flunkie check out the other two-men, one-woman complaints. He asked Wax how it felt, to be on the verge of greatness, if only by association.

"Okay," Wax said.

Wax was getting so depressed, he could have cried.

Charley English hung up the phone in the booth and wondered what his pals would think if his tip turned out to be the one that got the bank robbers nailed. They sure acted like average people, trying to hustle a few bucks despite overwhelming odds.

Whereas Charley English would be the first to put the cruncher on a dope addict, this was different. These people had done something everybody dreams about, which was get rich without hurting anybody. He didn't want their blood on his hands.

The lousy cops were too cocky.

You throw the book at a man for making an improper left turn, and then get him for no taillight, which happened last week, well, it comes back to haunt you.

He'd give them descriptions, all right.

The woman was 6'4", and the men were both short and bald.

Bernard Overby called back and asked Rotzinger what he thought of having his lead character, Greenbriar, get into a little dope smuggling, and Rotzinger said, "Bernard, son, god-damn it, you have got to get a grip on yourself, we're in the middle of a very serious investigation, here."

Bernard Overby said he knew it was only a sham, and that the reason Rotzinger had been so courteous and understanding before was because he was pumping information, and now that he had it, nobody cared what happened to a promising novelist. Bernard Overby said his agent's definition of a "promising novelist" was one who said, "I swear to God, the first chapter will be in the mail tomorrow." Bernard Overby also said he was starting to feel suicidal, homicidal, and insane.

"Hold on a minute," Rotzinger said.

"You sound *exactly* like my agent," Bernard Overby said.

Rotzinger told Wax there was a squirrel on line two, the guy at the hotel. "Talk to him, while I think."

"What?" Wax said.

Wax got on the phone and listened patiently as Bernard Overby outlined the first eight hundred pages of his Sweeping Novel of the North. Several times, Wax covered the phone and said to Rotzinger, "This guy is mad as a hatter."

Rotzinger concerned himself with what had happened after the robbery. The bank robbery was still a current event, and becoming more current all the time. Something becomes *history* only when you have counted and tagged the bodies. They had gone somewhere, and they had dumped the car they left the bank in, and they had taken a taxi toward the airport, until one of them had jumped from the moving cab. They were clearly out of control. They had scrambled into a bus, of all things, to God knows where. All Rotzinger had to do was put out an APB on all people frothing at the mouth.

There couldn't be more than a couple of thousand, at this time of night. Even though he was sitting in his office, the sensation of a chase was very real. It was like Rotzinger was breathing down these rascals' necks.

Rotzinger absent-mindedly rose from his chair and began picking up litter from the floor.

"With everything falling apart, now what would they do?" he asked nobody.

"What?" Wax asked.

"Would they continue to the airport? To a different airport?"

"This guy here on the phone, this Overby, is crying."

"Or would they hole up?"

"This guy has written almost a thousand pages of a book and doesn't even know where in the hell the setting is, and he hasn't even introduced all the characters. I'm going to hang up."

"We need to know a couple of things. We need to know, urgently, what bus they got on, and where they got off. Right, Wax?"

"Can I hang up on this joker or what?"

"What?"

Wax held the phone out.

Rotzinger took it. "Who is this? Oh yes. Overby. At the hotel. What, Overby? No, I think killing your lead character off in the middle of a novel is a bit theatrical. What I think you need is a nice, solid rewrite, top to bottom, all eight hundred pages. Fine, Overby, fine. You call me when it's finished."

Rotzinger replaced the receiver and told Wax to find the bus in question, and find the driver, and get him on a telephone immediately.

"There's one more thing, Wax. You're going to love it. I just thought of it. This may be on billboards at the convention in Las Vegas, right next to Sinatra's picture. In fact, the

HE'S HERE billboard might refer to me, not Sinatra. I want every airline called."

Wax frowned.

"We have four hundred forty-four telephones in this building."

"I know," Wax said.

"Every airline, every commuter service at every airport within fifty miles."

"That's a lot of airports and airlines."

"I'll bet there aren't four hundred and forty-four of them, Wax."

He nodded.

"We call the airlines and we check on the reservations for every flight from midnight, three hours ago, until, let's make it, midnight tomorrow night. Rather, tonight."

"Oh, boy."

"We check on every reservation involving two-men, one-woman packages."

Rotzinger punctuated this revelation with a serious, firm nod of his smiling head.

Wax was speechless.

"One would think that if they chose to flee the area, the reservations would have been made together, on the same flight. There can't have been *that* many one-woman, two-men reservations made."

"No."

"We get them, we check them."

"If they are going to different cities, we're in trouble, still," Wax said.

"Ah, but if they're not, their asses are in a very secure sling. Remember, Wax."

"Don't give them too much credit."

"Exactly."

Rotzinger said that people who jump out of cabs can be counted on to further blotch things. Assuming it *was* them in the cab, the once overwhelming head start had been greatly reduced.

"We get another fabulously current description from the bus driver. I doubt if they were still heavily disguised. Go, Wax, into the night, and get me the sons-of-bitches with valuable information."

Rotzinger pitched the french fries in the garbage can and ordered a container of cottage cheese and a glass of carrot juice. He called his wife and told her not to hock her designer golf gloves, just yet.

Grimm carried the suitcase with the money. Phyllis carried the clothes. Lackey walked with his hands on the wall, like he was drunk.

Phyllis choked down a glass of orange juice and a roll. She said she was beyond hunger and fatigue, and had no *real* feelings at all. She said it was like she had come off a binge. She couldn't concentrate.

"You're just tired," Grimm said, placing the suitcase full of money beside his chair.

"We've got beards," Lackey said, rubbing his chin, which was stinging with pain. "We've been up so long, we've grown beards."

The prospective passenger in the seat next to Lackey said she had had a terrible night, too, and had been forced to park two blocks from the terminal. Lackey looked at this woman, and didn't know whether to laugh or cry, so instead he yawned.

"Tell me," Phyllis said to Grimm, "did this really happen?"

Grimm, doing his damnedest to maintain morale and keep her spirits up, thumped the suitcase full of money and said, "Yep, it happened, all right."

"It seems to me that since we've quit trying, since we've just started floating around like driftwood, things have gotten better," Phyllis said, and yawned, which set off a chain reaction of yawns down the row. "I mean, we're here, at some gate. What are we doing here?"

"Beats me," Lackey said. The chairs in the luxurious waiting area were cloth, and suspended from chrome frames, and Lackey rocked gently.

"Trying to go to London," the woman next to Lackey said.

"Oh. Right. Thanks very much."

"What's wrong with you?"

"My side is broken."

"My!"

"Oh yeah," Phyllis said. "London. Great."

Russ Crane announced to the passengers that he would act as their spokesman and make sure God-given rights were administered, which prompted another of the passengers to remark, "Why don't you shut the hell up and sit down, you windbag."

Russ Crane pushed his sleeve up and threatened to punch out that passenger, a woman.

Lackey looked at the room full of people and said he felt like he was in one of the *Airport* motion pictures, where wings fell off and terminals were fire-bombed and the stewardesses flew the planes while the pilots watched porno View-Master slides.

It was 3:40 A.M.

The flight to England was supposed to leave in three minutes.

"I'd just as soon go home and forget the whole thing," Lackey said. "Except I can't walk."

"What home?" Grimm said, of his apartment that had already been rented.

"The flight to Cleveland was not *that* bad an idea," Phyllis told Lackey.

"If I had a good idea, it was an accident," he said.

"Well," Grimm said, "how we doing over there?"

Lackey and Phyllis yawned at him.

"I see," he said. The plan was, as Grimm saw it, to remain

calm and see what the airline had up its sleeve before making the next move.

Lackey said that didn't sound like a plan, it sounded like a thought. Not even a thought. A daydream. "It all looked so easy ten hours ago."

"Well," Grimm said quietly, "we've got our," and he started to say health, and then he started to say money, but he instead said "sanity," and then he said, "to a certain degree."

When you looked at the picture as a whole, all the dots except the one on the other side of the ocean had been connected. The pilgrimage to the airport had been accomplished, and it was only when you dealt with specifics that things began to wear thin around the edges. Sure, the trip had been a little erratic, but close only counts in horseshoes and, as Lackey said, death. They were where they were supposed to be, *with* the goods.

"What I can't believe," Lackey said, "among other things, is that we were at that bar, remember, Grimm, only a few hours ago. It seems like years."

"Put it out of your mind," Grimm told him.

"What about the car by the fire hydrant?"

"Put that out of your mind, too."

Lackey asked just what in the hell was he supposed to think about.

"Sun. Beaches. Girls."

"Christ," Phyllis said, snapping out of it a bit.

"And this," Grimm whispered, tapping the suitcase.

Lackey said he would trade his share, this second, for an injection of Novocaine, right in his brain. "How much do orthopedic surgeons cost?"

"A few thousand," Grimm assured him. "A drop in the bucket."

Grimm told Phyllis and Lackey that it was now time to summon something from deep within themselves and get a second wind, because everything that had happened before was meaningless without perfect execution down the home stretch.

Otis Boomershine tapped on a microphone and Lackey said, "Oh, God, they're opening fire."

The microphone screeched and Otis Boomershine made several important announcements, the first of which was that flight 742 would not take off in one minute and twenty seconds, as scheduled.

"Can you hear me?" Otis Boomershine asked. He continually mopped his gutless brow.

"You damn right, we can hear you," somebody said.

There really *is* security in numbers. You can push an average person around and tell him to take a seat for three hours or sell him a product made out of cheap crap or charge eighty-five dollars for fifteen minutes of labor, but if you try any monkey business with a group, there is somebody around to answer the question, "Why?" Then somebody says, "I don't know why they're doing that," then somebody else says, "They can't do that, let's get the son-of-a-bitch!"

Otis Boomershine knew that he was in the wrong place at the wrong time. He was aware that any judgmental error would result in a confrontation, and somebody might rip his wig off. He wanted so badly to tell these fine people that he was like them, one of the boys, and shouldn't be punished. It wasn't his fault the hideous computer had gone berserk. He didn't even enjoy working for this airline. It was just a job. If Otis Boomershine had his way, if it were up to him, gosh, he'd have everybody over for cocktails. But as Otis Boomershine looked out at this motley group, he was also aware that if he got one word out of place, somebody would yell, "Get the son-of-a-bitch," and he would be pummeled. The *real* villains who had been screwing these poor people hid behind computers and under grease racks. Otis Boomershine hadn't done a thing! God, he wished he was a record. Let them smash that, not me, he thought, mopping his brow.

"Ladies and gentlemen," he said.

There was a man on the front row, moving his lips maliciously, as Otis Boomershine spoke. He was calling somebody, Otis obviously, a dirty, stinking something.

"Speak up, you weasel," a woman toward the rear of the room said.

Otis Boomershine chose his words carefully.

He explained the problem with the computer—that it had malfunctioned—and had overbooked Flight 742 by nineteen lovely, gracious, deserving, God-blessed people. He thought he heard somebody off to the right mumble, "Get the son-of-a-bitch," but it must have been his imagination because nothing happened.

Milt Tune stood to Otis Boomershine's left, holding his nose with a hanky, looking fearfully at Russ Crane, who, from time to time, held up his right fist threateningly. Every time Russ Crane held up his fist, Milt Tune shrunk about an inch and took a step back.

As Otis Boomershine spoke, women continued to pass out French pastry and coffee and London guide books.

There was no need to get into the specifics of the computer failure, so Otis Boomershine merely said there was no reason to cry over spilled milk, and before anybody could say "Get the son-of-a-bitch," he continued, "We, the airline, have worked out a fair solution."

It was like he was holding a chair in front of some wild animals. Otis Boomershine again dried his brow, he was about to rub the wrinkles off, and he said, "I have just communicated with a senior vice-president, and this was his idea." Otis spelled out the official's name, then asked, "First of all, are there any people who would like to voluntarily relinquish their seats on Flight 742 for guaranteed space on the same flight tomorrow morning?"

Fat chance.

"With, of course, housing and meals provided by the airline."

"What idea?" Russ Crane shouted.

"A lottery," Otis Boomershine said. "The seats on the flight will be filled by a random drawing." He said it was the only fair way the airline could think of to get the airplane off the ground within an hour or so. Any other plan would take hours and hours.

Grimm did some quick figuring and determined that a person had about a 94 percent chance of landing on that flight. It takes a real pessimist to think you would land in the lower 6 percent of anything, so the passengers had a brief meeting conducted by Russ Crane, who said he thought the drawing was equitable enough, just so long as his name was drawn from the crock.

"What about my wife?" one of the passengers asked Russ Crane, who answered, "What about her?"

"What if one of us gets on, and the other doesn't?"

Russ Crane forwarded this question to Otis Boomershine, who was fidgeting like a cricket. "We'll just draw individual names," Otis said. "We'll book the other party on tomorrow morning's flight, with free room and board tonight in the airport hotel."

The passengers decided that taking a flying leap beat sitting around complaining all morning, so Otis Boomershine had some flunkies scurry off in search of buttons on which the passengers' names would be written, and a vat, from which the lucky names would be drawn.

"If one of us doesn't make it," Grimm told Lackey and Phyllis, "just get on the next flight. Whoever makes it will meet you at the airport."

"I wonder if they would put me up overnight in a hospital," Lackey said quietly.

"What are the odds on all three of us missing out?" Phyllis wondered.

"Astronomical," Grimm said.

While Otis Boomershine and his associates fixed the stage of the waiting room for the big drawing, Grimm, Lackey, and Phyllis thought positively and carefully plotted their next moves. After the last name was drawn, the passengers would have approximately thirty-five minutes to proceed to the gate and get on the flight.

"We go to the rest room and take the money from the suitcase and put it on our bodies," Grimm said. "Now, it's essential to keep our bodies from being searched. We can't carry anything through that would set off the metal detector."

"Magazines and papers are in the suitcase that had the money," Lackey said.

"Right," Grimm said.

"And we go into a rest room on the other side of the metal detector and put the money *back* in the suitcase," Phyllis said.

Grimm nodded. "We dump the papers and magazines in the bathroom. We take the suitcase full of money onto the plane."

"We check the big one with the clothes?" Lackey wondered.

"Right." Grimm asked Lackey and Phyllis to sit quietly a moment and think about getting to and on the airplane. Was there *anything* they hadn't thought of, anything at all? Something even completely unlikely or unbelievable? "The key is, we cannot be searched at the metal detector. If that happens, if they take us somewhere and remove our clothing, we go to prison."

Lackey thought a moment and said, "I've never seen anybody searched yet, just for the hell of it."

"No," Grimm said.

Lackey checked his pockets and had only change.

"We'll need some tape so we can stick the money to our skin," Phyllis said. "That's a lot of money to hide."

"Gift shop," Grimm said.

"Well," Phyllis said.

Lackey said it sounded fine to him. He said he would concentrate on not passing out. "If they rip my shirt open to listen for a heartbeat, we're through."

"I don't see any problem," Phyllis said. She put her hand on Grimm's knee.

"Here we go again," Lackey said.

"When it gets a little tense," Phyllis whispered into Grimm's ear, "I get a little excited, you remember?"

"Sure," Grimm grinned.

"When it gets nervous and things look good, it makes me want to hold somebody real close."

Grimm said, "Yes, I understand." He put his hand on Phyllis' leg.

"Aren't they cute," Lackey said to a kid wandering up the aisle. "Just married."

"We just might make it, sweetie," Phyllis whispered, "and if we do, I can promise you one thing."

"What?"

"What about me?" Lackey asked nobody. "What am I supposed to do, stand guard?"

"I can promise you the greatest thing in the world."

"Oh," Grimm said. "I deserve it."

"Me."

"I didn't know this would turn into a date," Lackey said. "There's only one thing keeping everybody from being happy ever after. Getting on that stupid plane."

Phyllis straightened up in her seat.

Grimm thanked Lackey a lot for playing the devil's advocate.

"It's a job," Lackey said.

Otis Boomershine reached into the vat, drew a name tag and said, "Za, Za, Zago, excuse me, Zu-goce."

What? everybody wondered.

Otis Boomershine cleared his throat and tried again.

"Za-go-cee?"

"They left," Russ Crane said. "Draw again."

"Anita Zgonc?" a woman from the back row asked. She

waved her hand. "Right here. Anita Zgonc. It's pronounced
Za-*ga*, on the last syllable."

"Yes," Otis Boomershine said. "That's it. That's the first
name. Please step forward."

Anita Zgonc collected her belongings and happily trotted
forward, where her ticket was stamped, her bags checked, and
her boarding pass issued.

"What kind of name is *that?*" Russ Crane asked.

"A lucky one," Anita Zgonc said, waving at the crowd, several of whom applauded weakly.

"I'll give you one thousand American dollars for that
ticket," Russ Crane said.

"Three, and it's yours," Anita Zgonc said.

"Honey," Mrs. Crane said to her husband, "there's hundreds of seats left. There's no need to panic."

Russ Crane sat down. Anita Zgonc padded off to the airplane. Otis Boomershine continued to draw names, about
one every 10 seconds. Extra flunkies had been called for, and
they were issuing seat numbers to the winners quickly.

Grimm kept the odds up to date.

Ten names.

Twenty.

Thirty.

"You ever won anything?" Lackey asked Grimm. As names
were removed from the vat, the remaining passengers became
increasingly nervous. Several swore viciously at each announcement. Russ Crane said that since he had booked first-
class passage, his name should be in the vat twice. There was
a slight delay as Otis Boomershine, Milt Tune and several of
the officials had a meeting. A more important official was
called, and it was conceded that passengers holding first-class
reservations were deserving of special consideration, so two
additional half-tags were deposited in the container, with the
obvious stipulation: both halves had to be drawn before said
persons got to board. Grimm tried to compute the odds on
having two halves drawn, but gave up.

"I hope it's your bottom half that gets on board," Lackey told Russ Crane, who seemed about to waive the you-can't-hit-a-cripple rule.

Lackey told Grimm that he had never won a single, solitary thing, never, ever.

Grimm said he had once won a free sitting for a portrait. If you wanted to *buy* the picture after you had sat, though, it was $75.

"I won a toaster," Phyllis said. "When I was nineteen."

"You'll both love Europe," Lackey said. "Write me in intensive care."

Forty names.

The odds were coming down to earth. In thirty minutes, Lackey said, they would be in a ditch. He never imagined that being wealthy was so nerve-racking. "In all the years I was poor, I never felt this bad, Grimm. I thought all the rich worried about was what color socks to wear."

"Robbing a bank is the only sane hedge against inflation," Grimm whispered.

"You remember when I was a postman?" Lackey asked. "I liked that. I should have stayed with it. Security, you know? You knew where you stood. You were on welfare, but *knowing* it made it all right. The bad thing about being a postman was guys hauling mail in Pocatello, Idaho, make the same as guys here in the city."

Lackey had quit his job at the post office because of the Gimp job.

"You can be a postman in England," Grimm said. "Be quiet."

"I feel old."

"You are old."

"I'm only thirty-six," Lackey said.

Grimm said things were going so bad in this country, the stinking "good old days" were only a couple of weeks ago.

They sat in silence as more names were drawn and called. This was the last domino, all right, Grimm decided. This one would fall right on their necks. He wondered what he had ever done to deserve this. Robbing a bank is certainly not grounds for this kind of mental anguish and harassment.

Otis Boomershine drew Phyllis' name, it was the fifty-third called, and she rose and said, "The hex is broken." She went forward to collect her boarding pass, took the suitcase of money from Grimm, and waited patiently in the hallway outside the lounge.

"Don't let some sneak thief steal the suitcase," Grimm said.

"I hadn't planned on it," Phyllis said.

"If we don't get on, you're going to have to hide all the cash on your body."

Phyllis looked around the room and said, "There's still time for you guys," and turned on her heel. She looked back and saw Grimm and Lackey holding hands, and flinching as subsequent names were called. It was damn sad.

"What if she gets on and we don't?" Lackey said. "What if she doesn't stop in London? What if she keeps going?"

Grimm turned around and watched Phyllis leave the lounge.

"Concentrate," Grimm said.

Lackey closed his eyes.

"Crane," Otis Boomershine said. "C-r-a-n-e. Eduardo Crane."

Russ Crane had risen from his chair at the sound of his name, and when it was revealed that it was some other Crane whose name had been plucked, the big-shot businessman gasped, turned pink, and fell back into his seat. His wife loosened his tie.

"If they call another Crane that isn't him," Lackey said, "his head's going to explode."

"It would help the odds," Grimm said. "How's your side?"

"Very bad," Lackey said.

"Concentrate."

"Jones," Otis Boomershine said.

Five people stood.

"Bob Jones."

Three sat down.

"Bob T. Jones."

"How was that for concentrating?" Lackey asked.

"Bad," Grimm said. "Stinking."

Names came and went. When they called a "Lacy," Lackey fell forward from his seat onto his hands and knees and Grimm had to help the poor fellow up. Things were going *so* badly—nobody within five rows of Grimm and Lackey had been called—Grimm almost missed it when his name was announced. It was name number 167. He looked around and when no other Grimm was seen standing, the correct Grimm leaped to his feet, cheering. Grimm got his boarding pass and waved it at the remaining passengers.

"Fuck you," somebody said.

"Yeah."

"Get lost."

The crowd was definitely getting restless. Otis Boomershine had summoned extra security, for when the drawing reached its final anxious moments.

Grimm put the boarding pass in his pocket and returned to where Lackey was sitting.

"Maybe you can have some fun now, without me," Lackey said, rubbing his eyes. "When this debacle is finished, I guess I'll catch a bus over to the Salvation Army, and then hit the free clinics and see if I can't get some tape for my side, here."

"Listen," Grimm said.

"You think you could loan me some money for tape?"

"We'll both be just outside in the hall, waiting, for when they call your name and you get your boarding pass."

"Crap," Lackey said.

"There are sixty, seventy more seats to be filled."

"Getting crippled was only a sign of things to come. I have a feeling it gets worse."

Grimm put his hands on Lackey's shoulders. Lackey looked

up like a sad puppy. Names were announced. None of it was real. Grimm didn't feel like himself, and this certainly wasn't a normal situation. It was another scene Grimm was acting out. This one was like out of a doctor movie. This was where the physician told the guy with the rare blood disease that you never knew with modern medicine, perhaps in the morning somebody would discover a cure. So Grimm told Lackey to have courage, to keep a stiff upper lip and to concentrate. Lackey looked at Grimm like, who's kidding whom, here. In the movies, this was where the sadly ill person rose to his feet and pledged to live every moment to its fullest. Lackey was supposed to go be a stock-car driver or snake charmer or sword swallower—stare death in the face, do things he had always wanted, make the minutes count.

Only Lackey couldn't move so good.

Had this moment been on television, millions of viewers would have gasped, because Lackey looked up at Grimm and said, "Screw it and you."

Grimm left Lackey sitting crookedly in his chair, and he rejoined Phyllis in the hall. He informed her that approximately sixty people remained in the room, competing for the forty-one seats. She handed the suitcase full of money to Grimm, it was heavy, then she suggested that he hold it more casually, and not like it had the family jewels inside.

"I hope he doesn't make it," she said. "He makes me nervous."

Grimm said that Lackey was in great pain.

"Let's go take the money out of the suitcase in the bathroom and get on the plane," Phyllis suggested, yawning. "I'm too tired to think anymore." When Grimm made a feeble comment about a second wind, Phyllis said she had hers back at the apartment when they tore Grimm's car apart, and that she was now on her thirteenth wind.

They leaned against the wall and drank coffee and watched people come from the drawing room.

"How's it going in there?" Grimm asked Mrs. Crane.

"Russ is having a hard time breathing," she said. "Every time they call a name, he starts wheezing."

It had been announced that Flight 742 would depart at 5:05, which was in forty minutes. Grimm and Phyllis finished their coffee and stepped back inside the room. The airline officials were busy at the front, consulting seating charts. Any error now might prove fatal.

"Lackey," Grimm said.

Lackey tried to turn his head right, but was overcome with pain. He leaned his head *back*, and looked at Grimm and Phyllis, upside down.

"How's it going?" Grimm asked. "How many more seats do they have left?"

Lackey said matter-of-factly that he thought the circus was over.

"The way it goes," Phyllis said. "Let's go to the gate."

"Thank you for your encouragement," Lackey said to Phyllis.

Grimm counted heads and said there were twenty people remaining in varying stages of disarray. Russ Crane was swearing in bursts. The veins on his forehead and neck were visible. "Bastards," he bellowed.

"Attention," Otis Boomershine said into the microphone. He had a clipboard in front of him. After flipping some sheets, it was announced that there was one seat left on Flight 742, a coach seat, row 11, seat D. Otis Boomershine again asked that those passengers bumped from 742 please remain seated so they could be processed for space on the next Flight 742 which left in, well, not *that* long.

The vat of name tags was thoroughly jostled, and ticket agent Milt Tune reached his hand down to pluck the final lucky name.

"If it's not me," Russ Crane roared, "I'll choke your goddamn chicken neck."

Milt Tune's knees almost buckled, and he stepped back from the vat to catch his breath.

"Twenty to one," Lackey said. "That's about like the milk bottle game at the fair."

Milt Tune reached into the container and came up with a name, which he handed to Otis Boomershine, who said, "And the winner in Hollywood is," which so infuriated Russ Crane, he had to be restrained by one of the security guards. Airport security guards have never been mistaken for *real* officers of the law, about all they do is stomp out burning cigarette butts, so it took four security men to subdue Russ Crane, who thrashed his large fists wildly in the direction of the podium, where Milt Tune was hiding behind Otis Boomershine.

It was becoming more obvious each second that Russ Crane was some variety of criminal who had to get out of town, fast. There was a lot of that going around, Lackey said. Whereas it was normal to be disappointed, even physically ill, about the overbooking, you wouldn't think a person would stoop to *murder* as a display of his dissatisfaction.

As Russ Crane was wedged back into a seat, he threatened to hurt everybody on the podium, in this room, and in the cockpit. He threatened to rip a wing off of Flight 742. The airline personnel stood nervously but quietly on the podium as the guards forced Russ Crane into a seat. Otis Boomershine held the last name in his right hand. Two guards held Russ Crane's shoulders. One held his head. One stood in front of Russ Crane with a nightstick.

"If we may continue," Otis Boomershine said. "Please."

"My name is not really Crane," Russ Crane yelled. "It's Lombino."

"Oh boy," Grimm said.

"I knew a Lombino in school," Lackey said. "He sold knives."

"Either you or me better be on that plane!" Lombino shouted.

Otis Boomershine looked from the last name tag to Lombino and he bit his lip.

"Get away from me, you bum," Lombino said to the security officer with the nightstick.

"Hey, Mr. Lombino, my name is Fetalichi, look here." The officer tapped his name tag. He holstered his nightstick.

Grimm detected an evil note to the proceedings and called out that the name tag had better be what was announced.

"Oh my God," Otis Boomershine said faintly.

"*What?*" Lombino asked. "WHAT?"

"Lackey," Otis Boomershine said. "L-a-c-k-e-y. Lackey."

"I'll be damned," Lackey said. "That's me."

"We did it!" Grimm said. "That last name. Unbelievable. The tide has turned."

Lombino turned his large head and said the tide was also fucking deep this time of year. Grimm helped Lackey to his feet, and they struggled down the aisle.

"This is the biggest miracle I ever saw," Phyllis said. She stood guard over the suitcases.

The security officers had released Lombino. He forced himself out of his seat and rose to his full height. He reached out a hand and stopped Grimm and Lackey. He said, quite calmly, "One thousand."

"Sorry," Grimm said. "Bad luck, pal."

"I need to be in London," Lombino said. "I need to be in London very bad." He was falling into a mean mood, Grimm noticed. "I need to be in London so bad that if I am not in London I am going to get very pissed off. Two thousand."

"Why don't you go get a pizza and calm down," Lackey said. "It's my seat. I deserve it."

Mr. Lombino said something in Italian that caused the security guard named Fetalichi to suck in his breath.

"Three thousand."

"If you'll excuse us," Grimm said. Lombino said you could tell what sorry shape this country was in when scum like that started turning down two and three grand.

"Three thousand, is it."

Lackey said there was a time when he would have gratefully accepted such a generous offer from such a nice man, but circumstances warranted the refusal, for, as desperately as Mr. Lombino wanted to get to London, he, Lackey, needed to get there even more urgently.

Mr. Lombino leaned over and said, "You better hope the plane goes down in the ocean because there will be a guy at the other end who will skin you like a fucking fish—with pliers." He took out a notebook and wrote down names and said, "This fucking world will be a better place to live this time tomorrow."

Mr. Lombino predicted a population explosion.

Lackey accepted his boarding pass, and the name tag for a souvenir.

Mr. Lombino had tired of being the volatile Russ Crane and was comfortable being himself. "You," he said to Otis Boomershine. "Over here." Lombino whispered into Otis Boomershine's right ear. Otis Boomershine collected some papers and hurried off to the gate. Milt Tune arranged for sleeping quarters and food for the losers.

"What do you think?" Lackey asked Grimm.

He said he wouldn't be surprised if Mr. Lombino made the trip instead of somebody like the second officer.

As Grimm said as they headed for the gate—it was slightly downhill and Lackey was able to limp along at a decent clip— anything else that could happen would be nothing more than a minor annoyance, and he was right.

It had slipped their minds that men and women don't use the same rest room. An hour ago, this revelation would have been grounds for panic. Now, it was perfectly understandable *life*. Anything painless and smooth was abnormal. Grimm, Lackey, and Phyllis handled potentially catastrophic trauma like it was duck soup; they simply scratched their heads and waited for things to cool.

They paused outside the rest room.

Lombino walked by, heading toward the gate. He gave Lackey a horrible growl.

"That guy is a psychopath and ought to be put away," Lackey said.

It was decided that Grimm and Lackey would enter the men's room and tape approximately two-thirds of the cash to their persons. The suitcase would then be handed to Phyllis, and she would stow the remainder of the money. The case would be filled with newspapers by Phyllis in the women's room, then they would proceed smartly to the gate, board Flight 742, and get the hell out of there.

"I'm starving to death," Lackey said. He was dispatched to a newsstand for tape, newspapers, and a candy bar. He said his side felt slightly better. It got worse when he was immobile. The stand was only around the corner.

Otis Boomershine and several other airline officials hurried toward the gate. The flight would depart in twenty-two minutes. One of the airport security guards was walking with Otis Boomershine, communicating with somebody on a walkie-talkie. It was not the Italian security guard. He had weakened under Lombino's oaths, and was replaced with what seemed to be an Irishman.

"It would be a crime if we missed the flight," Phyllis said.

Lackey was only gone about four minutes. He returned with a half a dozen newspapers, a large roll of Scotch tape, three candy bars, and another sack of unknown contents.

"The gate is just past the metal detector," Grimm said, checking his watch against the announced departure time. "No problem."

Lackey said outside of the stiff neck, he was at about 75 percent of full-speed.

"What's in the sack?" Grimm asked.

"Tape."

"The other sack."

"Oh, that sack. Nothing."

"What do you mean, nothing?"

"Time is flying," Phyllis said, "as you two stand here making small talk."

"Magazines," Lackey answered.

"Oh," Grimm said. "Okay."

Grimm and Lackey went into the men's room where, for some weird reason, the stall walls came all the way down to the floor, making it impossible to pass the suitcase full of cash underneath, from stall to stall, as God intended.

It was a typical rest room, otherwise, small and messy.

Except for the stalls, there was no place a man could comfortably and privately tape cash to himself.

"In here," Grimm said, and he and Lackey entered the first stall, together.

It was cramped, but there was room to work, with Grimm stradling the toilet. He opened the suitcase, and told Lackey they could admire the money later, it was time to get serious. Lackey theorized that the closer they got to Europe, the better he would feel. They agreed, a high percent of any injury is psychological.

"Running into a stand at thirty miles per hour *does* hurt," Lackey said.

"Yeah," Grimm said. He stuffed $15,000 in each shoe and had Lackey tape $20,000 to his ass. He taped quite a few grand on his arms and legs. He flexed his arms and was pleased.

"You positive they have a bathroom on the other side of the metal detector?" Lackey asked.

Grimm taped $10,000 to Lackey's calf, and $25,000 to the small of Lackey's back. "You think people catching flights about six blocks away use the bathroom in plants?"

Lackey said, "This is kind of hard to believe."

"Quiet," Grimm said.

Somebody entered the men's room and tried the first door.

"Anybody in there?"

"Of course," Grimm said. "There are other stalls."

"Every time I fly overseas, I use the first stall," the person said. "It's good luck."

"I'm going to be here about an hour," Grimm said.

"That's ridiculous. What in the hell are you doing in there?"

"Throwing up."

The man left and sought a first stall in another area.

When a little more than two-thirds of the cash had been disposed of, Grimm took some papers and stuffed them into the suitcase.

"Not that," Lackey said. "Those are my magazines and extra candy bars."

As they exited the stall together, a gentleman smoothing his moustache in the mirror over the sink said under his breath that it was a shame what this country was coming to, and that there ought to be a law that kept sissies from making a spectacle of themselves in public rest rooms.

Lackey told the guy to kiss his butt.

Grimm said that was probably not the right thing to say.

They found Phyllis just outside the men's room, handed her the suitcase and the remaining papers.

"Let's go," Grimm said.

"Not that," Lackey said. "Those are my magazines."

"What's so special about some stupid magazines?" Grimm asked.

"The good ones on the airplane always go fast and I wind up with something like *Popular Mechanics*."

"Here are your idiotic magazines," Phyllis said.

Lackey held his sack of magazines securely under his right arm.

Phyllis walked into the women's room.

"Feel all right?" Grimm asked Lackey.

"Some of the tape itches. The stuff on my rear itches real bad."

"Don't touch it."

"Right."

To keep the money firmly in place, they had wrapped the tape all the way around their legs.

"My right calf is getting a shade numb," Lackey said.

Grimm informed him that it would only be a matter of minutes until they were through the metal detector, in another rest room, and free of the irritating tape. From where they stood waiting for Phyllis, they could see the metal detector. At this time of night-day, there was little business. The security guards read magazines and sipped Cokes. A real city cop sat at a desk, reading the paper.

"It's not long until morning," Lackey said.

"I know," Grimm said.

"We're going to make it," Lackey said.

"Surprised?"

"Totally."

They checked their pockets for objects that would annoy the metal detector. Nothing. Lackey had a nail-clipper-knife that he pitched in a garbage can.

Phyllis was inside only about five minutes. She handed the suitcase full of papers to Grimm, who said, "Putting on a little weight, aren't you, dear?"

She smiled faintly.

"I always said your fanny was worth a hundred thousand dollars."

"Let's go," she nodded.

Nobody was in a particularly frivolous mood. This was serious business. Even Lackey, who had been battered to within seconds of unconsciousness, walked upright toward the metal detector. There is, they knew, a time and place for everything. This was not a time for bullshit. Once beyond the metal detector, they were home free, providing the airplane did not plunge pitifully into a building or the ocean. That would be a low blow. The plane dare not malfunction. There had been no sign of unusual police activity in or around the airport. The cops were evidently still stumbling in circles, not knowing whom they were looking for, not knowing where to look.

"We handle customs on the other end the same way," Lackey said. "The bathrooms?"

"Right," Grimm said. "We'll put the money on us. We'll dump the suitcase with papers, and just walk through. Tourists."

Phyllis had the passports in her purse, which she placed on the table. The security guard put the purse on a conveyor belt, and it was propelled through the metal detecting device without problem.

"So we'll need more tape," Lackey said. "For before customs."

"Oh Christ," Grimm said, as Phyllis walked through the metal detector. There was no sound from the machine.

Lackey removed an extra roll of tape from his jacket. He smiled. "I thought of that."

"Where were you all evening?" Grimm asked, jokingly.

"You got us this far," Lackey said. "It's time to share the responsibility."

Grimm went through the metal detector next, hundreds of thousands of dollars taped to his skin, and he was very relieved when nothing happened. He had handed the suitcase full of papers to a girl who nonchalantly plopped it on the conveyor belt. Another worker looked into an X-ray device and passed the suitcase on as though carrying a bag of papers was perfectly normal.

"Okay," the girl said to Lackey, and she nodded at the small tunnel you had to walk through. She had her hand out. Lackey looked at the hand and frowned. He walked toward the metal-detecting tunnel.

"Wait," the girl said. She moved her open right palm up and down.

Grimm and Phyllis were on the other side of the tunnel, looking back. Phyllis held Grimm's hand, tightly. She strengthened her grip as Lackey and the girl stood looking at each other. Grimm started to shout, "Give her the goddamn sack of magazines, you imbecile," but he didn't want to start a scene.

"Let's have it," the girl said.

"Have what?" Lackey asked.

"The sack," the girl said.

"Oh," Lackey said, looking at the sack, holding it up. "It's only magazines and a couple of candy bars."

"Sure, sure," the girl said. "Gimme it."

"Why?" Lackey asked.

"What's he doing?" Grimm whispered to Phyllis, who was squeezing his hand *very* hard.

"Going crazy," Phyllis said.

"Give it to her," Grimm said through clenched teeth. He was more or less talking to himself. "Give her the sack, you lunatic."

"Give her the sack, you jerk," Phyllis growled.

It was like they were watching a movie where the good guy was about to get blackjacked on the back of the neck.

"It's magazines," Lackey said again. "It's a sack of magazines. I just bought them over there at the stand."

"Listen, pal," the girl said.

The city cop put his newspaper down and looked up from his seat at the table. The other guy who looked into the X-ray device was also looking at Lackey, who was clutching his sack like there were thousand-dollar bills inside, not silly magazines.

"You don't think," Phyllis wondered.

"You *wouldn't* think," Grimm wondered.

"Are you gonna gimme the bag, or what?" the girl asked, loudly. Other passengers had lined up behind Lackey, about seven or eight people. They were watching and listening.

"It's magazines," Lackey said again. His face was white. "Put it through the machine if you don't believe me."

"I'm gonna *look* inside the sack myself, pal," the girl said.

"What's the problem, Milly?" the city cop asked.

"The guy won't give me the sack."

"Oh my God," Grimm gagged. "What's he doing?"

"He's a madman," Phyllis answered. "He should be in a home."

"Here," Lackey said. He half-heartedly held out the sack. Milly reached out to take it. Lackey wouldn't let go.

"I told you it's only magazines."

The cop had risen and was about ready to go over Lackey with mirrors and gadgets, and then Grimm and Phyllis would also be arrested and they would all be hauled off to jail, but at least, Grimm thought, they would be able to get some sleep.

Milly pulled on the sack. Lackey held firm with his half. The sack ripped open and the two candy bars and three magazines fell to the table.

Milly looked inside the empty sack and pitched it into the garbage.

"See," Lackey said. "I told you. Candy bars and magazines."

Grimm blinked.

Phyllis said, "Maybe he put some money between the pages."

Grimm said, "He would *never* do that. Nobody is that ignorant."

Milly picked up the candy bars, looked at them, and put them on the conveyor. They were scrutinized and found to be plain old candy.

Milly picked up one of the magazines. She looked at the cover, and then at Lackey, who was now bright red. He coughed nervously.

"Magazines," he said.

"God," Milly said, thumbing through the pages. About fifteen people were now watching Milly display Lackey's choice of reading material, which was soft-core porno. As Milly flipped through the pages, a centerfold flopped down, showing a hideously ugly woman standing on two chairs, one leg on each, as three preposterously ugly naked men looked up, like they might have been looking out a window to check the weather. Only they were looking up at the woman's underside, which caused Milly and several passengers to choke.

"What are you?" Milly asked Lackey, whose face was about purple.

Milly thumbed through the other magazines, pausing at particularly revolting photos, to give Lackey sorrowful, disgusting glances. On the cover of one of the magazines was a woman in a ballcap, holding a bat between her legs.

"God," Milly said.

The city cop looked over her shoulder, and winked at Lackey, who said, "It's a long flight."

"No wonder he didn't want to give up the sack," Phyllis said.

Milly held the magazines like they were dead fish, and she plopped them on the belt. They were taken off at the other end by another girl who was repulsed. The cop again winked at Lackey, as he picked up his magazines, rolled them, and concealed them under his arm.

The cop winked again.

"Well," Lackey said, "are we ready?"

"You should have put your head on the conveyor belt," Phyllis said. "And had it X-rayed, free."

"Why'd you buy that garbage?" Grimm asked.

"I like girls," Lackey said.

"Don't come near me," Phyllis said.

They all three scratched themselves, and started to walk to the gate.

Solving crime can get on your nerves.

Little things like missing a bus driver by five minutes can cause a man to want to rip out walls and smash chairs and kick in the glass.

Bud Heathcoat had checked his vehicle in at the yard, and

Wax said that when he called, the guy on the phone reported Heathcoat was driving through the gate at that very moment. "There he went," the night man at the busyard said. "Gone now."

Rotzinger digested this information, took a deep breath, and had officers dispatched to Bud Heathcoat's apartment. Rotzinger also had cars cruise the likely route Bud Heathcoat would take home.

Rotzinger roared at his bad luck and fingered the early editions of the papers with contempt. On each page the police got bad reviews. That the chief himself had been at the scene was prominently displayed. In one paper, Rotzinger was pictured shaking a large fist at the photographer. In another, he was scratching his head.

Rotzinger ran the phones like a bookie. He had another telephone jacked into his wall so he could feel the pulse of the investigation. He was on the phone with people at the airlines, people at the maintenance yard at the bus station, and Bernard Overby, who threatened to kill himself and leave a suicide note indicting Rotzinger as the reason he had blown his brains out. The chief dispatched an officer to Overby's hotel, where the night manager was found crouching behind his typewriter with a revolver. Overby was arrested. Rotzinger doubted that this firm policework would merit much space on the front pages.

It was verified that Bud Heathcoat's bus had made a sweep fairly near the airport, but then it veered away and passed through an area congested with motels.

It had taken twenty valuable minutes to pinpoint Bud Heathcoat's route. People who work at the maintenace yard between the hours of one and nine A.M. are not noted for their quick thinking.

The news from the major airlines at the airport was not good, because it was slow. It took Wax eleven minutes to get the person who could check *all* the reservations for this morning's flights at the first airline contacted, then it took the supervisor fifteen *more* minutes to report that from the hours of midnight to noon, eighteen sets of reservations had been made involving three passengers together. And the reservations did not always specify sex. You would think that three people running for their lives would, even if they booked the tickets together, avoid using Mr. or Mrs., wouldn't you? Wax thought.

Rotzinger assigned an officer to check each airline, and he had an officer named Brooks set up a command desk with the vital information.

"There goes another one," Brooks said, checking his watch. "Flight 202 to Guatemala or some goddamn place." Brooks had been dragged from his sleep to assist in this investigation. As Flight 202 to some place took off, Brooks put a big check by it, and said, "There were two three-person reservations on that one."

It seemed like such a good idea, Rotzinger thought, as phones rang and people reported in to Brooks. Checking three tickets booked at once seemed inspired.

"Flight 424 to Ireland leaving now has no three-ticketers," Brooks said.

"Praise God," Rotzinger said.

In the next hour, sixteen flights were scheduled to depart, nine to domestic cities, the rest overseas. Approximately seventy-one sets of three-person reservations were contained on the eighteen flights. This figure remained "approximate" because one airline reported computer trouble, and according to the supervisor, "God only knew who would be on the flights." The computer would be fixed "some day."

Rotzinger found it pathetically incredible so many reservations would have been booked in threes, and this opinion was verified by a supervisor from one of the airlines. On the average, the guy said, there was maybe one or two three-person reservations booked per flight.

"There goes another one," Brooks said. "Dallas. Zoom."

"What if," Wax said, during a pause in the phoning, "and this is pure supposition, mind you, the robbers took some insurance?"

"Flight insurance?" Rotzinger wondered.

"Figuratively. What if they called in a number of phony three-person reservations. The airlines give a person until several hours before departure to pick up the tickets. The reservations are not depleted from the computer memory bank until it is confirmed there was a no-show, that is, until the flight takes off."

"South America," Brooks said. "Twenty minutes and counting. Five sets of triple reservations."

"That theory obviously gives you a lot of pleasure, Wax," Rotzinger said.

Wax said it was a thought, and that if the robbers covered their escape consistent in concept with the way they took the bank, nothing would be too brilliant to assume.

Rotzinger had his massive arm cocked when the call from Bud Heathcoat came through. The call no doubt saved Rotzinger a prison sentence for manslaughter because Wax was in a position to have been knocked through a window thirty-two floors above ground.

"You don't know much about buses that run from midnight to dawn, do you?" Bud Heathcoat said in response to Rotzinger's question about whether anything unusual had happened during the shift tonight. "The only time anything *usual* happens is when it rains real hard and nobody gets on."

Bud Heathcoat told Rotzinger about the drunk with the guitar and the dice game. "People riding the bus at this time of night are not exactly the salt of the earth. They're more like the crumbs."

Rotzinger asked if Heathcoat remembered picking three people up, two men and a woman, carrying suitcases.

"I try not to look too closely at the fares," Bud Heathcoat said. "I might see weapons."

"They reportedly got on by the cab accident."

Bud Heathcoat thought and said all he could remember tonight was eleven cab accidents. He *did* recall a triple fare sometime tonight. You didn't see too many people get on in threes, together.

"With luggage?" Rotzinger asked.

"I think," Bud Heathcoat said. "People going to the airport can usually afford a cab. Yeah. Three people. A couple of bags."

"Airport?"

"Yeah. I come within a mile of it."

"Two men and a woman?"

"Yeah. One of the guys threw up, out the window. I saw it in the mirror but didn't want to say anything. They got on together, sat together, and got off together. They *did* say they were going to the airport."

"Excellent," Rotzinger said.

"You know what? They were pretty normal fares. No funny stuff. Too normal to take a bus to within a mile of the airport, you would think."

Rotzinger told Bud Heathcoat to remain at his apartment, an officer would be by in moments for a description.

"What did they do, anyway? They seemed harmless."

Rotzinger said they were merely wanted for questioning.

Bud Heathcoat said that when things were slow some night, the beat cop ought to let him know, he could arrest the whole bus and earn some nice easy collars.

Rotzinger hung up and informed Wax that the lunatics had been last seen *walking* in the direction of the airport. Twenty cops were quickly dispatched to the airport, with artist's drawings.

"Two hours ago," Rotzinger said.

Rotzinger checked with Brooks. In the last hour and a half, eight flights had departed.

"We need to get lucky," Rotzinger said.

"It's a big airport," Wax said.
"One more screw-up."
"If they're there."
"One of the men threw up on the bus."
Wax cursed the robbers under his breath. Taking a bus to
the airport! The way things were going, one of them would
fall down the ramp leading to the airplane into the arms of
an off-duty cop. Rotzinger had been right. The robbers were
coming unglued. Still, they could be airborne on any of almost a dozen flights, free and clear, virtually without a trace.

A Captain Holder was coordinating things at the airport.
Rotzinger ordered every inch of the place searched. An officer
was to be assigned to check every departing flight, concentrating on those flights with any reservation made for three
people.

"Slow down, you son-of-a-bitch," Rotzinger said to the
clock.

Surely, Wax thought, this rather obvious trail was part of
an elaborate scheme designed to cover the real escape route.
Surely, they were on a bus to Topeka or a boat to Hong
Kong.

Before Wax could finish his prayer, he and Rotzinger were
in the air.

"Can't this thing go any faster?" Rotzinger asked the pilot,
who was wearing earphones and couldn't hear. They were in a
helicopter, heading for the airport. Rotzinger sat next to the
pilot, an officer named Pine. Wax was in the back seat, hoping a building would end his misery.

Pine motioned to the speedometer and nodded, this was
top speed.

A call had come from the airport, reporting a disturbance
at one of the metal detecting areas, a disturbance involving
two men and a woman. Rotzinger told Captain Holder to apprehend the sons-of-bitches, he would be there shortly. The

disturbance involved quite a bit of shouting, and resisting a search.

"I knew it," Rotzinger said to Wax, who had to admit he sort of knew it, too.

Cars were sent for the pregnant teller Teresa Singleton, Charley English, the cab driver, and Bud Heathcoat, the bus driver. They would all meet at the airport and identify the criminals, the press would be notified, and then Rotzinger would find himself a good agent, for the talk shows.

"It's them," Rotzinger said to Wax, in the back seat of the helicopter.

Wax nodded.

"Faster," Rotzinger said to Pine, the pilot, who removed an earphone and said, "What?"

"Faster."

"It won't go any faster."

"Then don't slow down when we land, by God."

They came in low and landed by Gate 32, near where Captain Holder had detained the two men and a woman.

Rotzinger had brought three sets of handcuffs. They clanked together on his belt as he took the steps leading to the gate, three at a time.

The trip in the helicopter only took fourteen minutes. It was 5:20 A.M.

"Where the hell are they?" Rotzinger asked Captain Holder, who said, "This way."

They walked down the hall about thirty yards.

"In there," Captain Holder said.

Wax got the door.

Rotzinger stepped inside to confront the thieving bastards. It was funny, he felt like he'd known them all his life.

The room was a canteen area used by airline ticket clerks. The two men sat on one side of the table, the woman on the other. She was holding a wig in her lap.

"I want to press charges," she said to Rotzinger, who was out of breath. "I want these men pistol-whipped. They're crazy."

"But," one of the men said.

"Now honey," the other said.

"Don't honey me," the woman said.

"We're not crazy," one of the men said. "*She's* crazy."

"Put the cuffs on them," she said, looking at Rotzinger's belt.

"Those their bags?" Rotzinger asked Captain Holder, who nodded at the two suitcases. Rotzinger looked at the three people. They were not at all what he expected. It was like talking to somebody on the telephone for years, and then finally meeting them. He thought they would look a little more sophisticated, a little more cunning, the woman, particularly. She was terribly made-up. It looked like she had used about a pint of paint on her face. The men looked like, well, weasels, like they were about to be hit. Rotzinger walked around behind the woman and leaned over and looked at her legs.

"That's just about enough of that," she said. "I get enough of the cute stuff from *those* two."

Her legs were chubby. Firm. Good and firm. Face it, she had big legs.

"You mind standing up," Rotzinger said.

When she did, Wax whispered into Rotzinger's ear that it was hard to believe those legs had been described by various witnesses as good to great.

"What do cab or bus drivers know," Rotzinger said. "Get the bags."

"You leave the brown one alone," the woman said. "That's *my* bag. I have rights."

"You have the right," Rotzinger said, "to do what I tell you."

Wax lifted the bags to the table.

"I told you she had a big mouth," one of the men said.

"Yeah," the other man nodded. "You can't see the forest for the trees."

"You talking about my posterior again?" the woman asked.

"What happened?" Rotzinger asked Captain Holder, who called an officer named Bean inside.

"Tell the chief what happened," Captain Holder told Officer Bean, who was very young.

"Well, you know," Bean said, "I was on airport duty all night, you know, and, you know, I kept up with the bulletins on the bank thing, just like I'm supposed to."

"Good work, Bean," Rotzinger said. Then to Wax, he said, "Take a memo. Advanced speech class for all officers. Go ahead Bean. Try not to say 'you know' all the goddamn time."

"Well, you know."

"Bean."

"Sorry, sir."

"Go ahead, Bean. Please don't drive me crazy."

"Well," Bean continued, pleased with himself, "I got the update about anything with two men and a woman and, well, one of the airport security flubs called in the disturbance at the metal detector, and, well, I held them just like it said."

"I made the disturbance," the woman said.

"Name?" Rotzinger asked.

"Y."

"Because I say so."

The two men grinned.

Rotzinger's face reddened.

"What's your name?"

"Y!"

"What?" Rotzinger said.

"No." One of the men grinned. "That's her brother."

"Her sister's named Come Again," the other man said.

"See," the woman said. "See what I told you? They're slimy."

Rotzinger said to the woman, "Your name is Y?"

"Yes," she said.

"Y what?"

"Y Knott," one of the men said. The two men giggled.

Rotzinger said one more word from either of them and there would be hell to pay. The police department didn't accept Mastercharge, either.

"Y Montgomery."

"Name?" Rotzinger said to the men, who looked at each other.

"Joe."

"Joe."

"Are we under oath?" the first man asked.

"From this moment on," Rotzinger said. He was remembering just how much he hated routine policework.

"Tom."

"Tom."

"Both of your names are Tom?"

"Yeah."

"Right. Listen, sir. This is a very difficult situation."

"Shut up," Rotzinger sad.

"They're perverts," Y said. "Both of them."

The two men looked at the roof like little angels.

"It starts out as a routine date," Y said. "Right?"

Rotzinger looked at his watch.

"Well, almost routine. So it's a funny hour. So? These two vultures ask me out, so I say, fine. I'm a grown woman."

Rotzinger looked at her breasts.

"Typical," Y said.

"Out to where?" Captain Holder wondered.

"Houston," Y said. "I figure, if you have money, there's no difference in a date to Houston or a date to Arby's, right? Anyway, these two screwballs say why don't we zip down to Houston for breakfast, no funny stuff, just down and back. Separate rooms."

"Things like this happen all the time on the street," Wax whispered to Rotzinger, like the chief had been in a monastery the last five years.

"But we start to get on the plane and these two slobs, start talking dirty and grabbing my posterior. You should have heard what they said."

"Well," Tom said.

"Hell," Tom said. "I mean, what does a person expect, for God's sake?"

"A good, clean time," Y said. "Anyway, *that* one starts talking filthy, and it dawns on me, maybe these two aren't simple businessmen. Maybe they're dirty."

"She got pissed the room was pre-paid and all we have is credit cards," one of the Toms said.

"That's a lie! That one grabbed my butt."

"It was an accident."

"Oh, sure. Nobody grabs my butt."

"Her butt has been grabbed so much, it's like bicycle handlebars. It's got grip marks."

"Arrest them," Y said.

Keys were produced and identification and suitcases were checked, and it was revealed that Y was short for Yolanda, but that didn't mean a *damn* thing except her mother had a vivid imagination.

"Yeah," Tom said.

"Sure," the other Tom said. "Thank God this thing was nipped in the bud."

It was further revealed that one Tom's name was Eugene Jones and that the other Tom's name was Shelby Collins. Eugene Jones sold auto parts. Shelby Collins bought auto parts.

"That's perjury," Y said.

Yolanda Montgomery sold drinks at a bar, and at closing time, one thing led to another, and the rather exotic date was arranged.

"Houston?" Captain Holder asked. Rotzinger was beyond words.

"Convention," Eugene Jones said.

"You two were taking me to a convention?" Y gasped. She crossed herself and her legs simultaneously. "Bums."

The luggage contained normal things. As Yolanda Montgomery's bag was searched, and when the contents were spread on the table, Eugene Jones leaned forward and said, "There's no toothbrush."

"You talk about a close call," Shelby Collins said.

"I forgot it," Yolanda Montgomery said. "I was so excited about the big date with you big spenders."

"Sure you did," Eugene Jones said.

"You saying I don't brush my teeth?"

"I want to go home," Shelby Collins said.

Rotzinger collected his thoughts, which almost filled a Dixie Cup, and he went into the hallway with Wax, Captain Holder, and Officer Bean. A cop had been left in the room with the suspects, so they wouldn't steal the ash trays. Officer Brooks came out in the next helicopter, and he set up a command post in an administration office where he monitored the flights for reasons unknown to him. The helicopter flight made Officer Brooks madly ill, so he drank four 7-Ups and had to go to the bathroom three quick times.

"Well, you know," Officer Bean said. "I guess it wasn't them."

"Get that man out of my sight," Rotzinger told Captain Holder, who sent Bean off on a search of the lockers, which is probably illegal, but what the public doesn't know won't hurt them. On the average night, you can pick up maybe a dozen arrests, searching the lockers and finding machine guns and then waiting for somebody to claim them. Rotzinger had Captain Holder send twenty sleepy officers off into the morning with the up-to-date descriptions of the robbers.

Witnesses Singleton, English, and Heathcoat arrived in

about fifteen minutes. Teresa Singleton, the pregnant teller, looked at the most recent sketches of the alleged robbers and said, "That one is my Uncle Hal."

The alleged witnesses were led to the room just vacated by Eugene, Shelby, and Y, and they were offered coffee and doughnuts. After several minutes, cab driver Charley English asked Rotzinger, "What are we doing here?"

Bud Heathcoat asked for a pillow.

Rotzinger took a couple of calls from Officer Brooks's phone on the command desk. Brooks reported that the computer failure with the one airline had not been solved.

The first call was about hotel clerk Bernard Overby, who didn't have a damn thing to do with anything. That's the thing about a simple investigation—it opens up a can of fruit flies. Overby had been booked on several charges, including overwriting.

"Throw the fucking book at him," Rotzinger said somewhat humorously. "The dictionary."

The second call was about public relations executive Buzz Murdock who, when informed that the robbers were still at large, stuck a ball-point pen in his neck and was rushed to the emergency room.

The third call was from Rotzinger's wife who asked, "How's it going, dear?" and hung up when her husband didn't reply in forty-five seconds.

When the mayor called, he said it sounded like a good sign, Rotzinger was at the airport, unless, of course, he was catching a flight. Rotzinger said he was not there to arrest drunks.

"Keep me informed," the mayor said.

Rotzinger did *not* say that was what he had just done; rather, "Yes, sir."

Rotzinger asked Wax why it was that when a person said, "We're fucked," everybody assumed that was bad.

Wax had no idea.

Rotzinger thought. Were they gone? Were they here? Was it even them in the cab and bus?

"Two threesomes on Flight 222 to some damn place, leaving in nine minutes," Officer Brooks reported. "This is the airline with the computer trouble, so who the hell knows anything for sure."

"Well put," Rotzinger said. He dispatched a sleepy officer to Gate 18, with sketches. "If they look remotely like these three, bring them here."

"What about the flight?" the sleepy officer asked. "How can I stop it? What if they want to take off?"

One airline had already lodged an official complaint about delaying flights for no apparent reason.

"Fuck the flight," Rotzinger said.

"Yes, *sir*," the sleepy officer said sternly. "If it looks like them, fuck the flight."

"If it looks like them and the airplane starts moving, shoot it out of the sky with your pistol."

"Sir?" the kid said.

"Just tell them to wait a minute, and call us."

"Okay, sir."

"We need more than luck, Wax."

He nodded. The old boy was fading again.

"We need intervention from God."

"Don't arrest my Uncle Hal," Teresa Singleton said to the sleepy kid cop heading to Gate 222 with the sketches. "He has a bad heart."

"This is sort of exciting," Charley English said to Bud Heathcoat, in a faint Norwegian accent.

"If you think *this* is exciting," Bud Heathcoat answered, "you ought to ride the bus more."

The depressing break in what Rotzinger had hoped would be action but turned out to be nothing, came to an end when Captain Holder flung open the door and said to Rotzinger, "We have something!"

Charley English and Bud Heathcoat were feeling Teresa
Singleton's tummy because she had suggested her baby was
about ready to walk out. "If he wants to be a policeman, I'll
sue all of you," she said.

"Something's going on in there," Bud Heathcoat said.

"You ever deliver one?" Charley English asked.

"You kidding? All they bring on a bus under their clothes
is toasters."

"Me neither," Charley English said. He felt Teresa Singleton's tummy again and said the kid was jogging.

Rotzinger got the helicopter driver and told him to take
the pregnant teller to the hospital.

"He just ran the hundred in ten, five," Charley English
said, removing his hands from Teresa Singleton's mid-section.

"You married?" Rotzinger asked.

"That'll cost you," Teresa Singleton said, leaving with the
helicopter pilot, "if I live."

Captain Holder was standing with Otis Boomershine. The
captain said, "We got something big."

"How big?"

"About 250, 275," Otis Boomershine said nervously. "He's
mammoth. And mean. He scares me."

"It's Lombino," Captain Holder said.

Rotzinger squinted and thought. "Lombino?"

"Vince Lombino," Captain Holder said.

Otis Boomershine said this creature had bought his ticket
under the name of Russ Crane, and that he had socked agent
Milt Tune right where it hurt the most, on the moustache.

"Oh," Rotzinger said, somewhat despondently.

"That thug has more whorehouses and bookie joints and
dope runners than anybody on earth," Captain Holder explained to Otis Boomershine, who gulped. "The Grand Jury
wants to talk to him about polluting a couple of rivers, too."

"Goodness," Otis Boomershine said.

"With bodies. It's bad for the fishing."

"Where is he?" Rotzinger asked.

Otis Boomershine told them.

They had been after Lombino so long, he had aged naturally and hardly matched the last description.

"This is very big," Captain Holder said. "This is not a lousy bank robber. This is a *killer*. A dope peddler."

Well, Rotzinger thought, there was a lot to be said, in large black letters on the front page, about apprehending a dope-dealing killer. You're not talking lives with this bank robbery. You're talking inconvenience and forms to be filled out. With Lombino, you're talking blood and guts and veins. You're talking headlines. Take this louse out of circulation, the mayor might name a day for you, or at least an afternoon.

"I thought he was in Arizona," Rotzinger said. "Playing golf and having face-lifts."

"He's here," Captain Holder said.

"Call the newspapers," Rotzinger told Officer Brooks.

Lombino handed a girl who was about eighteen some bills, patted her on the head, and accepted her boarding pass. The girl looked at the money, kissed it, and walked back toward the coffee shop.

"She never even heard of two grand," Lombino said to Lackey. Lombino extended his hand and said, "No hard feelings."

"Not yet," Lackey said.

"Russ Crane," Lombino said.

"Sam Billabong," Lackey said.

They were standing directly outside the tunnel that led to Flight 742.

Lombino told his wife to hop the next flight. He kissed her and pinched her on the butt. Lombino offered his boarding pass to ticket agent Milt Tune, who jerked his head backward at the motion and banged his skull on the wall. Tune's moustache looked like a dead fish. He tore the stub from Lombino's boarding pass.

"Listen, no hard feelings," Lombino said. Milt Tune extended his hand like it was something to be examined for a rash instead of taken, so Lombino ignored it and walked down the tunnel to the airplane.

Grimm, Lackey, and Phyllis were the last passengers to get on board. They had replaced the cash in the suitcase, at great pain and itching from the tape, and all was as well as anybody could expect. Lackey had also dumped his soft-core porno in the men's room, after being severely scolded by Grimm, who said Lackey was at his dead-level worst when things were going well.

"I'm just not used to fame and glory," Lackey said. His neck was still stiff, but the pain in his side had subsided to the extent that his shirt no longer stung his skin.

Grimm told him the ocean cured everything.

They handed their boarding passes to Milt Tune and were nodded toward the tunnel. Phyllis stopped halfway to the aircraft and kissed Grimm on the mouth, and then, Lackey on the cheek.

"That's more like it," Lackey said.

Phyllis reminded them that 90 percent of all traffic accidents happened within twenty miles of home, so although things looked extremely good at this point, a person could never be too careful. She was looking at Lackey as she said this, and he again apologized for the magazines.

"After all these years of bad jobs and starvation," Lackey said. "After all the times of about going to prison. After all the times when we about got killed."

"We never about got killed," Grimm said. "And I wish you two would quit making it sound like those jobs were idiotic."

"They were," Phyllis said. "But practice makes perfect, honey. This one makes up for everything." She kissed Grimm again on the mouth. "It's not *only* your mind I love."

"After jobs that never worked, jobs that about got us maimed," Lackey continued.

"He has a way with a toast, doesn't he?" Grimm said into Phyllis' lingering kiss.

"After getting tranquilized tonight, after accidentally hitting the car horn while you were making the call back to the bank, after taking the wrong turn, after your car was demolished with axes by the fire department, after jumping out of the cab, after shooting dice in the bus, after the overbooking, after *all* that."

"Don't forget the magazines," Grimm said out of the side of his mouth.

"Shut up and kiss me," Phyllis was saying.

"After the magazines. After everything, things that would have brought mortals to their knees, by God, *we made it.*"

Grimm squeezed Phyllis there in the tunnel, as Lackey shook his weary head and marveled at being moderately wealthy.

"Carry me across the threshold," Phyllis said, and Grimm did, stumbling onto the airplane, hanging onto the suitcase full of cash with his right hand.

"Lo," the stewardess said, "welcome aboard. Good to have you. Nice to see you. Can I take your bag? Give me your bag."

"No," Lackey said.

Grimm put Phyllis down, gave Lackey a dirty look, and said, "I'll just keep it with me, under the seat."

"Why?"

"Important papers," Grimm said.

"What is this, a third degree?" Lackey asked.

"It would be a lot more comfortable," the stewardess said, "if you took the papers out and put the bag here in the damn luggage compartment."

"Did you say *damn?*" Lackey asked.

The stewardess was about forty, and tired looking. The discrimination laws have hit the airlines hard, so you find a lot of tough mothers patrolling the aisles, married women, *strong* women, instead of all the little flirts who were so helpful in taking your mind off the fact that for the next seven hours, you would have no control over your life. There are some jobs, Lackey thought, where beauty and legs *should* be a consideration. This stewardess reminded Lackey of a mechanic, and consequently his thoughts drifted toward the bizarre; like, what if we crash?

"Everybody's tired, pal," the stewardess said to Lackey.

Pal?

"And because of the mess with the computer, there are bags all over the place. Take the papers out and leave your bag here."

"I think not," Grimm said.

Lackey asked for a card you filled out so he could comment on the service.

The stewardess looked at the bag, at Grimm's white knuckles, and then at Grimm's face. "Who cares?" she said. She told them where their seats were, and then went into the cockpit.

"Don't order hot coffee," Lackey said. "She'll throw it in your face."

Phyllis said, "Ignore her," and they walked into the airplane in search of their seats which, because of the computer, were not together. Phyllis was in about the middle of the coach section, roughly halfway between Grimm, who was toward the front, and Lackey, who was back by the tail, which was the first to incinerate if they crashed.

The plane was a mess. Because of the computer malfunction and subsequent ticket raffle, people traveling together had been seated far apart in most instances, and there was a lot of shuffling and bumping going on, as two seats next to each other were being arranged. The three stewardesses trying to handle this mess looked like they had been wrestling. Their shirttails were out and hair was in their eyes.

"What do you want?" one of the stewardesses asked Lackey, who answered, "Could we work out three together?"

Some of the passengers booed.

People were crowding past each other in the aisle.

"Go sit down," the stewardess told Lackey. "Please?"

"Where'd you pick up that word?" Lackey asked.

"Listen, buddy," the stewardess said.

"My name is Pal," Lackey said, and he plowed toward the back of the airplane, banging people sitting on the aisle, pushing people walking forward.

Grimm and Phyllis wedged into their assigned seats, and waved at each other, once they were secure.

Phyllis was on the aisle, next to a fat man who scooted his left knee onto Phyllis' right knee.

"Get your goddamn knee off me," Phyllis said.

"This is going to be a great flight," the fat man said.

Grimm was in the middle of a row, by a boy who was yelling "Mommie!" To Grimm's left was a woman who could not get her seat belt fastened. "So why are you going to Europe?" the woman asked. She was obviously a talker.

"I'm deaf," Grimm said. "Sorry."

"You're what?"

"Deaf."

A switch was made so the boy's mother could sit in Grimm's seat, and the talker moved forward and Grimm got the aisle seat.

Lackey worked two switches and got to the row behind Grimm, and Phyllis wound up to Grimm's left, directly across the aisle. A stewardess announced on the intercom that there would be no more changing, then the captain came on and said that because of the late bag-checking, the departure would be delayed approximately fifteen minutes.

Lombino was to Lackey's left, across the aisle.

Lombino leaned across, grabbed Lackey's knee, and said, "How's the kid?"

"Just great," Lackey said.

"I'm glad to hear that," Lombino said. "There's nothing

like a trip to cleanse the soul. Change of pace. Different scenery. Like that."

Lackey reached forward and removed the air sick bag from the seat compartment, and he read what was on the wrapper.

"I'm in the import-export business," Lombino said. "How about yourself?"

"No thanks," Lackey said.

"I mean, what business you in?"

"Harmonicas," Lackey said, surprising even himself.

"You're kidding."

"No."

"You *sell* harmonicas? People overseas *buy* harmonicas?"

"By the million," Lackey said.

"Why?" Lombino asked.

"To play," Lackey answered. "And give as gifts."

Lombino said he would be darned.

"What do you import and export?" Lackey asked.

"Mostly myself," Lombino answered, smiling wickedly. "Harmonicas?"

"Boxes. Crates. Shipsfull."

Lombino made a note of that and settled into his seat.

Grimm had the suitcase with the money on his lap. The kid two seats to his right was asking his mommie if she was sure they weren't going to crash in a firey ball, or hit electric lines on the way up, or blow a tire on takeoff and run through a freeway. The kid told his mommie he had been having a dream where the airplane took off but couldn't find an opening to come up through the utility wires and had to keep flying fifty feet above ground.

Grimm and Phyllis held hands across the aisle, which somebody a few rows back thought was the sweetest thing she had ever seen.

Lackey asked for a magazine and received a *Popular Mechanics*.

One of the stewardesses blew a tangle of hair off her fore-

head and said under her breath she wished more than anything in the world that she was pregnant so she could quit this
diabolical job.

They came on board like pirates.

Before anybody knew exactly what was happening, they
were through the first-class section into coach, weapons
brandished, just like on TV when they run the sirens, giving
the criminal time to leap through the window and head down
the fire escape, which always turns out to be much more dramatic than had they snuck up, picked the lock, and nabbed
the crook while he was sleeping.

Rotzinger was *also* after good ratings. He looked like a Ma-
rine or something.

Phyllis saw them first and said, "Look." She released
Grimm's hand and covered herself, like she was about to be
mugged.

Grimm swallowed and put the suitcase full of money on
the floor by his feet and tried to look innocent as a newborn,
and he did a very good job. A tear ran down his right cheek.

The kid on Grimm's row stood up and screamed, "It's
cops!"

Lackey stood suddenly from his seat and ripped the seat
belt from its socket. He put his fists in front of his face
parodying a prize fighter, and said, "You sons-of-bitches will
never take me alive!"

People screamed.

It came off more or less the way it had been predicted.
There was more blood and less routine than had been pro-
jected, but as Rotzinger had told his forces before the inva-
sion, "Fear is a mighty foe."

When the reporter left, Rotzinger said, "The mean bastard
is liable to do anything."

The reporter had been flown to the scene by a police helicopter, so this moment could be appropriately and accurately preserved in history. As Rotzinger told the reporter, "It is not every day a force as sinister as Vince Lombino is, is . . ."

"Harnessed," Captain Holder said.

"No," Rotzinger said.

"Defanged," Officer Brooks said.

"No."

"Apprehended," Wax said.

"Is apprehended," Rotzinger nodded.

So the reporter stood back and took notes as Rotzinger led his men onto Flight 742. Wax had been quickly dressed as a flight attendant, which he didn't care for at all, and he had been sent on board to mill around behind Lombino and, if things got rough, choke hell out of the guy.

Rotzinger would lead the way, which he did, followed by three uniformed officers.

Lombino had no weapon.

When you got right down to it, he was a sitting duck.

Lombino was reading *Time* magazine and didn't know anything was out of the ordinary until Lackey stood and yelled, "You sons-of-bitches will never take me alive."

Lombino looked up and saw Rotzinger about five rows away.

"Police," Rotzinger said. "Don't move."

Lackey stepped into the aisle and backed away from Rotzinger and his pistol. Lackey bumped into Wax, shielding him from Lombino, who was still sitting there. Wax said, "Get out of the way," and he pushed Lackey forward. Lackey tripped and fell at Rotzinger's feet. Rotzinger stood on Lackey's back, still aiming the pistol in the general direction of Lombino.

"You're killing my back," Lackey groaned, and he tried to get up, throwing Rotzinger off balance and into Grimm's lap. The officers took up the slack and moved forward, stomping on Lackey's shoulders and back. He slithered up the aisle on his belly. Rotzinger lost control of his pistol and it fell over by the kid who had been worrying about crashing.

The kid picked the pistol up.

Rotzinger, sprawled forward on Grimm's lap, grabbed the suitcase full of money by the handle, and pushed himself up, off Grimm's knees.

Lombino unfastened his seat belt and elbowed Wax in the stomach. Wax had his nightstick over his head at that moment and was very vulnerable to such a blow. Wax coughed and simply sat down in the aisle.

Lombino moved into the aisle and turned around toward Wax. Lombino picked up the nightstick. Rotzinger clumsily removed himself from Grimm's lap, balanced himself in the aisle, and swung the suitcase full of money in a vicious swoop that missed Phyllis' head by six inches at the most. The suitcase caught Lombino as he was turning around, right on the temple, producing a loud thud. Lombino fell back into Wax's lap. Wax had recovered enough to put a weak choke hold on Lombino. It didn't matter. Lombino was out cold. Rotzinger rushed forward to apply the cuffs and inform Lombino that he had certain rights, one of which was the right to resist arrest some more, so it's your decision, Rotzinger said.

Lombino mumbled something about how the city would be in ruin this time tomorrow. He was hauled to his feet and pushed toward the front of the airplane. His feet were in chains so he had to step on Lackey's back. Twice.

"Get this man up," Rotzinger said to an officer, of Lackey.

"My back is broken," Lackey said.

Wax, still holding his stomach, stepped around Lackey.

"Can I have my suitcase?" Grimm asked Rotzinger.

"What?"

"That was my bag."

"Oh. Right."

Rotzinger nodded to one of the officers, who stepped over Lackey, picked the suitcase from the floor, and handed it to Grimm, who said, "Thanks."

The suitcase was one squeeze from bursting. There was an indentation where Lombino's skull had been hit.

The officer said that if there was any damage, stop by with the suitcase and fill out a couple of hundred forms and within twenty-five years, the city would reimburse him.

"It's okay," Grimm said.

He made a mental note to invest some of his bankroll in Samsonite. He remembered the day he had bought that bag. You pay a little more for quality, the saleswoman had said, not giving a damn about quality, but rather trying to hustle a few more commission bucks. Grimm remembered thinking, what the devil. He had been *that* close from buying the cheap bag, which would have obviously come unhinged when applied to Lombino's head. The saleswoman had a glass eye and was pitiful, and that was why Grimm bought the good bag.

Grimm leaned across the aisle and whispered to Phyllis, "Let's name our first child Sam." He patted the bag.

"Huh?" Phyllis said. Tears were dropping off her chin.

"It's okay, baby," Grimm said.

Her eyes were closed. "Is it over?"

"Yeah," Grimm said. "For the time being."

Phyllis rubbed her pink eyes. She saw Lackey sprawled facedown in the aisle. "Did they shoot him?"

"They stomped him. Accidentally."

Grimm explained that Lackey had panicked, not that he blamed him, and had become sandwiched between two cops. The cops had shoved Lackey to the floor in order to arrest that thug.

Stewardesses were bending over Lackey.

Otis Boomershine thanked the ladies and gentlemen for their cooperation and said that Flight 742 would be departing in less than fifteen minutes.

A physician who had been sitting forward was with the stewardesses, instructing them not to move Lackey because of possible damage.

Lackey got to his hands and knees and said, "Woof." He

backed down the aisle to his vacant seat. Grimm bent down, put his arm around Lackey's shoulders, and helped him upright.

Lackey was able to stand up three-quarters straight, and the physician felt around the spine and said he didn't think there was serious damage, after all.

"Charge it," Lackey said of this advice.

"Can you move your neck in small circles?" the physician asked.

Lackey put his hand on top of his head, and moved it slightly right and left.

Grimm carefully lowered Lackey back into his seat.

The stewardess named Lucy said, "All seats must be upright for takeoff," and she depressed the button on the arm of Lackey's chair, flinging him forward. He managed to put his hands out to keep himself from cracking his head open.

"My seat belt doesn't work," Lackey said, handing it to Lucy.

Lackey was helped to Lombino's seat, and buckled in.

Phyllis had stopped crying.

Grimm lifted the suitcase from his knees to show Lackey that they were still on schedule.

Grimm winked at Lackey.

Lackey winked back.

He kept winking.

Lackey's right eyelid was out of control.

Rotzinger was gracious in victory.

Other members of the press arrived and there was an interview.

A press conference is like a little symphony. You conduct it. Rotzinger planted a shill on the second row. This kid worked for a tabloid and, in return for asking certain loaded questions, got some minor scoops from Rotzinger and the department. It is always better to make your statement as an answer from a reporter, so the kid from the tabloid hinted that

Lombino was the most wanted criminal of the decade. The kid suggested that Lombino had a hand in some ten gangland killings, and also suggested that Lombino's organization supplied drugs to every junior high this side of the Adirondacks. Rotzinger said there were indeed many, many questions that would be asked of Mr. Lombino.

When the kid reporter replied that Lombino's arrest might save the life of hundreds of America's youth, Rotzinger shrugged and said only time would tell.

The arrest was made possible by "sound investigatory technique," Rotzinger said, and he let it go at that. He did *not* mention that Lombino was so mad at being denied a seat on Flight 742 that he shouted his real name.

One of the reporters from a wire service asked why Rotzinger had a hand in the arrest, "To take everybody's mind off the bank robbery?"

Rotzinger forced a smile.

"Escape" is a funny word and concept he said. It is relative. Because a fugitive has not been captured within a few hours of a crime does not mean he or she "escaped." Rotzinger said that although the bank robbery was the farthest thing from his mind, he was being kept up to date on that particular investigation, and from his associates, he had learned that the trail left by the robbers was pointing in a very specific direction, and that although certain members of the press specializing in "slanted, sensational journalism" thought that the robbers had left no trail, well, that was not quite the case.

Since the reporter *had* mentioned the robbery, Rotzinger felt obligated to express his feelings about the matter. Now everybody knows that a crime is a crime. Each violation of the law is treated seriously. An officer will perform his duty to the best of his ability, whether the complaint is a domestic squabble or a mugging. Certain violations are pursued more intently. We have so many men, and must weigh the seriousness of the crime as it pertains to public safety, as it pertains to numbers of persons involved, as it pertains to the safety of our by God sons and by God daughters! As a rough estimate, the arrest of an alleged rotten son-of-a-bitch like Lombino was ten, twenty, or fifty times more important than the arrest of some idiotic, amateurish bank robber.

Rotzinger quoted some figures about robbers. Even when an arrest is not made within twenty seconds of the robbery, there is little likelihood the robbers will remain free. Granted, any robbery is painful for the victim, but until the robbers were captured, the investors at the bank were protected by insurance, but who, in the name of God, insures this country's young people against narcotic addiction, pornography, gambling, and atrocities like that?

Rotzinger's shill led a smattering of applause.

Rotzinger did *not* tell the ladies and gentlemen of the press that he had been very close to several nervous breakdowns this evening, and that because of the bank robbery, he had been popping Valium, eating french fries, and kicking his office apart.

He said Lombino would be closely guarded because there might be a couple or three thousand people who would just as soon the prisoner kept his mouth shut.

The arrest was described as "routine."

They had received word Lombino was flying out of the country, and they merely represented the taxpayers to the best of their ability.

There were no more questions about the robbery.

As the press conference was winding down, Rotzinger wondered if he would be the first police officer to receive the Nobel Peace Prize.

His summation about the current relentless crackdown on organized crime was interrupted by one of the stewardesses from Flight 742, which was preparing to depart.

The stewardess said, "Is this yours?"

She was holding Rotzinger's gun.

The boy sitting on Grimm's row had turned the pistol over to the stewardess after twirling it on his finger like a cowboy.

Rotzinger reached inside his coat, felt the empty holster, and remembered how the gun had been lost when he had fallen.

"A child found it," the stewardess said.

Rotzinger accepted the gun, put it away, and said the press conference was completed.

It was like the door to hell was closed, and they had nothing more to worry about. Grimm turned to Phyllis and said that the cabin door had been shut, could she believe it?

"It gets to a point," Phyllis said, "when you have to balance things out. You have to add up both columns. You have to determine whether what has happened was worth it. Look at this."

Phyllis stretched the skin around her eyes down.

"They're hardly even blood-shot," Grimm said.

"The wrinkles. I can feel them deepening. This night has aged me five years. I started this day in my prime. Right now, I feel like I'm very elderly."

Grimm said she looked fine to him.

Phyllis was still across the aisle from Grimm. Lackey was lumped in a seat behind Phyllis.

"Things are going to have to go perfectly for a long time, to balance the books," she said, yawning. "I'm so tired I could cry. Except I've already cried. Did you see the police come down the aisles with guns?"

It was some coincidence, Grimm had to admit.

"How's that one?" Phyllis asked, nodding her head backward to where Lackey had been last seen.

"I'm not *one*," Lackey said. "Not a *thing*. I'm a human being."

"How is the human battering ram back there?"

"Poor," Lackey said. "For openers, I cannot control my eyelid. There is a catch in the lower left portion of my neck, and I cannot seem to turn my head more than approximately a quarter of an inch. And furthermore, I think my back is bro-

ken. I cannot move my ass in any direction. Other than that,
I am fine, thanks."
Phyllis said she would rather be hurt than old.

Grimm looked at them both and couldn't understand how
anybody could have the nerve to be depressed or tired at such
a historic moment. The sound of the closing cabin door was
confirmation that the ball was finally in their court, and now
it was time to dribble hell out of it. Sure, they had been
fouled a couple of times, but the mark of a champ is to stay
in the game. Grimm was seeing personality traits in Phyllis
and Lackey that he didn't particularly care for, not at all. She
was adorable, all right, and a great one to have in your corner
after somebody had landed an uppercut to your chin. Several
times during the evening, Grimm had been able to compose
himself by merely placing his hand on Phyllis' wonderful bottom. Phyllis also had a wonderful mind. She was truly a re-
markable female companion, always full of fire and life. And
God bless Lackey. His contributions were immeasurable. As
long as Lackey was around, Grimm felt better. It was a rather
heartless point of view, but just seeing Lackey press on while
in the grip of excruciating pain, well, it had given Grimm the
courage to ignore minor inconveniences like the indigestion
he got after the sandwich in that filthy bar, right after they
missed the freeway. After what Lackey had been through, indigestion would have made him laugh. Lackey proved that as
long as a man is remotely in control of his mind, or even part
of his mind, anything is possible. The thing was, Phyllis and
Lackey were acting as though it hadn't been worth it. Grimm
wanted wine. He wanted to celebrate. The successful robbery
and subsequent escape meant an end to an obvious life of
hustling, of working for corrupt relatives, a life devoted to trying to break even!

Grimm leaned across the aisle, touched Phyllis' leg and
said, "You're a doll."

She looked at him, and back at Lackey. Well, at least I
know myself better, Phyllis thought. I always thought I

would do anything for money. I did. Now, was it worth it? It worried Phyllis that as brilliant a mind as Grimm's could have lapses, like with Lackey. That one back there was a curse. The job at the travel agency was no big deal. The guy with the Giants was a jerk. Grimm was a darling. Guys like that don't come along too often, either. He is so cute, you just want to hug him and curl up with him. It was something to think about. Had she cast her lot because of the idea or because Grimm was always so much fun to be with? Had some ugly guy suggested the bank, she would have laughed him out of town. So what it meant was, she was in love with *Grimm,* not his damn ideas. She had more or less proved she would follow him to the ends of the earth. The money was nice. Grimm, he was nicer. It was a startling awakening. She had not done anything for money. She had done anything for that guy across the aisle; he was grinning. They had by God *lucked* into a fortune! Phyllis also grinned. Getting *paid* for loving a guy is heaven.

Phyllis reached over and messed up Grimm's hair.

She turned around and asked Lackey if he needed a pillow. Any friend of her sweetie's was a friend of hers.

Perfect, Lackey thought. Maybe the pilot can marry them. He didn't know this goddamn *thing,* this goddamn *robbery,* was simply something to break the ice, something to *talk about* so they could justify running around the apartment with no clothes on. A computer dating service probably suggested the bank. Lackey decided what he would do with his share during the cooling off period in Europe. Motorized wheelchair. Monkey bars leading from his bed to the bathroom. Fulltime chiropractor. He might even have enough left over to put a down payment on an ambulance.

The bored stewardess named Lucy put an end to their dreams of heaven and hell.

"Put the suitcase under the seat," she said to Grimm. "We're about to take off."

Grimm released Phyllis' warm hand and said he would be glad to oblige.

Although it was not a king-sized suitcase, it was still too wide to slip bottom-first under Grimm's seat, so he said "No problem" to the stewardess, and he turned the bag and tried to cram it under his chair the other way, with the handle to the side.

This strategy very nearly worked.

Lucy, the stewardess, popped her knuckles as Grimm tried to stuff and pound and cram and wedge the bag under his seat.

"There," Grimm said, red-faced.

The suitcase was too fat to fit under the chair. About two inches of it was concealed, and the remainder was directly under Grimm's feet, which is a violation of FAA rules.

"It has to go under your seat," Lucy said, "or in the rack above you, or up front. Nothing can be loose in the aisle or under your feet."

"Why is that?" Lackey asked.

"I don't make the rules," Lucy said. "I make the coffee. Let's go, friend."

Grimm put his feet on the suitcase full of money, trying to reduce its bulk. There was a noise. The portable boarding ramp was being drawn back toward the airport. Engine sounds came from the wings. Lights in the airplane went off and on.

A passenger whistled.

The suitcase would not go under Grimm's seat.

Lucy sighed. "We've got two choices here. One, take something out of the bag so it will fit. Two, give it to me. I'll put it in the luggage closet up front. There's a third choice. You and your bag can get off."

"What ever happened to manners?" Lackey asked the stewardess.

"Damn," Phyllis said, slapping the seat in front of her. "Damn, damn, damn!"

"We're moving," Lackey said.

"Gimme the bag," Lucy said.

"Hey, for God's sake," somebody a few rows behind Grimm yelled. "Give her the bag so we can finally take off."

"Yeah."

"What's the deal up there?"

Lucy reached down to take the suitcase; Grimm wouldn't release it.

Lucy tugged and Grimm held firm.

"That's it," the stewardess said, releasing the bag. "I'm stopping the airplane." She walked toward the cockpit.

Grimm closed his eyes.

"What's in that bag, anyway," the kid by the window asked Grimm. "Money? Or dope?"

Phyllis leaned into the aisle and whispered, "Give her the stupid bag."

Lackey leaned up and whispered, "From back here it's like I'm a member of the audience. If this is what we have looked like all night, it's really very funny."

"This oversight," Phyllis hissed, "is unforgivable." She said she had just fallen out of love with Grimm, forever.

"Oversight?" Grimm moaned. "Oversight? What oversight?"

"The suitcase," Phyllis said. "The seat."

"What?" Grimm said.

"What kind of dope?" the kid by the window asked.

"Bobby," his mother said. "Hush."

"Smugglers," Bobby said.

"Hey," Grimm said to the stewardess. "Here." Grimm held the suitcase with hundreds of thousands of dollars in cash up. He told Lucy he had removed the important papers. No big deal.

"He didn't remove a thing," Bobby said to his mother.

"Hush, honey," she said. She scooted closer to her son, away from Grimm.

Lucy was not born yesterday. It was more like thirty-eight

or thirty-nine years ago. She had blocked the exact year out of her mind. It was inconceivable that she could have been born so long ago, when *Hitler* was alive, for heaven's sake, so of late she had been pretending it was all a big mistake and that she was, say, thirty. She tanned herself lavishly, exercised fanatically, and saved her money for a face-lift, which the guy said would add eight years to her sex life. That's a good investment, but at her current rate of saving, Lucy wouldn't be able to afford the lift until she was forty-four and a half. She had been a stewardess seventeen years. She was older than most of the planes she rode. She hated her job. The good thing about being a stewardess was that you meet plenty of rich men, but the bad thing was that they were all worthless. Lucy had married two of her passengers. Both had flown first class. That's not always a true indicator of a person's wealth. The first one she married, Bill, had been on an expense account. He was a salesman. He was all right until they were married, but then had a bad attack of jealousy, and he flew about every place Lucy did. Relatives of stewardesses get a nice break on the fare, but Bill finally bankrupted them, trying to keep an eye on his wife. Her second husband was a fat, balding oil man who snored. He was charged with selling old oil as new, and was arrested. The sky is full of success stories, though, so Lucy had been hanging in there, doing her sit-ups and facial exercise in hopes that some day she would meet a normal man, who would get her the hell out of this mess. You fly seventeen years, you get to know people. People on airplanes are more expressive than people walking down the street, more vulnerable. For example, you can tell by their eyes when a woman is carrying a dog in her purse, or when a guy is smuggling whiskey on board, or when somebody is running from something. The one with the suitcase, for a very good example, was hiding something in that suitcase. Lucy could tell this by the way he moved his eyes from side to side rapidly, and by the way he wouldn't let go of the bag. She wondered what, animal, mineral, or vegetable? The bag was solid and heavy. As she took it from the character with the nervous eyes, she squeezed the suitcase slightly. The contents had a very interesting feel, slightly flexible, but not much.

"What are you doing?" the guy asked when Lucy squeezed the bag.

"Feeling for cats," she answered.

The guy's eyes were the size of golf balls.

"You got a cat in here, fella?"

"No," he said. "Of course not."

Lucy took the suitcase forward and she placed it in the luggage compartment, just inside the first-class section. The luggage rack was across from the kitchen area. As the airplane taxied toward the runway, Lucy pulled the curtains between first class and the peanut gallery. Couldn't have the peasants back there leaning into the aisle, gawking toward the high-rent district. Spoils the scenery. The big spenders in first class pay dearly for their right to privacy. The curtain hadn't been pulled thirty seconds before the guy who owned the suitcase was standing there, breathing hard, wondering what the hell was going on. Lucy informed him that he was breaking three or more FAA rules at the moment, plus probably he could also be nailed for loitering near first class. He wanted to know where his precious bag was. Lucy opened the door to the luggage rack and showed him. Just wanted to make sure a name tag was on it, the guy said. Sure, Lucy said. Course. The guy watched Lucy shut and bolt the luggage rack door. He returned to his seat, after looking over his shoulder several times.

Lucy *really* wondered what was in that bag.

Grimm fell back into his chair and buckled himself in.

"This is without a doubt the rottenest airline on earth," Lackey said. "Why in the hell didn't we pick a normal airline?"

Phyllis reminded Lackey that when their "vacation" plans were made, the time of the flight's departure was an important consideration.

"Oversight?" Grimm asked.

"Do I know you?" Phyllis wondered.

"With the lottery for these seats," Lackey said. "They had nineteen too many seats booked, right? Well, it seems to me, instead of drawing names to *fill* the spots, it would have been easier and quicker to draw nineteen names of people who couldn't get on."

Phyllis said that this was indeed a historic moment. Lackey was making more sense than Grimm.

"You expected me to measure the suitcase and then board an airplane and measure the distance from the floor to the bottom of the seat?"

Phyllis read a flight magazine.

"You expected *that?* The bag was about one-tenth of an inch too fat. You expected me to think of *that?*"

"Yes," Phyllis whispered maliciously. "I certainly *did.*"

"Well, that's a hell of a note because I *didn't.*"

"Do tell."

"What's in the bag?" the kid asked Grimm. "Heroin?"

The kid and his mother leaned toward the window.

Lucy told the passengers in coach what to do in case the aircraft plunged into the ocean, but she said it nonchalantly, as though the airplane wouldn't plunge into the ocean or, if it did, it didn't make a damn *what* you did, really.

Emergency door here, door there, oxygen thing up there somewhere, read the card, write your Congressman, what the hell. Seat up, belt fastened, chin up, relax, see you later. The pilot said something cute about the delay, and he gunned Flight 742 and it rose quickly off the runway and steeply into the air. Grimm, Phyllis, and Lackey watched the city disappear through the clouds. The top of the clouds had a pink glow, like cotton candy.

"It's a new day," Lackey said. "It really is. It's fucking morning up here!"

A mother asked Lackey to please watch his foul mouth.

The pilot had obviously just come from an extensive

layover in Las Vegas. Once above the clouds, he said, "Thank
you very much," like he had just done Sinatra and was going
into his famous Cagney. "We just made up twenty-five seconds on the rise from takeoff." He doubted whether they
would be able to make up the two-hour delay but they'd do
their best. If there was anything the crew could do to make
their flight more enjoyable, well, just let 'em know.

John Wayne.

For some strange reason, Grimm did not feel as though
they were in a position to control their destiny, just yet.
What the hell, this beat being arrested.

A joker with a medallion around his neck touched Lucy on
the hip and asked what sign she was.

"Forget it," she said.

It took a lot out of the guy. He nervously buttoned his shirt
all the way up, coughed, and put his right hand by his bald
spot.

Grimm went forward twice during the first half hour of the
flight, checking on the suitcase.

He blamed the frequent trips on a second-class bladder.

Rotzinger doubted if the arrest of the gangland mug would
rub the bank robbery off the front pages, but it sure would
put matters in perspective. The arrest would be across the
tops of the papers in fat headlines. The robbery would be old
news, down at the bottom.

Rotzinger was in fabulous spirits when he returned to the
command post where Brooks was still monitoring flight de-
partures. The mayor had sent his congratulations. Rotzinger
called his wife and told her of the glorious turn of events, and
she made plans to leave for The Club to soak up the glory.
Nothing like this had happened since a member named
Schmidt had won $200,000 in a lottery.

Officer Brooks had things organized. He had all the flights
scheduled to depart within the next six hours neatly col-
umned on a blackboard. A policeman with the newest draw-

ings of the suspects would be at every gate. Flights where two men and a woman had booked passage together were marked for careful observation. Brooks estimated that within the time frame of when the alleged robbers were known to have been walking toward the airport, until the police began checking flights, approximately twelve airplanes had departed without notice. Now if the robbers were on any of those flights, Brooks said, we were in a little bit of trouble here. Brooks gave Rotzinger the unchecked flights and their intermediate stops and destinations.

"You're doing a sparkling job," Rotzinger said.

"It's hard in your sleep," Brooks said. "If they're here, if they're together, if they look like those drawings, we have a chance."

"Very good," Rotzinger said.

Wax was checking things with the small, commuter airlines. He reported that because of the remote departing areas of the commuters and charters, officers were having trouble finding the right gate or hangar or set of steps.

"All we can do is our best," Rotzinger said. He had undoubtedly set a very uncomfortable precedent, and would be the subject of some scorn at the convention in Vegas, when he delivered his essay on how to catch gangland figures. Most chiefs would resent Rotzinger's personal contact with criminals. It's not normal for a man with such responsibility to mix it up with thugs. A chief is more executive than officer. When a chief draws his gun, it should be at a cocktail party to show ladies.

Rotzinger would compare himself with somebody like Patton. Risking life and limb in front of the troops is definitely good for morale. Then Rotzinger would make a joke about how associating with known criminals shouldn't become habit forming.

"Isn't it a shame about Anita Bryant," Rotzinger said to Wax, who said, "What?"

"Isn't it a shame about Anita Bryant?"

"Why?"

"She can't get her hair done."

Wax looked at Officer Brooks, who looked at Captain Holder, who frowned, smiled, and cleared his throat.

"How come?" Officer Brooks asked.

"Well for God's sake," Rotzinger said, eliminating this joke from his Vegas repertoire. "There's no more question. That was the joke. That was *it*. The joke was, Anita Bryant can't get her hair done."

"Oh," Officer Brooks said.

Then he said, "Why?"

"Take a memo, Wax. Bring a comedian to talk to the recruits at rookie school."

Rotzinger said that Anita Bryant can't get her hair done because the guys who *do* hair are, for God's sake, strange.

Wax said that according to a recent survey, 18 percent of the law enforcement officers in this country, and this includes city, county, state, and federal, are gay.

"I don't want to hear that word again," Rotzinger said. "They're not gay. They're strange."

Wax also suggested that a few of the chiefs in Vegas might be, uh, competitive, so perhaps a more appropriate attempt at humor would be advised.

Big city jokes always went over real well.

"You hear about the guy, this tourist, who comes up to a native and asks, 'Can you direct me to the Statue of Liberty, or should I go fuck myself?' "

"That's very funny," Officer Brooks said.

"Then why aren't you laughing?" Rotzinger asked.

"I heard it about two hundred and fifty times."

"Well, what do you suggest, Brooks, sending out cards into the audience, asking what jokes they've heard?"

"They probably haven't heard it west of the Rockies," Brooks said.

"There is hardly anything of value west of the Rockies, Brooks."

Rotzinger told Wax he wanted the best new joke in the city on his desk, first thing Monday morning.

Rotzinger excused himself from the command post for a walk. It was morning, all right. Rotzinger stepped on the mat of an electric door and went outside for a breath of fresh air. He stretched. The air here is good from 6 A.M. until 6:45, when the cabs and buses get cranked up. Rotzinger filled his lungs, stood on his toes, and wondered what the poor people were doing.

There was not much business at the unloading areas this time of morning. The day shift was arriving. Porters were reading the sports page.

Rotzinger watched a squirrel come down the trunk of a tree. This tree was in a parking lot. It was the only tree in sight. When they built the parking lot, they left a base of about five square yards of dirt. The tree was more of a reference point than scenery. A person could find his car by going four thousand paces straight and two thousand paces right, of that lousy tree. The squirrel looked like it weighed about six ounces. It was very ugly. The only explanation was, this squirrel's family had been in that tree since before there was an airport. The skinny squirrel inspected an empty paper cup at the base of the trunk.

Rotzinger stepped off the curb and picked up an old hotdog bun, and he threw it over the railing, down into the parking lot, toward the tree. The bun sailed left and came to rest about ten yards from the tree. The squirrel sat on its back legs, rubbed its front feet together, looked at the bun, at Rotzinger, and then jumped from the curb. As the squirrel ran for the bun, it was run over by a kid on a motorcycle. The animal wasn't exactly run over. It was hit. Bumped. The kid on the motorcycle swerved right, bumped the squirrel, lost control of his motorcycle, and crashed on his ass. The squirrel limped back to the curb, struggled up it, tried to climb the trunk of the tree, and fell on *its* ass.

Rotzinger decided that the moral of this story was, you do your best and let the chips fall where they may.

He forgot who said it, maybe Confucius: the hell with it.

Rotzinger went back inside the airport, ordered a cup of coffee at a snack bar, and solved the bank robbery. It was so obvious, he was surprised he hadn't thought of it before. He laughed. That would be the reaction of the person who discovered a cure for the cold, a laugh. I can't believe I didn't think of that, the doctor will say. Why didn't I think of testing bone marrow from healthy mice before? We just threw the mice away. Shot them full of disease, tested *sick* mice, and then put them down the garbage disposal. God. How funny.

Rotzinger walked and thumbed through his book of worthless criminals, guys who would steal pencils from blind people, guys like Mario Bizanti.

From where Rotzinger stood, there by the newsstand in the airport, it sure looked like the Seabolts had robbed the bank. Rotzinger had known the Seabolts many years, even before he became a captain. As a lieutenant, he had sent four or more of the Seabolts to jail at least a dozen times.

The Seabolts were not even honorable enough to be a gang. They were a mess, thrown together like a mess of beans or eggs. Some of the Seabolts were not even Seabolts, they were Donellis and Ferragamos, cheap crooks who moved in with the Seabolts, thinking there was security in numbers.

When Rotzinger first came across the Seabolts, they were unloading golden chalices and crosses stolen from Catholic churches. There was *some* security in numbers because there were so many brothers and sisters, they were able to rotate prison sentences, and surrender the Seabolt with the least offenses to the authorities. This game of musical offenses kept the more sinister Seabolts on the street.

Once, the Seabolts turned in a ten-year-old brother to keep

a thirty-year-old sister out of jail for stealing cars. Most of the Seabolts had similar physical characteristics, huge chins, so when they were caught pimping or stealing, the law was offered the pick of the litter.

The file on the Seabolts was approximately two single-spaced feet high.

Eddie Seabolt was the head of the household. Because of his leadership, the Seabolts specialized in crimes too time-consuming to prosecute, things like lifting quarters from a blind man's mug. Eddie would insert a coat hanger with gum on the end into the blind man's cup, and nickel and dime the guy to death. Eddie believed it all added up. His favorite game was robbing crooks. He and his family would hang around susceptible liquor and grocery stores and whack robbers on the verge of getting away, when a person's guard was down. He made a lot of money that way, but every once in a while, Eddie would get stupid drunk and try something out of character, like robbing honest people.

Eddie Seabolt's last venture into the world of creative crime—with criminals, coming up with something innovative is half the fun—was blow-torching off the tops of parking meters. Actually, it was a fairly decent game. Eddie came up with this idea one night when he was drinking. You get this powerful torch and cut the money part of parking meters off and then you place the top in a sack and move to the next meter. Eddie could have made a lot of money deheading parking meters if only he had the legal-minimum amount of brains. Only he didn't. After the first night, when the Seabolts ravaged about thirty parking meters, he took up right where he left off, at the very next meter, like the beat cop might not notice the thirty naked poles, there. The police hid across the street the second night and shot about fifteen minutes of black-and-white film of the Seabolts drunkenly torching off the tops of twenty more meters. The third night, five cops stood around watching the Seabolts drive up to where they had left off. The cops told the Seabolts to stop it. Eddie Seabolt wondered why he and his relatives hadn't been arrested on the spot.

There was a very good reason.

"I want to talk to Eddie Seabolt," Rotzinger said. He had called from a pay phone in the airport.

"He can't come to the phone," a female said.

"Why?" Rotzinger asked.

"He's dead."

Rotzinger identified himself and said that if Eddie Seabolt didn't come to the phone, there would be trouble.

"He's not dead after all," the female said. Then, "We all watched television last night."

"*Whose* television?" Rotzinger asked.

"None of your business."

"Lo."

"Eddie."

"Lo."

"This is Rotzinger."

"It's all a big mistake," Eddie said, out of habit.

The money could be a problem, but a minor one. It happens all the time, nabbing robbers and not the money. There was a way around that. That a robber would have misplaced or lost almost a million dollars is a little hard to digest. Having the robber get robbed is slightly more feasible and moderately ironic. Giving it to the poor is always a possibility. If the money was hidden, it takes the glow off an arrest, but when you're dealing in lies, you can't have everything.

"We got you on film, killing the parking meters," Rotzinger said.

"Meters?" Eddie asked. "What meters?"

"Parking meters."

"Can't afford them."

"We also have you and your brother Johnny stealing playground equipment. We've got enough to have a Seabolt film festival. My favorite is where you and Henry stole the wheel-chair over in the park."

"I couldn't have done any of that," Eddie Seabolt said, "because I'm not arrested."

"We're coming to that part, Eddie."

"I thought it was my chair, right? When we found out it wasn't, we took it back. Left it in the same spot. Somebody must have restole it. Honest mistake."

Rotzinger said it would be a, well, *crime* to go to prison for cheap crap like that. "Sometimes it works out that you get the same time for stealing pennies from a meter as you would have for something big, like, well, a bank."

"Bank?"

"It seems a man could sleep better at night knowing he had a little something socked away."

"What is it you're getting at?" Eddie asked. "What you're talking about, those other things, it could have been my brother Buddy or even my sister Martha. We all look alike."

"These aren't silent films, Eddie. These are talkies. Your brother says, 'Eddie,' so we have to think he means Eddie."

"So?"

"Eddie," Rotzinger said, "we need a few good men."

"Great. I figured."

"Actually, two good men and one good woman."

A person has to think that money is more important than fame. Nobody robs anything for the glory, except actors, on television or in the movies. Every once in a while you come across a psycho who cuts somebody up and subconsciously wants to get caught. Robbers with hundreds of thousands of dollars want to get *away*. So there the robbers are, on some beach, holed up—somewhere—and they pick up a paper and see the robbery has been solved. This means they're home free. It is doubtful they would ask for equal time. This was one of those unique situations where everybody wins.

"So Eddie, what it boils down to is you go to jail for five

years for stealing pennies out of parking meters, or you go to jail for five years for robbing a bank. If you choose the latter, you will be handsomely rewarded."

"This is so crooked, I can smell it all the way here."

"I know lawyers and judges who don't like guys who rob churches, orphanages, and blind people."

"How much?"

"Fifteen a head. It doesn't matter whose head."

"That's ridiculous. My family is in its prime. Fifty a head."

"Twenty."

"Forty."

"Twenty-five a head," Rotzinger said, "and good night."

"It's morning," Eddie Seabolt said.

The fine thing about confessions is that they don't tie up the courts. Somebody says he did it, he says *how* he did, you match the guilty party up with a witness like, say, public relations man Murdock, who would identify a dog to save his skin, you have a nice, neat conviction. With all the disguises the real robbers used, nobody really knew who looked like what, anyway.

"It would help," Rotzinger said, "if you had somebody who had a normal jaw."

"I got cousins that look like Marilyn Monroe," Eddie Seabolt said.

"As popular as the robbers are," Rotzinger said, "whoever did it will probably be heroes. You give me some nieces and nephews without records, they'll be out before anybody knows it."

Eddie Seabolt said he didn't know.

"The idea will grow on you," Rotzinger said.

"Like a fungus," Eddie said. He wanted to think it over. Rotzinger gave him thirty seconds. Eddie Seabolt decided $75,000 had a nice ring to it, and he promised to call roll that evening and come up with some good, clean-cut bank robbers.

Rotzinger said he was about to say something that didn't need to be said, but he would throw it out, anyway. If at any time within the next hundred years, word of a possible conspiracy gets out, Eddie Seabolt would be fed to some Doberman pinchers, an arm and a leg at a time.

"What you hadn't ought to forget," Eddie said, "is we would do anything for money."

Rotzinger and Eddie Seabolt agreed to meet later in the week to arrange the capture. Rotzinger could personally fix it so that ten grand or so would be found in the robbers' possession. The eighty-five grand would be a solid investment in the future. Eddie Seabolt wanted a gentleman's agreement in the deal stipulating that if Rotzinger became mayor or governor while some Seabolt was still in the can, or if Rotzinger got a raise, Eddie Seabolt would get a 10 percent commission.

"You drive a hard bargain," Rotzinger said.

It was also agreed that if the real robbers were apprehended before the Seabolts went to jail, there would be a two grand surcharge for services unrendered.

Rotzinger said, "Done," because just between him and the rest of the world, it looked like the real robbers had pulled a once-in-a-lifetimer. For the first time all evening, Rotzinger could sit back with his feet up, like the rest of the population, including the police, and admire the sneaky sons-of-bitches.

Eddie Seabolt hung up and told one of his brothers to break out the bubbly.

"And just what the hell for?" brother Johnny asked. "They shut the bath water off ten days ago."

There were many intangibles to this game, Eddie Seabolt knew, beyond the dead-certainty that he would offer his guinea pig cousins or nephews only ten grand, thereby clearing sixty-five grand himself. Who knew for sure, things around this dump had disintegrated to the extent that prison would look like a Howard Johnson. Maybe Eddie would take five years himself, in the joint. He could use a nice vacation.

Simply being associated with something as smart as the robbery would be so good for business. The Seabolts might be called in on some really big games, from here on out.

"Not bubble *bath*," Eddie Seabolt told his brother Johnny. "Break out the *champagne*."

"Break it out of where, Eddie, the store down at the corner?"

Rotzinger returned to the command post and arranged for fresh officers to replace the ones who had been at it all night. He gave Wax the day off. The same procedure was to be followed the rest of the morning. An officer at every gate. From now on every two-man, one-woman threesome was to be searched prior to boarding.

The witnesses, Bud Heathcoat and Charley English, were released.

"We have done our best," Rotzinger said to his men. "There is no substitute for sound investigatory technique."

He said that in the end, justice would triumph. Press on. Stiff upper. Like that.

If needed, he could be reached at The Club, brunching with his wife.

The captain announced that the land off to the left side of the aircraft was the last they would see for about four hours, and he made a sharp right turn. Boats on the water looked like bugs.

Grimm was so tired and sleepy. He felt like he was just coming out of a bad drunk. Nothing had any definition, any *feel*. His body tingled. He seemed incapable of resisting the slightest force. He tilted with each movement of the airplane. When Lucy handed Grimm a pillow, it fell through his arms as though it were a sack of cement. Any emotion was also too strenuous. After four checks, he was too exhausted to get up, or worry about the suitcase.

As Lackey had said, the only thing to worry about was a crash.

We made it, Grimm thought.

"A bloody mary," Grimm told Lucy the stewardess. "And a straw."

Lucy woke Lackey to ask if he wanted a cocktail, and then on the way back to the kitchen, she again roused Lackey to ask if he wanted breakfast. Lackey asked Lucy if, when she was a little girl, if she could remember back that far, somebody kept sneaking into her room, waking her up?

"You want breakfast or not?" Lucy asked.

"Not," Lackey answered.

"You want music?"

"No," Lackey said.

"What's wrong with your neck?"

"Not a thing," Lackey said.

"It's crooked."

Lackey asked for and received a stewardess-evaluation card. On the line requesting an evaluation of the cabin crew, Lackey wrote, MY STEWARDESS WAS WRETCHED. SHE SHOULD BE PUT OUT TO STUD IMMEDIATELY. Lucy took the card, tore it in half, and put it in her apron.

Phyllis had breakfast.

Lackey had a sweet roll and asked to see the chef.

Grimm had three bloody marys.

He told Phyllis and Lackey to relax, he would take the first watch.

"You sound like Sergeant Preston of the Yukon," Lackey said. He put his seat back, flinched at some pain, and went promptly to sleep.

Lackey snored.

Phyllis had another breakfast, four milks and three orange juices, said, "I feel a little better," and passed out. Grimm got a blanket and put it over Phyllis. He touched her cheek. She smiled.

Lackey said, "Listen, doc, do the operation, I have the money."

Grimm shook him. Lackey turned his head left, shut up, and slept.

The third bloody mary flooded Grimm's joints with fatigue. He checked the suitcase again, under the guise of wanting more coffee. The bag was fine.

"I think I will just rest my eyes," Grimm said to nobody. The first sheep trotted out of the gate. It looked at Grimm, and stopped. The sheep walked up to Grimm, and looked into his eyes from about a foot away. Realizing that Grimm was already out of it, the sheep returned to the pen; no need to waste any energy.

Feeding the animals is one big bitch. The steaks are not cooked well, medium, or rare, they're just cooked, so everybody bitches about that. Walking up and down the aisles is like a swimsuit competition. All those bald heads leaning toward the middle reminded Lucy of a cantaloupe patch. It's funny how all the normal-looking ones sit by the windows, and the drunks sit on the aisle.

One of the other stewardesses, Annie, who had been flying ten years, reported that the hamburger in 22-A was playing with himself, that two guys on 31 were holding hands, that the moose in 26-D had unbuttoned his shirt another notch and had said he was a bra salesman, that there was a bona fide white-knuckler in 18-C (an elderly woman who was on the verge of hyperventilating), that the fat, bald loud-mouth on 26-A had his arm in the aisle and was ass-grabbing, and that there were some possible swingers on 35, asking for blankets and whipped cream.

"You think *that's* bad," Joyce said. "I have a guy who is about to hiccup himself to death." Joyce had first class.

"I would a lot rather have a guy hiccup than throw up," Annie said.

Lucy said the flight would not be a total waste. They had a guy in coach going for the world's record. He had been to the bathroom six times and they weren't even two hours out.

"The guy who had the suitcase?" Annie asked.

"Yeah," Lucy said.

"What's with him, anyway?" Annie asked.

"Who knows?"

The girls agreed they would have something to write home about—the violent arrest before departure.

"Listen to that," Joyce said. "The guy sounds like a popcorn machine."

"I read that if you time the hiccups like labor pains, you can tell how serious they are," Annie said.

"Where'd you read *that?*" Joyce asked.

"I think *National Geographic*," Annie said.

"You read *National Geographic?*" Joyce asked.

"Sure," Annie said. "I've saved every copy for about fifteen years."

Lucy whistled. "That's really something. Every copy. There probably aren't more than five or ten million people saving *Geographics.*"

"What's wrong with *her?*" Annie said to Joyce.

"Sorry," Lucy said. "Just tired."

Annie said it was all over now, but the hiccuping. Breakfast had been served, the remains collected and stowed, coffee had been sloshed, and the weirdos were settling back into merciful sleep.

Lucy walked the aisle in coach.

If anybody ever wondered why the more mature female attendants worked the long flights that left in the middle of the night, the reason wasn't because the airline was afraid to display these veterans in the light of day. The attendants with the most seniority got to choose their flights. That's why you see the big-breasted, long-legged feisty teenagers or thereabouts on the Dallas–Oklahoma City–Tulsa–Ft. Smith–Little Rock–Nashville–Mudville–Memphis tests of courage—flights that seem to bounce instead of fly. Serving a Coke and peanuts in thirty-five minutes is not much fun. The people who know the ropes prefer flights that leave at, say, 2 to 4 A.M. Feed and water them, and it's simple after that.

"Bruce, you simply have to get ahold of yourself," Lucy said to this flight's male attendant. Bruce sounded like a wind chime when he walked off flights. He was not opposed to having a nip now and again, and he stole quite a few hundred thousand million complimentary whiskey bottles. Bruce had been on a flight a few months ago that blew a tire on take-off and went through a fence into a field. The poor kid was never the same. The male flight attendants are manufactured in a warehouse outside of the Dallas–Ft. Worth airport, which is a big, centrally located complex. Quite a few passengers, as many as 98 percent, think that the male flight attendants are human, which just shows how technically proficient this country really is. The male flight attendants are robots. No kidding. They are assembled piece by piece in the warehouse in Texas, and sold to the domestic airlines at a price of $15,750, which seems like a lot of money. But the average robot-span of these creatures is 3.5 years, with a one-year service-and-parts warranty. When you figure that the *real* female attendants are paid an average salary of fourteen grand a year, plus all the food, whiskey, and men they can steal, it doesn't take a genius to figure that if an airline can get 3.5 years from a male flight attendant robot, this is cheaper than using the flesh and blood. The place in Dallas started catching a little heat several years back because they weren't using enough imagination on the robots, and they all looked alike. People were getting tired of seeing virtually the same male attendant on every flight, so the company in Texas started mixing it up a little bit, putting out one robot with a little longer moustache, and the next one with a sprinkle of silver hair, and maybe another version of model MFAR would come off the assembly line with a lisp. The robots still look basically the same, black hair and black moustache, but if you look closely, you might notice a slightly longer fingernail on the latest model male attendant.

You take a punch at one of these attendants, you'll break your goddamn hand.

"Keep 'em honest, Bruce," Lucy suggested. "Talk to some girls, too."

"It's a free sky," Bruce said.

Lucy had a feeling Bruce might need his points changed.

They wouldn't have to break out the sleeping powder or saltpeter this trip. About everybody was asleep or, after the ordeal in the airport, too tired to complain. The white-knuckler gave Lucy a shopping bag that was coming apart at the seams, and requested that it be stored in a safe place for the remainder of the flight.

"Okay," Lucy said. She took the shopping bag full of gifts by the bottom. "You can relax," Lucy told the little woman. "Everything is under control."

"Do you have a Bible?" the woman asked.

"A what?" That was a first.

"Holy Bible."

Lucy said she would check. The man hiccuping in first class had his head in a pillow.

"We have a Bible?" Lucy asked Joyce. Joyce blinked and asked, "What's wrong?"

"A lady wants a Bible."

"She know something we don't?" Joyce asked.

"No," Lucy said. "She just wanted to check in while she's in the neighborhood, I guess."

The closest they could come was a *Reader's Digest*. As Lucy stood checking the magazine rack for something remotely religious, a man opened the rest room door. He tried to close the door quickly, but couldn't hide the smoke. The guy got the door slammed shut, but smoke still came out through the "Occupied" latch.

"What the hell?" Lucy wondered.

"Um, uh, listen," the guy said.

Lucy opened the door and was flabbergasted by *more* smoke, lots more.

"Gosh," the guy said. "Uh, we're, my wife and I are, uh, back in non-smoking, because you see, I've quit smoking, generally speaking."

"What?" Lucy wondered again.

"If, uh, she knew I was still smoking, well, we quit together, the same time and, I had a couple there in the john."

"You smoked two cigarettes in there?"

"Two, three. Maybe four."

"Good God," Lucy said. "There's no smoking in the rest rooms."

"Yeah, well, uh."

"Please go sit down," Lucy said.

The guy smelled of so much smoke, somebody on the aisle in first class woke up coughing.

"There's smoke coming out of that guy's pores," Joyce said. She got some air-freshener and shot it into the rest room, then sat down for a little nap, she hoped.

Lucy bent down. Her knees popped. She opened the luggage compartment and tried to wedge the little woman's torn shopping bag inside. She couldn't get the door closed. She put the woman's shopping bag to her side and removed a box, an overnight case, and Grimm's brown suitcase.

She put the shopping bag inside the compartment, replaced the box and the overnight case, then stood up. Her knees popped. She looked around. She bent back down. Her whole *body* popped.

She put Grimm's brown suitcase back inside the luggage compartment sideways. It fit. Before closing and latching the door to the luggage compartment, Lucy thought, what the hell, we're all gossips at heart, and she reached inside and slid a button on the brown suitcase, left to right. That side of the bag opened with a slight click. So much for the high drama. Even psychos lock up their valuables. Lucy changed positions, looked around, saw nothing, and nudged the other locking button, which also opened. Lucy lowered half of the suitcase toward her, revealing the contents:

Money.

Furthermore:

American money.

And more importantly:

Several square feet of it.

She looked at the money maybe ten seconds. She leaned back on her heels and looked left and right. Nobody. She touched the money. She closed the suitcase. She opened the suitcase. She removed a pack of fifty-dollar bills from one of the stacks, and put it in her bra. She closed the suitcase and snapped it shut, and tried the lock buttons again, gritting her teeth at the opening sounds. She closed the suitcase a third time, closed the door to the luggage compartment, and she stood up. She didn't notice it, if anything popped.

She went into the rest room and removed the fifties from her shirt and studied them under what light there was. The bills had a good feel. She put the fifties—$500 worth of them —in her bra.

I deserve it, she thought.

Lucy felt her way out of the rest room, through first class, into coach. She balanced herself on the chairbacks and walked to where Grimm was sleeping. She kneeled down and looked closely at his face. Grimm's head jerked in his sleep, and Lucy about fell over backward.

Lucy also studied Phyllis and Lackey.

Everybody in the area was asleep or reading.

The plane even sounded like it was snoring.

Lucy turned and walked back to the mini-kitchen area, where she patted some cold water on her face. Annie returned from the farthest extremities of coach for the coffee pot.

"Hey," Annie said to Lucy. "What's the matter? You look real sick."

"Thanks," Lucy said.

"Listen, I don't mean anything by it," Annie said. "I was just trying to help."

"I know. You did. I mean it. Thanks."

"You better lie down, Lucy."

"I feel pretty bad," she said. "Down here." Lucy touched her stomach. "It's worse when I'm still."

"Oh Jesus," Annie said. "It sounds like appendix to me. I roomed with a girl in college and she about *died* with appendicitis!"

Lucy said she would probably be okay.

While Annie and Bruce worked the coffee pots, and the other attendants took turns dozing, while everything was very quiet, Lucy kept busy by rearranging the suitcases in the luggage compartments to her satisfaction.

Grimm woke up when he felt the airplane drop slightly. He looked at his watch. Since it was still more than an hour before the scheduled landing, and since the airplane was *definitely* going down, Grimm decided that it might be a good idea to ask somebody if they were crashing.

He had slept a couple of hours and was surprised to still feel so rotten. If anything, he felt tireder now than when he had dozed off. Perhaps his fatigue had something to do with the dream. Grimm had dreamed sheep attacked him.

He felt dull.

Phyllis was sleeping sideways in her chair.

Lackey had a pillow on his head, placed there by his neighbor because of the snoring.

"Are we crashing?" the kid on Grimm's row asked.

"Of course not," Grimm answered.

"Then what are we doing? We're going down to the water. It's too early to land."

"He's going to wash the plane," Grimm said, and he waved at a stewardess, who was collecting coffee cups. For an instant, he thought the worst, which was *not* a crash. What if they had turned around and were landing back in the States? Although Grimm was not comfortable with panic, he had at least gotten to know it a little better during the last twenty-four hours, so he remained calm and reasoned his way through this nervous thought. He checked the position of the sun and determined that they were still flying east. There was nothing on *that* horizon that could cause any trouble.

"What's going on here?" Grimm asked the stewardess with cups.

"Just relax, sir," Annie said.

"It's hard to when the aircraft you're on is going down in the middle of the ocean."

"We *are* crashing," the kid said, waking up several people on the rows in front of him.

"Please," Annie said to Grimm and the kid. "Nothing's wrong. There will be an announcement in a moment. Everything is perfectly under control."

"We taking the turnpike the last hour?" Grimm asked, as the airplane continued to drift downward.

"Sir, we're landing in Ireland because of an illness on board," Annie said. "It's an emergency, a possible case of appendicitis."

"Oh," the kid said.

"Oh," Grimm said.

Grimm wondered if he ought to mention the delay, because Lackey wasn't known for his ability to cope with minor annoyances. Grimm reached back and pinched Lackey's foot.

"Lackey."

There was no response.

"Lackey." Grimm pulled on Lackey's foot. Lackey instinctively grabbed the arm rests and braced himself.

"Lackey, wake up."

"*Let me go, you,*" Lackey screamed. He opened his eyes and looked at Grimm rather apprehensively.

"It's me, pal."

"Grimm?"

"Yeah. Listen."

Lackey blinked. He looked around and realized where he was. "Why is everybody looking at me?"

"You woke up loud."

"I thought it was the devil, Grimm, pulling me into hell."

"Listen. Nothing's wrong."

Lackey straightened himself in the chair. He rubbed his face. He looked at Grimm. "So?"

"I just wanted to let you know."

"What?"

"That nothing's wrong."

"You woke me up to tell me nothing's wrong? I was sleeping. There has never been anybody who needed rest more than me."

Grimm explained the reason for the unscheduled landing. "I thought you might wake up and feel us going down and check your watch, and maybe panic."

Lackey said he was too tired to panic. He closed his eyes. "I can't sleep now," he said after a few seconds.

"Count sheep," Grimm suggested. "But be careful. They're mean."

Lackey closed his eyes and reported periodically that he could not sleep. He even tried counting his cash.

The captain made his announcement.

"Ladies and gentlemen, this is Captain Rook. I have some good news and some bad news."

"What the hell is this, amateur night?" Lackey wondered.

"The good news is, we have made up four minutes and thirty-five seconds of the two-hour delay we had back in the States. The bad news, we're going to lose about twenty more minutes. We're in the process of landing in Shannon, Ireland. I'm going to put the seat belt sign on in about seven minutes, and the no smoking light will go on in about fifteen. We have a very sick young woman on board, and we're putting down in Shannon briefly so she can get some immediate medical help."

Passengers leaned into the aisle, looking for the culprit.

"We'll only be on the ground a few minutes, so we're asking that everybody please remain seated. We're going to fly right up the mouth of the Shannon River. The Irish countryside is something else, this time of morning. Sorry for the inconvenience, folks."

Grimm was out of his seat before the captain switched off his microphone. He was the first one to the rest room. He told Bruce, the male flight attendant, that he wanted to check his bag, it sometimes came open unexpectedly. There were valuable papers inside.

Bruce opened the bottom door to the luggage compartment, Grimm got down on his hands and knees and located the brown suitcase. It was about the third one inside the compartment. Grimm reached inside and felt the locks and he pushed against the side of the bag. He nodded to himself and got up.

Lucy was in a little seat that folds down from the wall, where stewardesses sit during takeoff and landing. She was wrapped in blankets. She was doubled over slightly. Her face was red.

"Well, hang in there," Grimm told her.

She looked up feebly and said that was what she was trying to do.

The landing was rough, but forgivable, because the runway was obscured by fog.

Lackey did a play-by-play, announcing every thirty seconds, "I cannot see a thing." When Lackey *did* see the runway, he only had time to announce, "Oh, God!"

The airplane played hopscotch for about a block, shuddered to a halt, made a left, and stopped. They sat there a few minutes.

The airplane presently followed a cart to what was probably a gate, who could tell. Through the mush, you could see the flashing light of an ambulance. In the glow around the ambulance, you could see the stricken woman being helped down the stairs. Her belongings were loaded into the back of the ambulance, and that was that.

The cabin door was quickly closed, and the ambulance sped away.

"I know why this place produced so many poets and writers," Lackey said.

"Why?" Grimm asked.

"There's nothing else to do."

Lackey said the weather also explained the potato famine. Nobody could find the damn things.

The captain got a shove backward from a little truck, located a runway, gunned the engines, and released the brakes. Lackey leaned over two seats, looked out of the window, and blamed the roughness on small shrubs, which were growing up through the cement runway. The takeoff over some wires was achieved, Lackey said, with a good ten feet to spare.

Although Grimm thought London was the most beautiful place he had ever seen, Lackey was not as impressed. He said it looked a lot like Wichita, Kansas, where he visited, once, to bury an uncle. The burial was incidental. Lackey made the trip because of the will. That uncle left Lackey a Pinto and $500. The Pinto broke down four times on the drive back and Lackey finally sold it to a junk dealer for $139. Considering the air fare and two nights at a motel, plus meals, Lackey cleared $310.

You couldn't see all that much of London because of the fog.

"When we land, men in raincoats will probably present us with complimentary flashlights," Lackey said, comparing this arrival with one to a more exotic locale, for example, Hawaii, where naked women run up and kiss you and give you flowers.

Grimm reminded Lackey that Hawaii was a member of the United States of America, and that shuttles ran continuously to California, transporting escaping criminals back to the mainland.

"Oh yeah," Lackey said. He looked out the window. "It looks like we're under water."

Grimm didn't want Phyllis to sleep through such a momen**t**us occasion, so he roused her, shaking her gently by the shoulders.

"I love that," she said, without opening her eyes. "I swear to God, I love that with all my heart, and I want you to keep doing it."

Grimm was getting nervous, so he reached across the aisle and pulled Phyllis' eyelids up. "Wake up, honey."

Phyllis screamed.

Grimm recoiled.

Passengers looked.

Phyllis blinked herself back to consciousness and said, "Oh. It's you."

Grimm smiled. "We're landing."

Phyllis stretched. "Why is everybody looking at me?"

"You're attractive."

"Oh." Phyllis yawned. "That's a hell of a way to wake somebody up, just prying their eyelids open. I didn't talk in my sleep, did I?"

"No," Grimm said.

"I was dreaming."

Grimm said they could discuss it later, if absolutely necessary.

"About you," Phyllis said.

"Oh?"

"And me. On a beach."

"Was I in it?" Lackey leaned up and asked.

Phyllis wrinkled her pretty brow. "Come to think of it, yeah."

"I was drowning in the ocean while you two were making love, right?"

"No. You were in traction. Right there on the beach, in one of those hospital beds, in traction."

"Well," Lackey said, "at least I lived."

The airplane descended in great gulps, and finally leveled off. Lackey smiled, looked out the window, and said he took back everything he had said about the pilot, that was the smoothest landing he had ever been involved with.⬛Then when the airplane *continued* to drop, Lackey looked out the window and said, "Oh hell, forget it, we haven't landed yet."

When they touched down, Grimm whistled loudly, Lackey praised the Lord, and Phyllis said the first thing she was going to do was take a shower. Lackey said this could be done relatively simply on the way to a taxi because it was raining like hell out there.

"Welcome to Philadelphia," the captain said humorously. "Just kidding. On behalf of the cockpit and cabin crew, welcome to merry old England and London. It's one of the friendliest cities in the world. Your free sauna is waiting just outside the aircraft." The captain clicked his microphone off so the laughter from the cockpit wouldn't pierce the eardrums of the passengers. He came back on and gave the current time and temperature, and asked that everybody please remain seated until the aircraft had reached the gate. He apologized for the computer malfunction and subsequent delay, hoped everybody had a pleasant flight, apologized for the stop at Shannon, and asked that everybody please fly this airline again in the near future.

"Your father's moustache," Lackey yelled.

The airplane taxied a great distance. The captain came on again briefly and said they were now entering France, ha, ha, and then in about five more minutes, they finally stopped.

There was cheering by most of the passengers.

Many of them had jumped out of their seats during the ride to the gate. Before the airplane had stopped, there was a line in the aisle thirty deep. Grimm was the first on his feet. He told Lackey and Phyllis to stay put and wait until everybody got off, he would get the bag and wait for them, up front.

When the cabin door was unlatched, it was as though somebody had opened a can of condensed people, the way the first passengers popped out of Flight 742. Bruce, the male flight attendant, reported that stewardess Lucy Smith was not seriously ill. They had received that radio message from Ireland just before landing.

Grimm was the first one to the opened luggage compartments, and the moment the plane stopped rolling, he reached inside and grabbed the handle of the brown suitcase. He hauled the bag toward him, scattering other luggage into the aisle, making a complete mess of flimsy shopping bags. Presents and things from the shopping bags were kicked all over the place.

"What's *wrong* with you?" Bruce asked Grimm, who answered, "Now that we're on the ground, why don't you mind your own business?"

Grimm clutched the suitcase to his breast and stepped into a row as people moved toward the exit.

The captain stood at the door to his cockpit, hat tilted back, and he nodded as people got off.

Grimm, Lackey, and Phyllis were the last three to leave.

"Take your time," the captain said to Lackey. "There's no hurry."

Lackey turned to Grimm and said, "That's this airline's motto." Lackey's back was stiff and he was slightly bent over.

"Have a," Bruce, the male flight attendant, said.

"Nice day," stewardesses Annie and Joyce said.

"Give my best to Uncle Donald," Lackey said.

Bruce, Annie, and Joyce didn't get it.

"Huey, Louie, and Dewey are these ducks, see," Lackey said.

"Come on," Phyllis said.

"This is important," Lackey said. "I don't want them to think I'm crazy. Donald is their uncle."

"Disney," Grimm said.

"Right. Disney. The kid ducks, it takes all three of them to make a sentence. Can we, Huey says, go to, Louie says, the bathroom, Dewey says." Lackey nodded. "You guys are as good as they are."

The flight attendants scratched their heads as Grimm, Lackey, and Phyllis marched through the connecting tunnel to the airport. Lackey thumped the suitcase with his finger, patted Grimm on the back and said, "We forgot magazines to stuff in the suitcase, if they open it at customs."

"You can stop panicking now," Phyllis said. "We made it."

Grimm bought eight newspapers from a puzzled salesman, accepted the extra roll of tape from Lackey, and the three of them followed the CUSTOMS signs. Phyllis had the passports in her purse.

"I'll feel a lot better when we're through customs," Lackey said.

Grimm impressed upon Lackey what a shame it would be if, after all they had survived, some idiotic and mindless mistake cost them their liberty. Lackey held his arms out like a scarecrow to show that he had left his reading material in the bag in front of his seat in the airplane. "There was a woman on my row and I didn't get to read anything."

"Read?" Phyllis asked.

Grimm told Lackey as an afterthought that he had heard they had rats as big as beavers in some of the jails here. "If you have ever in your life looked innocent, let it be now," Grimm said. The fatigue and bloody marys had worn off, and he was his old self, thinking hard, plotting, scheming.

"No matter what is said at customs," Phyllis sternly lectured Lackey, "no matter what happens, do *not* panic." She had a lot of travel agency material in her purse and, if necessary, would make a comment about how they were here to update hotels for future tours. "Don't act *too* innocent."

"Act normal," Grimm said. "Okay. We go in a rest room and transfer the money. The papers into the suitcase. We go to the baggage area, around the corner there, and get the other luggage. We go through customs. Taxi. Hotel. That's it."

"I'll wait here," Phyllis said, "while you guys go in.

Straighten up as much as possible, Lackey. You can carry more cash."

"So," Grimm nodded at the rest room door.

"It stinks," Lackey said.

"Let's go," Grimm said. He took a step and stopped. "What stinks."

"The whole thing," Lackey said.

"What whole thing?"

"This whole thing."

"Goddamn it, Lackey, I'm in no mood for this."

"It stinks."

"*What* stinks?"

"This?" Phyllis asked.

"Yeah," Lackey answered. "This. The whole thing."

The conversation almost made no sense.

Lackey explained to the best of his ability.

"Taking the suitcase full of papers through customs stinks. Nobody gives a damn, getting *out* of the country. They'd probably pass through cheese and crackers in a suitcase. But coming *in* worries me."

Grimm said they had talked about this part at least ten times. Why hadn't Lackey said anything?

"I was too hurt to talk. They open the suitcase and see eight copies of the same paper, well, they might stop us. I was working in customs. I saw that, I would."

"It is a little thin," Phyllis said.

Grimm licked his lips. "Well, then, the hell with the suitcase. We'll leave it in the bathroom. We have the other bag full of clothes."

"Three people coming from overseas to a foreign country with one lousy bag? I was working customs, I would wonder why."

"It's a *big* bag. Maybe we're not going to be here long."

"Yeah," Phyllis thought. "That might be better than trying the suitcase with papers. Here for a couple of days. I like that better than papers."

"Okay," Grimm said. "Okay."

"We could make it to a hotel with the money on us easily enough," Phyllis said.

"Or we could take an empty bag through," Lackey suggested. "Like we were going to fill it with presents or something."

"Happens all the time," Phyllis said.

It was decided that they would go with the one large bag, and dump the empty one in the rest room.

"We should have brought more clothes," Lackey said. "And more bags. It's making me sick, thinking about this."

"Let's go," Grimm said to Lackey. "Wait here," he told Phyllis.

Phyllis kissed Grimm on the cheek. Also Lackey. "Remember," she told Lackey, "don't panic."

"You can count on me," he said.

The rest room was small and damp, with open stalls, which was a problem that hadn't been counted on, but you have to take the bad with the rotten, so Grimm and Lackey set up shop beyond the stalls, by the sink. Grimm put the brown suitcase on the sink, and told Lackey he would be right back. He went outside and explained the lack of privacy to Phyllis. She was instructed to use her best washerwoman, British accent, and tell anybody trying to get into the rest room that it was out of order.

Grimm went back inside, to the sink, where Lackey had his shirt and jacket off. He had removed a section of tape from the roll and told Grimm, "You hold the money on me and I'll tape it."

"Right."

Grimm opened both latches.

"We never locked it?" Lackey wondered. "I'll be damned."

Grimm pushed the top of the suitcase up; he and Lackey stood there, without comment. There was no way to describe what they felt.

Lackey was the first to leave the rest room.

Phyllis turned her head toward him and said she had scared
two guys off, one of whom remarked that the janitors in London sure dressed good.

"How am I doing?" Lackey asked.

"About what?" Phyllis wondered.

"About not panicking?"

Momentarily, Lackey leaned backward against the wall and
grabbed his stomach. Phyllis stepped up and supported
Lackey's shoulders. Then she felt downward a bit, like she
was frisking him. Lackey sank to the floor and sat there.

Phyllis rushed into the men's room, asked Grimm, "Are
you all right?" and walked around the partitions of the open-
end stalls.

Grimm was facing the mirror, where the bag was opened.
His feet were some three feet back from the sink, but he was
leaning forward with his hands on the front rim, like he was
about to be ill.

Grimm slowly looked at Phyllis.

He said, "No," and his voice cracked. "I'm not all right."

Phyllis' eyes went from Grimm's face, down his extended
arms, to the sink.

She looked at the contents of the suitcase, opened her
mouth to say something, but walked to the sink, instead. She
picked a towel out of the suitcase, and threw it over her
shoulder; she did the same with a washcloth, a half dozen
napkins, and a large blanket, which had been wrapped around
dozens of knives, forks, and spoons—silverware from the airplane.

At the bottom of the tightly-packed suitcase was a small
pack of money, maybe $500 in fifties, maybe not, and approx-
imately twenty-five flight magazines. Phyllis threw all of this
garbage over her shoulder, all but the $500, and she kicked
the silverware out of her way.

"The stewardess," she said.

Grimm blinked.

Phyllis made a fist, but decided not to slug Grimm. She felt her way along the partition hiding the sink from the door, as though she were blind. She sat down on the first stool, with her head in her hands, and she didn't move until a man entered the rest room. This person pushed some silverware away from the door with the side of his foot.

He stopped, naturally, and glanced down at Phyllis.

She looked up, but didn't say anything.

"I like England already," the man said.

It was still a cool and gloomy and moist day.

And it was a sorry little bank in a scuffed part of town. Grubby people were depositing pay checks, holding back a few pounds for a pint or two on the way home.

Nobody smiled. There was nothing funny about trying to stay within 10 or 15 percent of even, whatever the rate of inflation was this afternoon; they seemed to adjust it by the hour, anymore.

The bank was colorless, except for a red tie one of the tellers wore. From his expression, he had already been reprimanded by a superior for dressing out of character. The walls were gray and the wood was almost black, and everybody wore dark suits and subdued dresses. It was a trick of the trade: always dress down to the customers so they will think the staff was as poor as they were, which was true enough.

The whole out-of-the-way little neighborhood seemed angry. Doors didn't close; they slammed. All the signs on the shops and pubs were in block letters. People didn't walk, they stomped; they spoke exclamation points. Anybody living in the middle of this depression deserved exactly what he got, the one with the bad back thought. He would occasionally stretch. His neck was stiff.

"Nothing," he said to the woman with superior legs.

"Who cares?" she said.

The guy with the hurt back pitched the newspaper into a garbage can. There was nothing about the big bank robbery in America.

"Not a paragraph. Not a word."

"Go away," the woman said.

"I better have a look," the guy with the aching back said. "Something might have happened to him."

"No such luck," the woman said. She nodded toward the front window.

There was a tired clown plodding along the sidewalk across the street. His shoulders were slumped and his head was down. A dog nipped at the clown's baggy pants; he kicked the dog in the rump, and accidentally released the balloons.

He watched them float away.

The clown shrugged, put his hands in his pockets, and jaywalked toward the bank.

HUGH ESTES, the guard, continued to work for the bank until he knocked out a fourteen-year-old boy who was carrying a transistor radio in his back pocket. Hugh Estes thought the radio was a bomb, and he knocked the kid unconscious with the back of a gun. Hugh Estes' nerves were never the same after the robbery, and he was fired for assaulting the boy. He became a "maintenance engineer" for an old apartment house.

BUZZ MURDOCK, the public relations expert, had a nervous breakdown, and couldn't get arrested in advertising. The word got out that if Murdock wrote about your product, it was screwed. He wrote billboard copy for a while, but was fired when a large display advertising perfume collapsed onto a Toyota, resulting in a multimillion-dollar lawsuit. He got on with a newspaper, writing sports.

TERESA SINGLETON, the teller, had a large son, without complications. She took advantage of the bank's maternity benefits, then quit. They never found out that she stole $4,500. When the guy in the clown suit had announced the robbery by firing a bullet into the water sprinkler, Teresa Singleton had stuffed some cash into her purse.

MARGO, the fat woman who had that awful bar, torched her place and used the insurance to settle up with her bookie. With what was left, she bought the bar across the street. She turned over a new leaf, and bet *against* the Blue Jays every night.

MOUNTBATTEN, who had worked on jobs with Grimm before, the one who got thirty grand to keep his mouth shut, opened an automobile service center over in Connecticut by a retirement community, and is cleaning up.

ART THIEF MARIO BIZANTI was paroled. He was shocked to learn what inflation had done to his nest egg. He went to see Rotzinger about a cost-of-living supplement, and was never heard from again.

CAB DRIVER CHARLEY ENGLISH went to work for a chauffeur service, assisting his income by providing the police with information about drugs and celebrities, usually rock musicians.

BUD HEATHCOAT was involved in an accident with a police car and an ambulance. He was suspended. He found employment with a cab company, but had his license revoked when he ran over a seeing-eye dog. He went in with another suspended bus driver, and they bought a carriage and they give rides around the park to tourists for twenty dollars a pop, and they're doing all right.

PROMISING NOVELIST BERNARD OVERBY completed his Sweeping Novel of the North. His agent charged an extra $250 for reading the finished product, due to its extreme length. When the agent then requested a rewrite, Bernard Overby pulled a gun and shot the guy in the arm. Bernard Overby is serving a few years in jail, and is on page 220 of his new book.

TICKET AGENT MILT TUNE had some of his moustache pulled off by a passenger who was bumped from a flight to Dallas because of overbooking. Tune shaved the moustache off and this turned his whole life for the better.

VINCE LOMBINO spilled his guts out about every gangster and payoff and crime he had ever heard of, which resulted in hundreds of arrests. He and his wife were relocated. Lombino was given an operation to change his appearance. He works at the fifty-dollar window at a horse-racing track in Nebraska.

WAX quit the department and went to work for a detective agency.

EDDIE SEABOLT, a female cousin with great legs, and a male nephew were arrested for the Crime of the Century. A publisher bought the rights for a book from Eddie for twenty grand. The Seabolts served their time without regret. Compared to where they had been living, hell, prison wasn't bad at all.

ROTZINGER received a standing ovation at the convention in Las Vegas. He was named national Law Enforcement Officer of the Year, and he made all the talk shows, explaining how crime didn't have a prayer. With the expert assistance of a ghost writer, Rotzinger whacked out a paperback about his most magnificent investigations. Rotzinger came out looking very good in Eddie Seabolt's book, and vice versa.

ROTZINGER'S WIFE was elected president of The Club. She was the first woman ever to hold such a snazzy position.

LUCY, the stewardess, got well quickly. She caught a series of flights, the last of which put her inside the shadows of South America. Rich men were usually lined up halfway around the block of her villa, hoping for a date. She never did much, but she sure did it well. The deluxe face-lift was worth it. A gentleman farmer named Rico guessed her age at thirty. Not quite, she told him. He was humiliated, and got her a nice diamond, as an apology.